Toxic Waters

David G. Ferguson

Published by
North Channel Novels

Copyright © 2016 by David G. Ferguson

Published in Canada by North Channel Novels
Toxicwaters001@gmail.com

ISBN: 978-0-9939522-0-3

This book is entirely a work of fiction. Names, characters and
incidents are either the product of the author's imagination or are
used fictitiously. Any resemblance to actual events or persons, living
or dead is entirely coincidental. While the Canadian Coast Guard has
permitted the use of its corporate name and the names of its vessels
and Marine Communications and Traffic Services facilities in this
story, in no way does this imply its endorsement of this work; nor has
the Canadian Coast Guard contributed in any way to this book other
than by granting the permission noted.

Cover photo copied with the permission of Tim Downs

To Pat:

Thanks for your enduring patience throughout this prolonged process.

Novels by David G. Ferguson

Toxic Waters

Rob McNabb and Samantha Williams Wildlife Crime Series:
Bear Runners
Up Halfway Creek
Double Back Fur Run

Early Reviews for TOXIC WATERS

"…. exciting, fast paced, containing tension, action and surprise …. great introduction of all the elements that would eventually come together.

"Having been a Game Warden like Dave, and a boater on Georgian Bay, I found he painted a realistic picture of the job, of boating and behavior of the elements. His attention to these details was not only accurate, but I believe will make the reader feel like they are sailing or in court or at the mercy of the weather."

Norm Brown, retired Ontario Conservation Officer

"Absolutely riveting. Hated to put it down. Can't wait for the next book."

Carolyn Perry, Fish and Wildlife Tech, Nova Scotia Department of Natural Resources

"It feels as if the story was custom written just for me."

Tim Downs, experienced transatlantic and Great Lakes sailor

Acknowledgements

I owe many thanks to the following good folks: Carolyn Perry, for urging me to finally get this book finished. I had started my story on our Commodore 64 back in the 1980s, and Carolyn had read a skeletal version in 2004. She'd recently urged me on so she'd finally get to find out how the story ended; Jennifer Schwartz, environmental engineer. Her background in groundwater contamination remediation was most helpful in providing me with the necessary guidance in the field of toxic waste — particularly in selecting toxins best suited to the story; Jack Purvis of Purvis Marine Limited, along with his company's website for providing material related to tugboats and some of the operational basics of towing; Martin Beaupré of the Canadian Coast Guard for arranging permission to use the name of the Canadian Coast Guard, and the names of active CCG vessels and the Thunder Bay Marine Communications and Traffic Services facility in my story; And finally, special thanks to Marnie Ferguson of *Note* Editorial and Publishing Services (http://noteeditorialandpublishing.ca), for her professional editing expertise and for guiding me through the maze that lies between the keyboard and the end product.

1. DISCOVERED

July 18, 0320 hrs

The urgent voicemail message was still ringing in her head as Erin Franklin turned her late-model Toyota Corolla off the gravel township road. She cautiously guided the car up a grass-covered track that was an abandoned farm lane. At such an early hour, the glow in the southern half of the sky was the only evidence that she was close to civilization. That glow was the reflection of night-time Toronto, showing in the hazy heavens.

The caller said it was imperative that she remain anonymous in order to protect both her job and any future updates she might provide on the developing situation. It was obvious, from the specific nature of the details she provided, that the caller was an employee at Mid-Con Waste Management. According to the caller, the company was about to ship hazardous waste chemicals it was no longer licensed to handle. And based on Erin's previous experience with the arrogant SOB who ran the place, it likely meant that a load of toxic materials was about to be illegally disposed of. He'd already been convicted of abandoning poisonous products in remote locations before.

She parked her car between a pair of ancient apple trees in a long-neglected orchard. Locking the doors, she walked to the back of the car and removed a small dark blue backpack from the trunk. After double-checking its contents, she swung it over her shoulders and quietly closed the trunk lid. She made her way on foot through the dew-soaked grass back to the gravel road and headed south — the direction from which she had just driven.

The distinctive sound of loose gravel crunching under her old department store joggers silenced the chorus of nearby frogs. The inhabitants of the roadside marsh paused to wait for the perceived danger to pass before resuming their night song. Although she carried it ready in her hand, she did not use her flashlight; there was enough ambient light in the sky from the moon and the city's glow for her to see her way. She did not want to announce her presence. She wore dark blue jeans and a black sweatshirt, blending seamlessly into the hazy darkness.

The humid night air carried the organic aroma of the marsh, blended with the sweet smell of wild grasses and flowers growing in the idle farm fields nearby. But the closer she came to her destination, nature's perfumes gradually took on a hint of the pungent odours of industrial activity. There were no frogs sounding off by the time she approached the high chain-link fence that enclosed the headquarters of Mid-Con Waste Management Inc. The lingering smells there were distinctly chemical in nature.

As she walked down the road toward her objective, Erin thought about the voicemail message again. After taking down the information, she had made half a dozen calls to the government's environmental spills hotline. Unfortunately each attempt had led her through the same voicemail maze leading to an endless loop instead of connecting her with a live operator. Technology lets you down when you need it most, she thought. Worse still, the handful of environmental conservation officers she'd regularly dealt with all had unlisted phone numbers and none of them had cared to share his with her.

A call to the nearest regional police detachment had left her with the unsatisfactory answer that they were having a really busy night, but would try to check out her complaint in the morning — if they had time. With no way to call in the cavalry, she knew she had to look into the matter herself. And that was why she was about to go sneaking around a toxic waste warehouse yard at such an ungodly hour of the morning.

Standing five feet seven inches tall, Erin was slim — but not skinny — and modestly proportioned. She was physically fit, thanks to her active lifestyle rather than any structured fitness program. She wore her black hair in a 'mushroom cap' hair cut, her bangs almost down to her eyebrows. Her cosmetic-free face could radiate a brown-eyed smile that would melt the hearts of most men. But there were presently no men in her life other than her father. In fact, other than her father, she ranked most men, especially those in her own age group, as a bunch of self-centred, video-gaming, immature morons. A boyfriend was just not in the cards for her.

Her mother died when Erin was only fourteen. An only child, she had been raised by her father since then. In reality, she and her father had shared the effort of her upbringing.

Her mother's death had hit them both really hard. Her dad carried the guilt of having taken his wife's role as a stay-at-home mom too much for granted. For Erin, her mom's death simply came at the worst possible time — puberty. Even during those awkward early teen years, as sick as her mother's cancer had made her, she had remained a patient and understanding mentor. Erin had often wondered afterwards, if she had shown her mom the appreciation she deserved during those final trying months.

Suddenly left on their own, she and her dad had had to

learn household management from scratch — cooking, cleaning, shopping, laundry — everything that her mom had always managed to do so seamlessly. Erin did have an edge however, when it came to ironing her dad's shirts. She had watched her mom breeze through that job right from early childhood. But on learning how finicky a task it really was, she vowed that she'd never take a career like her dad's, where clothes with knife-sharp creases were expected at work.

Despite her disdain for quality business attire, she had adopted as absolute, her father's strong principles for doing what is right. Often found sitting in the back row of his courtroom during school holidays, Erin was always amazed how he could see through the varied stories told in the witness box, sorting truth from fabrication with apparent ease. At the end of each case, he always seemed to be able to make what she felt was the right decision while affording very fair treatment to the people he convicted. Those he felt had a chance to redeem themselves were given ample opportunity to do so, but repeat offenders and unrepentant criminals sure got the punishment they deserved.

At twenty-four she had graduated from university with degrees in both law and environmental science. She could have accepted one of several corporate jobs offered to her after graduation, but instead she had spent the past five years working as a self-styled environmental crusader. She was not looking to get rich; she just wanted to save the world from human stupidity and industrial greed.

Much to her father's chagrin, Erin had no particular business plan in place when she launched her self-employed career of tracking down companies engaged in illegal dumping. But it was her idea and her business, and he just hoped she wouldn't get trampled by the opposition along the way.

Her company name, Ontario Envirobusters Ltd.

sounded a bit gimmicky now, but it had gotten her established, so she accepted that she was stuck with that handle.

At the beginning, she had no significant financial backing, but lived frugally on a portion of inheritance money she had received from her maternal grandmother. However, after making some headline-grabbing victories, she began to receive grants from several big-name environmental activist organizations — rewards for having slain some particularly repugnant corporate dragons.

She turned over evidence she gathered to environmental investigators at the Ministry of Natural Resources. The MNR, even after taking over the former environment ministry, was so overworked and understaffed it still didn't have the resources to go looking for additional offenders. And although some of the officers at MNR were not entirely enthusiastic about her investigative activities — something to do with a civilian meddling in ministry affairs — the detail and high quality of her research enabled them to successfully prosecute the cases she presented to them. In fact, Erin had quickly become recognized by the courts as a credible witness. The ministry's conviction rate in the cases she brought to them, ranked right up with their own investigations.

Unfortunately, her stubborn, in-your-face tenacity had gained her the nickname, 'Iron Maiden of Envirobusters' with most of the COs she knew — usually behind her back, but not always — and her reputation probably had something to do with them withholding their phone numbers from her.

She stepped off the road and followed a short gravel ramp down to an unused chain-link gate and paused to listen. She had visited the site earlier in the night and had returned only after coming up with the means of dealing with two canine sentries she'd found in charge of yard security. Just before parking her car she had bribed the big Rottweilers with hamburger patties modestly laced with sleeping pills. Not asleep yet, but definitely docile, the big dogs were now quite willing to make friends. More treats offered through the mesh of the steel fence helped to seal the deal.

It was a standard swinging gate, hinged to a steel post at one end and latched and locked to another post at the other. And of course, like the rest of the fence, it was topped with four rows of vicious looking barbed wire. Fully closed, there was no way for Erin to pass between the gate and the post, nor squeeze underneath — it did have to be dog-proof after all — and a concrete sill precluded digging.

However a broken eye-ring on the gate was replaced by a chain. And whoever had last secured the chain had carelessly left a little slack in it when attaching the lock. It wasn't enough slack to gain the dogs any advantage, but by raising the lower end of the loop of chain, Erin gained a few extra inches of opening. She pushed the bottom corner of the gate inward to its limit and shoved her backpack through. There was just enough flex in the gate's tubular frame that with some unusual contortions she was able to squeeze herself sideways, low to the ground, between the gate and the post. She was in.

The first stages of morning twilight allowed her to move easily across the unlit storage yard. Aided occasionally by the judicious use of her flashlight, she was able to read the labels as she searched for the specific batch of drums described by her informant. She found them at last, in a far corner of the yard. There were sixteen wooden pallets. Ten pallets sat on the ground in two rows, six feet inside the fence; the other six were stacked on top. On each pallet sat four black steel 45-gallon drums labelled, Petroleum Distillates – Waste class 213-I. The exact product inside was unknown to the caller, but she had said that the contents were far more sinister than simple used petroleum products. She suspected PCBs.

Erin knew she would be handling hazardous chemicals, so she had a pair of long rubber gloves, a disposable plastic apron and a clear plastic face shield in her backpack. She randomly chose half a dozen barrels from the group for her samples. Fortunately for her, the company employees had been meticulous about keeping the exterior surfaces of the barrels uncontaminated. They too had a personal interest in avoiding contact with the toxic contents.

Using a barrel bung wrench padded with a rag to minimize the chance of being heard, she set to work. Opening each drum she had selected, she used a large syringe to extract a sample and then carefully injected the contents into small glass jars. To avoid breathing in any potentially noxious fumes, she simply held her breath for the entire time it took her to open a drum, draw a sample and then recap the drum. Even then, she would step away several paces from where she had been working before allowing herself the luxury of inhaling once more. It was not standard laboratory procedure, but with the early morning air hanging motionless, it was the best she could manage under field conditions.

Gathering just those six samples was a painstakingly slow operation, and a hungry swarm of early morning mosquitoes didn't help any either.

A friend of hers, who worked under contract at a university chemistry lab, would be able to determine at least the class of chemicals in this batch on short notice. Armed with that information, she could alert the authorities. A full detailed analysis would have to wait for the moment. The important thing was to mobilize the MNR people as soon as possible.

Erin had just finished drawing the last sample when three workers emerged from the vast cement block warehouse with a forklift and headed across the yard in her direction. She hadn't expected an early shift — at least, not this early and she was alarmed when the men started loading pallets from the very batch she'd been sampling. Desperate to avoid being discovered, she crouched in the tall grass between the barrel stack and the fence.

The pallets were picked up one at a time and driven up a ramp to a loading dock where there was a tarpaulin-covered stake truck waiting. The forklift disappeared with its load into the back of the truck. The workers took their time and secured each pair of pallets to the truck bed with heavy cargo straps before loading the next pair. Even as they worked, they took more than enough smoke breaks for Erin's liking. And every other smoke break seemed to require at least one of the crew to stop for a piss break — usually within yards of where she hid. She was within an ace of being discovered several times.

Only a cessation of the loading activities, brought on by the arrival of a food vendor's truck, gave her the opportunity to recap, without being detected, the last drum she had opened. Fortunately, none of the loading crew had noticed it.

Now there were only ten pallets of the steel drums remaining to protect her from being discovered. There was no way out. The long grass appeared to peter out on either side of the pallet stack. Attempting to cross the open ground between her present cover and the next nearest stack of drums would be inviting immediate capture, and boldly walking through the yard and out the front gate was definitely a non-starter. Erin's only hope was that the truck might not have room to take the last few pallets.

Hiding at the back of the ever-shrinking stack of drums, she was beginning to wish that she had left this particular battle to save the environment until she had professional backup.

July 18, 0655

Willard Reiger parked his aged Chevrolet Impala in its usual space in the staff parking lot at the headquarters of Mid-Con Waste Management Inc. He was the sole owner of the company. He had built it from scratch into a thriving business serving the Great Lakes region, once known as the industrial heartland of North America. Though many North American manufacturers had moved their dirtiest operations offshore in recent years, there was still plenty of business to keep his company going. But the economic slowdown that followed the 2008 financial meltdown had put significant pressure on his bottom line. 'Growth' was no longer a byword of the trade.

Walking through the general office area, he acknowledged the obligatory greetings of the three middle-aged clerks, with a simple, "Good morning ladies." Everyone started early in the summer months as a concession to the lack of air conditioning in the building. By three in the afternoon, it would be like an oven in there.

Entering a dimly lit hallway at the rear of the main office, Reiger passed the lunchroom, several supply rooms and the accountant's cubicle before arriving at his own spartan office. The room had two entrances — the one he'd just used to enter from the front office and another that led directly out into the warehouse and the processing plant.

Once inside, he set his brown bag lunch and the business section of his morning paper on the plain oak desk. Scanning his in-basket for the first job of the day, he closed the door and sat down in one of the few luxury appointments in the entire building — a well-padded, brown leather desk chair.

Reiger was in his mid-sixties. He stood just over six feet tall and was of a slim, but rock-hard build. His hair was turning from silver toward white. Piercing grey eyes set in a weathered

9

but clean-shaven narrow face, gave him a perpetually stern look. He rarely smiled. Even if he'd tried to smile, he would have looked no less severe.

He used to have a wife, but she had moved on. Living with a man who was a slave to his business and, most of the time, an absolute bore at home had worn thin after fourteen years. But it was his mean temper that had been the deciding factor in her departure. She now lived comfortably with her girlfriend in a Florida condo with an ocean view.

His employees barely tolerated him. The fact that he expected a full hour's work for each hour of pay was not the issue. It was the persistent rumour that a couple of men, caught slacking on the job, had been summarily fired and when they demanded severance pay, his security chief had taken them out behind the warehouse and brutally beaten them, both at the same time. Reiger, who stood by watching, threw them each a two-dollar coin when Gant was finished. "There's your severance — spend it wisely," he'd said before turning and walking back into the building. True or not, it hardly made for a healthy workplace environment.

The man was driven by an inbred need to achieve increasingly greater levels of efficiency and profitability — even in a shrinking market. That attitude came from his family background. His parents, forced to give up a flourishing manufacturing business in eastern Europe, had fled to Canada during the early years of the Cold War. A festering hatred of communism, nurtured by his father, had surfaced early in young Reiger. On his eighteenth birthday he quit high school in Toronto and caught a bus to Buffalo, New York. There he enlisted in the U.S. Marine Corps.

During his first tour of duty in Vietnam he narrowly escaped with his life from a vicious firefight in the hotly contested Mekong Delta. Rather than leaving at the end of his tour, Reiger reenlisted and went on to become a decorated participant in an unpopular war.

Upon his discharge from the service, following the American withdrawal from that ill-fated conflict, Willard Reiger had returned home to Canada. For lack of any better offers, he had taken a job working at a large funeral parlour in Toronto's west end. That career was not long-lived — he'd seen more than enough dead bodies in Vietnam. But a curiosity about the handling of effluents generated by the embalming process led him to the world of hazardous waste management.

Within ten years Reiger had started his own waste disposal company. As various state and provincial jurisdictions created and tightened their environmental protection regulations, his business grew rapidly. Although there were considerable expenses involved in either processing waste products at his own facilities, or paying others to process products for him, it took only simple math skills to add up his costs and throw in his markup.

His clients paid him well. In exchange, he dealt with the waste products that various governments no longer allowed industries to dump down their drains. Reiger had made a great deal of money getting rid of other people's unwanted waste.

Much of his initial financial success had come because he managed to keep his overhead low. His personal car was just one example. It was almost thirty years old, and his mechanic kept telling him that he'd get better fuel economy with a newer one. But Reiger countered that this one only cost him a few hundred dollars a year in maintenance. At today's prices he'd have to lay out close to thirty thousand dollars for a new one, which would have to run for a good many years for the fuel savings to make up the difference. He managed his corporate fleet on the same principle.

Mid-Con Waste owned two older-model, full-sized

cargo vans used for local pickups of any product that could be carried and loaded by hand. Several five-ton stake trucks carried the larger, pallet-mounted loads, and a retired tandem-axle fuel tanker handled the bulk liquids. Any product requiring an even larger vehicle was contracted out to commercial carriers. The newest vehicle in his fleet had been on the road for twelve years.

Maintenance was the key to running a low-budget fleet — maintenance and the understanding burned into the mind of each of his drivers that there would be unholy hell to pay if he was found to be driving in anything but a careful and conservative manner. And there was of course, the one inducement that kept most of his employees duly diligent about their driving habits; if involved in a crash, they could end up awash in spilled product — some of the most carcinogenic fluids known to mankind. To a man, they were all very careful drivers.

However, in an era of shrinking markets, frugality could go only just so far toward helping Reiger's bottom line. He had become obsessed with improving his profit margin, and as competition from similar waste disposal companies increased, he felt compelled to take the occasional shortcut through fuzzy areas in the law. And when he found that he could get away with bending the law just a little bit, he arrogantly began to brush the regulations aside completely. His shortcuts eventually gave way to the outright illegal disposal of some of the most toxic waste products created by modern science and industry.

While maintaining a high-volume trade in legitimate, low-expense products, Reiger began to repackage, for special treatment, some of the more toxic chemicals he was being paid a premium rate to handle. Falsely listed on shipping manifests as more benign products, these dangerous toxins could be easily transported and simply dropped off somewhere when no one was watching. After all, he reasoned to himself, why pay a third-party good money to destroy the product when, for almost nothing, I can ship it out and just leave it somewhere using my own resources.

Abandoned industrial facilities used to be a favourite destination, but more and more of these were either being fenced in or repurposed into condo developments. Dumping along seldom-used country roads in rural areas had been another favourite. But those areas too, had become increasingly risky. Many such locations, formerly sparsely populated, were now being developed as residential or recreational properties by city folks looking for a place to get away from it all. Now the chances were far greater of getting caught by an irate landowner than by any government environmental officers, or even the police.

It was exactly one such circumstance that had led to convictions against the company several years ago and had resulted in a ban on handling several of the most lucrative classes of waste. This had not stopped Reiger's illicit activities; instead, it had driven him to even darker endeavours. Even after being caught a second time, he continued to seek out highly toxic, prohibited products that some businesses held without the appropriate permits. For a premium price, he would take these off their hands and employ a variety of tactics to move and illegally dispose of them.

The most successful solution to Reiger's disposal problem so far, had come to him by chance. Several years earlier, he had read about container ships frequently losing deck cargo overboard during storms on ocean crossings. It didn't take him more than a moment to realize that since his own company already shipped barge-loads of legitimate product across Lake Huron to Michigan for destruction, it would be easy enough to lose some unauthorized product overboard along the way. Huron was a big lake, after all.

July 18, 0700

Erin Franklin breathed a sigh of relief as the forklift was shut down and the yard crew finished securing the load in the back of the covered stake truck. She lay in a space between the eight remaining pallets of drums. When the crew moved to another part of the yard, she tried phoning for help, but Mid-Con had some sort of signal-blocking device running — Reiger found it a useful tool for stopping his employees wasting time texting and making personal phone calls. Her cell phone was useless here.

It looked as though she was just going to have to wait it out — lie there all day until darkness fell. Then she would steal away with the samples she had gathered and get the ball rolling with the ministry people.

Her attention was suddenly drawn to the two guard dogs, now fully awake after their tranquilized nap. The big dogs began to approach her position, but not maliciously. They were likely looking for more treats. They located her with no difficulty, and no amount of hushed 'shooing' would send them away. Eventually she was able to convince them to lie down. Perhaps the workers wouldn't notice.

"Between a rock and a hard place, eh?" A big voice, coming from behind her, startled Erin. Before she could even begin to react, she was grabbed by the ankles and roughly dragged over the gravel, out from her hiding place and into the open daylight. Looking up, she saw the largest giant of a man she had ever seen, staring down at her.

Forty-one-year-old John Gant was the chief of security for Mid-Con Waste Management. He was six feet seven inches tall and possessed a bodybuilder's physique. With his black hair cropped in a severe crew cut and his face wearing a permanent five o'clock shadow, Gant was not an attractive man.

Ever since childhood, his sheer size had predestined him for roles as an enforcer. He had protected the bullies in the schoolyard, played aggressive defensive positions in hockey and football, and worked as a bouncer in local bars even before he had reached legal drinking age. He was ideally suited to the role of encouraging people to toe his employer's line. While he could follow the boss's instructions to the letter, he did not possess the imaginative mind of a leader.

"Who are you and what are you doin' here?" he demanded, picking up Erin's backpack and rifling through its contents. He raised his eyebrows at the sight of the sample bottles, the barrel wrench and the protective gear in the bag. She was too shocked to reply, or even to move.

"I think it's time to go and see the boss," he said seriously as he reached down and grasped Erin's upper arm with a hand the size of a baseball glove. Without as much as a grunt, the big man 'helped' her to her feet. Wincing, she knew she'd have an ugly bruise on that arm later.

July 18, 0815

Willard Reiger was reviewing a waste oil disposal contract for a major U.S. trucking firm when he was interrupted by a commotion outside the warehouse door. He was about to shout through the closed door for some peace and quiet, when John Gant entered.

"Look what the dogs dragged in boss." Gant grinned as he directed Erin Franklin into the office and shoved her into a straight-backed chair in front of Reiger's desk. "She was snoopin' 'round the shipment for the barge," he added as he dumped her backpack casually on Reiger's desk. The glass sample bottles she'd filled so carefully, clinked loudly together. Fortunately, none of them broke.

"What, your dogs lost their teeth?" Reiger asked. "I thought you got them because of the damage they could do to intruders. There isn't a scratch on this woman!"

"I don't understand that either. Seems they took a likin' to her …." Gant's voice trailed off sheepishly.

"Well, Christ!" said Reiger, turning to fix his gaze on Erin. "Miss Franklin here has caused me a lot of trouble in the past couple of years. And tomorrow the saga continues … in your father's court, where I have to defend myself against the frivolous charges they laid after the last time you broke in here. I should have you charged with trespass and get a court order to keep you away from me."

"I had nothing to do with the last time you were caught," Erin stated bluntly. "The COs learned how to do it all by themselves once I pointed you out to them. And my father would have disqualified himself from hearing your case tomorrow if I'd been the one to turn you in. You should know that." Leaning forward over Reiger's desk, she went on the offensive. "All of that information will be in the brief the prosecutor disclosed to your lawyer. Can't he read?"

But Reiger hadn't known — he had just assumed she was the one, based on her performance the first time he'd been caught. She had been the original informant and he'd pointed that out to his lawyer.

He sat silent, perplexed, for several minutes; to Erin it felt like hours. Obviously the lawyer hadn't read the brief, Reiger thought, beginning to do a slow burn. This was bad news. They had been planning on claiming a conflict of interest — anticipating the likely prospect of Franklin being disqualified from presiding over the trial because of his relationship to the informant. That would have bought more time and given them a chance at being tried by a more lenient judge, and just about any other judge would be more lenient than James Franklin.

If Reiger was convicted again, he was certain that all of his licences would be revoked, and he would be hit with some stiff fines. The COs were tougher than the people at Environment had ever been. That would be the end of his company. They could even send him to jail. That's how strict things had become. Damn that stupid bastard lawyer, he thought, fuming. He's supposed to anticipate these problems. What am I paying him for anyway?

Now Reiger desperately needed a new plan. Staring right through Erin, he began to speak slowly, while allowing the seeds of an idea to germinate in his mind. "I told you the last time we met, to stay off my property for good. But, maybe . . ." Reiger paused, his thoughts expanding quickly now on the concept of his new plan.

He turned to Gant. "Miss Franklin is going to be staying with us for a while. Make her comfortable in the basement storeroom, and for Christ's sake, don't let her get away. And don't breathe a word to the women in the office." He didn't dare let them get even the slightest hint of this situation; they'd turn him in for sure.

Reiger turned dismissively back to the work on his desk signalling an end to the conversation. As soon as Erin had been led unceremoniously back out the warehouse door, he began to formulate a plan to use her as leverage in tomorrow's court battle.

July 18, 0825

Led down a basement hallway with her arm once again in Gant's firm grip, Erin came to the full realization that her life was in very real danger. Things like this just aren't supposed to happen, she thought, her panic growing rapidly. But she knew in her gut that she had pushed Willard Reiger too far. Now he was a desperate man who would apparently stop at nothing in his attempts to get himself out of his legal difficulties.

At the end of the hall she was pushed through a doorway into a dark and musty room. Empty metal shelves lined the unpainted concrete walls. Gant flicked on the lights and did a quick but efficient check of the room, looking for any items Erin could use to attempt an escape. Satisfied that there were none, he turned and left, closing the heavy steel door behind him. She could hear him sliding closed the large bolt she had seen on the outside of the door.

An unseen cold hand closed around her heart as she heard a heavy padlock snap shut to secure the bolt. Other than the bare shelves, the room was empty. A single row of fluorescent lights running across the twelve-foot ceiling made that obvious. There were neither windows nor ventilation grates through which she might escape. Erin had never felt so terrified or alone in her life.

2. ULTIMATUM

July 19, 0920 hrs

It had been a long and uncomfortable twenty-four hours. Erin Franklin was huddled on the concrete floor in a corner of the cool, musty storeroom. It smelled even worse now because without so much as a bucket to pee in, she'd had to go in a corner. She felt absolutely miserable. She could hear someone in heavy work boots approaching the steel door, and she listened with a mix of both anticipation and dread as she heard the padlock being removed and the bolt slid back.

Reiger's security man, Gant, pushed the door open and motioned to her to accompany him. She was not gripped by the vice-like hand this time, but she knew she was in no position to escape.

Gant showed her into a tiny basement office furnished with a plain grey steel desk, two matching chairs and a filing cabinet, which was also grey. The desk had nothing on top but a pad of lined paper with something written on it and a standard black desktop telephone, a relic of the 1970s.

Erin's backpack lay on the floor in one corner of the little room. She wondered, with little hope, if there would be any opportunity to sneak her cell phone from the pack. But that wouldn't happen; she was seated in the opposite corner and both the giant and his desk lay in her path. And then too, there was the signal jamming she'd have to overcome, even if she was able to get her phone. These guys thought of everything.

Gant looked at his watch, then picked up the handset on the phone and punched in a number.

July 19, 0930

Judge James Franklin was in his chambers at the courthouse in Parry Sound preparing for the day's trial. The government had filed environmental charges against a corporation and its owner. He finished gathering together his daybook and the various law books he suspected he might need in the courtroom and was about to slip into his judicial robe when the phone rang.

The caller was brief. The voice was male. "Your daughter Erin is alive and well ... for now. A dismissal in the case against Reiger and Mid-Con Waste would be wise if you want her to stay that way." And then there was a click, and the line went dead.

Franklin was aghast, a cold knot formed instantly in the pit of his stomach. This was every parent's worst nightmare. It didn't matter that she was an adult — she was his only child, and he was horrified by the thought of any of the potential outcomes that could result from her abduction.

Thinking quickly, Franklin had the presence of mind to dial Erin's cell phone number. After waiting through seven interminably long rings, he was about ready to hang up when the same male voice came on the line. Reiger had left a note on his prewritten script reminding Gant to turn off the cell phone jammer before making his call.

"Just a minute, I'll let you talk to her," he said with scarcely a pause.

"Dad? It's me. They want you to dismiss the case. Don't do it. I'm at …" she was quickly cut off, and the original caller came back on the line.

"Now, do you believe we have her? Believe this too: you call the police and there won't be anything left of her to find. Got it? When you dismiss the case, we'll call you about getting her back." Click.

Fearing dreadfully for the safety of his daughter and infuriated at being so helpless to do anything about it, Franklin reviewed the situation. The first thing he had to do was to call off today's sitting … no, that wouldn't work. They'd have to keep Erin until a new trial could be scheduled. A day or two might give him time to work out a solution, but rescheduling a trial involved accommodating numerous other professionals' calendars, and would end up being months away. No, today's trial would have to proceed as planned.

A myriad of thoughts churned through the judge's mind as he finished his preparations for court. The Mid-Con Waste people, or whoever was acting for them, had no concept of how the law or the courts operate. If he dismissed the case without valid legal grounds, there would no doubt be an appeal launched by the crown attorney and a retrial granted. For the defendants, as a way out of their legal problems, that just wouldn't work. Within a year they'd be back in court again, still facing the same charges. Unfortunately, desperate criminals frequently fail to see the obvious flaws in their hastily conceived plans — that was why they generally ended up in front of him in the first place. The judge had seen evidence of that same lack of foresight in almost every major case he had ever adjudicated.

As court was called to order, Franklin was left with the chilling thought that he was dealing with rank amateurs — desperate ones at that. It was a sure recipe for a tragic outcome, particularly if he didn't handle this correctly. In all his experience, James Franklin had rarely seen a case of this nature end with the age-old phrase, '*happily ever after.*' The thought left him in a cold sweat.

Even before the clerk announced the case against Willard Reiger and Mid-Con Waste Management Inc., Judge James Franklin had made up his mind. Ensuring the safety of his daughter was the single most important element in this whole mess. This was not the time to worry about his career on the bench. When it came down to making his choice, there was simply no contest. Besides, as he had already reasoned just moments earlier, the perpetrators would eventually be brought back to face to justice. For now, he would have to go along with the demands of Reiger and company and hope to buy enough time to figure a way to rescue his daughter.

The first step was to find an obvious hole in the prosecution's case — just for appearance's sake — at the moment he pronounced his verdict. Even this would not be easy considering that the investigation had been conducted by one of the most thorough environmental conservation officers he'd ever had in his court. And then there was Bill Samson, a top-notch crown attorney who would be prosecuting today's trial. The two of them frequently worked together and they formed an almost unbeatable team. They just didn't build holes into their cases.

July 19, 0935

Erin felt sick. Not only was she herself in extreme danger, but now her father too was being drawn into the mess with her. She knew that regardless of what transpired in court today, her dad would go to the ends of the earth to try to save her, and he'd probably place his own life in grave danger by doing so.

As the heavy door of her storeroom prison slammed shut once more, Erin crumpled, in tears, back into her corner.

July 19, 0945

In the Parry Sound courtroom, the crown and the defence counsel each made brief opening statements to the bench. Fortunately for Judge Franklin there were no juries used in provincial offence trials. He would get to make this decision on his own.

The first witness for the crown was Environmental Conservation Officer Richard David Webb. He was wearing his number one dress-khaki uniform which included a well-tailored tunic, freshly pressed trousers and a pair of brown oxford shoes buffed to a gleaming spit and polished shine. A fit thirty-five-year-old standing a couple inches short of six feet, Webb projected a very professional image. Despite the stifling heat — there was no air conditioning in the old oak-panelled courtroom — he strode to the witness box with the ease of a man entirely confident in his role.

In response to a brief introductory question from crown attorney Samson, Webb launched into a well-ordered testimony of his investigation as the case had evolved.

"Yes, your honour, at 0730 on February 23 of this year, acting on information received, I attended a site on Highway 518, three kilometres west of Orrville in Parry Sound District."

Webb went on to describe the discovery of twenty 45-gallon drums recently dumped into the bushes on the edge of a wetland at the bottom of a steep snow-covered road embankment. A set of four tire prints marked the snow-plowed bank where a dual-wheeled truck had backed to the edge of the road immediately above where the drums were observed and photographed and only a small amount of traffic had crossed the tire tracks since they had been made.

He also testified that the drums contained unknown liquids and without opening them at that place, he had sounded them — rapping them on the upper ends with his knuckles — and had judged them to be largely full. All of the drums were still attached to their shipping pallets by heavy-duty one-inch steel banding, four drums to each pallet. Despite some moderate denting, the drums were not damaged to the point of leaking. All of the drums bore painted markings identifying them as a common brand of solvent.

"I also observed," he continued, "that on the top end of each drum there was an adhesive paper label, but each of these had been painted over with black paint. However, using a rag soaked with acetone, the paint was easily removed, revealing a bar code on each label — all of them bearing the same set of numbers."

Following up on an address obtained by running a vehicle licence number provided by the informant, Webb and fellow officers from his ministry conducted a search of the buildings and storage yard of Mid-Con Waste Management Inc. in Toronto before the morning was out. Thirty additional drums with the same bar code were located at this facility. Four of those drums were also filled with unknown liquids, and the tracks left in the snow adjacent to those full drums indicated that five pallets had been recently removed from that spot.

"The drums we located there were also arranged four on a pallet, Your Honour," Webb explained, wanting to add that the five missing pallets would have carried twenty drums between them. But he knew that it was up to the judge, not the investigating officer, to draw such conclusions, as obvious as they might seem.

Continuing on with his testimony, the court learned how

Webb had traced the bar codes back to a company named Northern Petro-Chem, the original producer of the product indicated on the drums. They had willingly provided him with the tracking documentation related to this batch of product, an industrial strength, petroleum-based cleaning solvent. There were originally one hundred drums in that particular lot, fifty of which had been sold to one company, ABC Heavy Machine Industries Ltd., and smaller numbers, all of ten drums or less, to various other businesses. Only clean new drums were used to ship their product, and a chemical formula for their solvent was willingly provided to the investigators for the purpose of comparing the original contents to the unknown liquids found in the drums seized during the investigation.

Further investigation revealed that ABC Heavy Machine Industries had indeed purchased, and over time used that solvent for cleaning grease and oil sludge off the heavy construction equipment that they rebuilt. After the solvent lost its ability to dissolve heavier greases, it was returned to its original drums and picked up for disposal by Mid-Con Waste Management Inc. ABC's records, also willingly provided to the officer, indicated that the last of that particular batch of drums had been picked up two months before the appearance of the drums at the roadside in Parry Sound District.

That was the end of the examination-in-chief of Officer Webb. In cross-examination, the lawyer for the defence asked a couple of lame questions, the first being, "Is it possible that the drums fell off the truck without the driver being aware of it?"

In his enforcement training, Webb had been taught not to fear the 'is it possible' question while under cross-examination. It generally meant that the defence was at a loss for an insightful question. But he was so surprised by the total naivety of the question that he glanced toward the Judge, as if asking 'does this really need an answer?' A slight nod from His Honour told Webb to proceed anyhow.

"Just about anything is possible sir," Webb began. "But in this case it would be highly unlikely. You see, the road was straight and level above the place where the drums were found. Judging from the imprints in the snow, the pallets bearing the drums rolled down the bank perpendicular to the direction of the road; damage was minimal and not one of the steel banding straps was broken. If they had fallen off of a moving vehicle one would expect at least some, if not all of the barrels, would have broken free from their pallets. Each filled drum weighs over four-hundred pounds — rolling down the bank at speed would apply a great deal of strain on the nails that fasten the steel strapping to the wooden pallets.

"Furthermore, if they had fallen off a moving vehicle, one would expect them to have tumbled down the embankment at an angle. If they had fallen off a moving vehicle, one would expect them to have landed spread out over some distance at the bottom of the embankment, not be piled all together as they were."

"Mr. Webb," the defence began his next question, and the judge scowled. The 'Mr.' salutation was an insult to the officer's professionalism. Such arrogance was not appreciated in Franklin's court. "If they didn't fall off the truck, just how on earth do you suppose five pallets, each loaded with four drums of liquids, could be thrown off the back of a big truck? The truck in question has seating for only three adults, doesn't it? Each pallet would be very heavy I'd assume."

"Yes sir. Each loaded pallet would weigh over sixteen hundred pounds or seven hundred and thirty kilograms. That would certainly be more than three strong men could simply throw, as you say, off of the truck platform. But one man could have easily accomplished this job.

"You see, the stake truck in question is equipped with a tipping body — it is a dump truck. The driver alone, after removing his cargo ties, could simply back the truck to the edge of the road embankment, as the tire marks suggest, and raise the dump and off they would slide."

James Franklin's spirit sagged. Only a lawyer grasping at straws asks questions he doesn't already know the answers to, and Webb had handled the questions well. It was obvious that this defence lawyer was out of his league in an environmental case. In fact, the poor fellow was obviously not a trial lawyer of any sort.

The parade of witnesses carried on for most of the morning. A government chemist identified the contents in the discarded drums as trichloroethylene (TCE) containing a consistently uniform mix of heavy metals. They had been the by-products of a metal electroplating process. The TCE alone was a known carcinogen especially tied to cancers of the kidney, liver, cervix and lymphatic system.

He further testified that the drums found in the bush contained the identical product to those found at Mid-Con's facility. And that the product in both groups of drums had to have been generated at the same facility.

The production manager from Northern Petro-Chem provided corroborating testimony about the one hundred drum batch of industrial solvent, half of which went to ABC Heavy Industries. And the shipping supervisor from ABC Heavy Industries testified to the shipping of the used solvent, in its original drums, to Mid-Con Waste Management.

The defence continued to perform poorly throughout, and the judge continued to feel discouraged. But finally it was the Mid-Con lawyer's turn to present his defence.

"We call Willard Reiger to the stand Your Honour."

'The owner, and co-defendant . . . not normally a wise

move for the defence,' thought Franklin. 'But sometimes it works out. He's got to have some scrap of hope for me, surely.'

After the preamble, Reiger was asked about the events leading to the discovery of the product found abandoned by the roadside.

He told the court that the truck had been loaded with the drums described by the officer in preparation for transport to the company's Britt transshipping facility. During the night of February 22, someone had borrowed the loaded truck without his permission. The next morning the truck was empty, parked in the yard where it had been sitting loaded the previous evening.

"Look, here is the vehicle log. Mr. Mitchell, the regular driver filled in the log at the end of his pickups on the twenty-second, and the next morning he brought me the log and said that the truck had gone three-hundred and seventy-two kilometres since he had brought it back to the yard. See, here it is in the log your honour," he said, offering a dirty, tattered, company record book that appeared to have spent most of its time on the floor of the cab under the driver's boots.

Franklin thought to himself, 'this might be the only hole I get to use for a dismissal. I sure hope they don't screw it up.' But deep down, he knew that the crown was too shrewd to let them make any gains on a feeble defence like that.

"Mr Reiger." The prosecutor, beginning his cross-examination moved to stand beside his table. "Did you report the theft of the truck? Borrowed without permission is theft you know."

"No sir. We were just glad to get it back without damage."

"Do you not lock the gates of your compound at night?"

"Oh yes sir, every night. But it must have been forgotten that night."

"Did you report the theft of the load of product to the authorities?"

"No, by the time we realized it was missing, the officer and his storm troops were already searching my plant and accusing me of contaminating the environment." Reiger combined a look of hurt, with his palms raised in a forlorn 'poor me' gesture, just begging for the court's sympathy. "We are just glad that someone found it all, and as soon as Officer Webb and his department are through with it, we will be moving it immediately to the re-processor's plant."

"Was that, Officer Webb the storm trooper? Or Officer Webb, the savior of the day?"

"Objection, Your Honour."

"I'll move on, Your Honour," Samson apologized, seeing Franklin's raised eyebrows. Turning back to the defendant he said, "Mr. Reiger, why are there erasures and re-entries in the vehicle log for the days of February twenty-second and twenty-third?"

"Oh, Mr. Mitchell must have made a mistake and then corrected it later."

"Made all the rest of his entries for that month left-handed but the corrections with his right? No left-hand dominant person who writes that poorly in the first place, can write so neatly with his right."

"I don't know why he would do that sir."

"Alright then Mr. Reiger, returning to the mysterious truck trip, let me get this straight. Do you expect the court to believe that on the one night that someone forgot to lock the gate, a five-ton stake truck was stolen...."

"Just borrowed sir."

"... was taken then, from your facility, driven over 150

kilometres north, unloaded of its undesirable cargo, driven back south and returned to your compound undamaged?"

"Oh, yes sir."

"That's just incredible, isn't it?"

"Yes sir."

"I have no further questions for this witness, Your Honour."

"Uh, redirect Your Honour?" Counsel for the defence was quick to grasp that one. "What do you take the expression 'that's incredible' to mean Mr. Reiger?"

"That it is surprising, or amazing, I guess."

Franklin knew that the Crown's intention was to convey the original meaning of the expression: that it cannot be believed, and in a way, Reiger fell into the trap, but few people these days use the English language well enough to know that.

There were no further witnesses, and both sides quickly went through their final arguments. The ball was now in Franklin's court.

"Seeing as how it is just minutes away from noon, we'll recess for lunch, during which time I will consider the evidence. Court will reconvene at two o'clock." That was Franklin's standard procedure in these short trials, and in order to keep up the appearance of normality, he figured he had better follow the template.

'Webb and Samson are going to be livid when I hand down this judgement,' he told himself. 'At least they shouldn't have any trouble appealing for a retrial.' But that thought was cold comfort with the much bigger issue of Erin's abduction still hanging over his head.

At two-fifteen that afternoon, having pronounced his ruling on the case, Judge James Franklin adjourned court for the day, leaving the prosecution team stunned, their jaws hanging open after the blatant dismissal of their case. Neither

Webb nor Samson could finish a sentence as they stammered on about various pieces of evidence that the judge had completely overlooked.

"Man, that really pisses me off," Webb muttered, keeping the conversation between the two of them. "I never saw a judge fall for that one in the presence of so much clear evidence."

"I should have grilled Reiger further… run him into a corner…" the crown lamented.

"No Bill, their weak defence wouldn't normally have worked on Franklin. You know as well as I do that he'd never buy such a line of crap. But did you see him? He really seemed to be off his game … like his mind was in another place for most of the trial."

"Hmmm, it wasn't just me then. I was thinking that for a man who normally projects such an impressive image, he seemed a number of sizes smaller today. Oh, hell … maybe he's just got that summer flu that's been going around."

"So, as crown counsel, is there some way you can discretely ask him if we messed up somewhere? I mean, he didn't really scold us about screwing up. He just suggested that our evidence left room for some doubt. He's never summarized a case like that before. Usually, either the defendant gets a royal chewing out as he's being convicted, or we get reamed for screwing up a case and wasting the court's precious time."

"I'll look into it Rick, but don't hold your breath. Judges can get pretty testy with young prosecutors who ask questions outside the courtroom. In the meantime, I'll start the ball rolling for an appeal. Winning should be pretty straight forward … if you can wait a year."

3. CAST OFF

It was another hot, breathless day in a summer of record-breaking heat waves. Rick Webb, sweating profusely, laboured down the dock with the last bags of supplies he'd bought for his vacation. His burden wasn't getting any lighter, but each step he took toward the boat was one step closer to getting under way. He swelled with pride as he stepped aboard *Water Baby*, his classic sixty-year-old sailing yawl.

He set his load down in the cockpit and began stowing equipment and supplies in various lockers. *Water Baby*'s cockpit was not quite six feet long — somewhat small by modern cruising boat standards. It was crowded with piles of goods he'd already brought aboard.

The new spool of rope he'd bought to replace his aging dock lines went into the lazaret locker aft of the cockpit. This deep storage area occupied the aft-most five feet of hull space under the poop deck. When under way it would be filled to capacity with dock lines and fenders, shore power cords and spare sheets and guys — the lines necessary for trimming some of the eight sails found in the old yawl's inventory. His seventy-five-pound toolbox was nestled beside the spare sails under the port cockpit seat.

After opening the companionway hatch leading down

into the cabin, Webb carried the remaining goods below. Having been closed up while the sun was at its highest, there'd been no airflow through the elegant cabin. There wasn't any relief from the stifling heat down there, so he made a quick trip through to the forward cabin where he opened the fore-hatch. That started a slow exchange of the stifling air inside for the marginally cooler air out on deck. Without waiting for complete relief, which wouldn't occur until the boat was moving, Webb turned back to the job at hand. He cursed the sweat dripping off his face and arms as he stowed the supplies in their proper places.

Much of the food was stowed in the small U-shaped galley on the port side of the cabin at the base of the companionway steps. When he was finished, the tiny twelve-volt electric refrigerator and its accompanying two-cubic-foot freezer were filled to capacity. With just one person aboard, Webb wasn't planning on having to do any shopping during the next several weeks.

A couple of new Great Lakes nautical charts he'd bought were placed in the wide drawer under the chart table in the navigating station. That was situated on the starboard side, right opposite the galley. Canned goods and other bulk foods, as well as two bottles of premium scotch, went into lockers under the seats around the dinette table in the salon, just forward of the galley.

His shaving kit went into the head, forward of the salon on the port side of the yawl. Across from the head, was the clothes locker — stocked days earlier. Forward of this in a cabin of its own was the V-berth, which he'd already made up ahead of time with clean linen.

By the time everything was finally secured, Webb was desperate to cool off, so he rewarded himself with a cold beer from the fridge as he headed for the companionway steps.

Carrying the cold, condensation covered bottle up on deck he made his way forward to the bow, where he hosed himself down with lake water from the deck-wash pump.

Framed by short, sandy brown hair and neatly trimmed sideburns, his deep blue eyes were set in a rugged tanned face. He only shaved on workdays and was now already sporting second-day stubble that would form a thick, reddish-brown beard by the end of his vacation.

Standing barefoot on the teak deck and holding the end of the ship's garden hose over his head, Webb allowed the generous flow of cool water to soak him from head to toe. Without deflecting the water's flow from his face, he occasionally tipped back a swallow of the ice-cold beer. The tension and stress that had built up over the past few months gradually began to subside.

He was done with work for a while, and he planned to cruise to the northern end of Lake Huron. For three weeks he would relax and take in the beauty and seclusion of the hundreds of islands and coves lying between Blind River and the Bustard Islands. Other than that, he had no set itinerary; day by day he would let the wind direction determine his destination — if indeed he moved at all.

He stared blankly through the forest of sailboat masts in the marina, and despite his promise to just let it go, Webb found himself, for the umpteenth time, going back over the strange events in court yesterday. It had been a straightforward case and being a meticulous investigator, most of his cases resulted in convictions. Yesterday he had expected none other than a victory for the good guys. The Crown attorney too, had been confident of winning this case — he wouldn't have even considered prosecuting it if he hadn't been. It had come as a jolt to both men when the "not guilty" verdict had been handed down. Webb was still angry — and bitterly disappointed. He'd put a lot of time and hard work into that investigation.

Judge Franklin, who Webb had come to respect in the past as being very supportive of environmental cases, had appeared distracted throughout the trial. What on earth was he thinking when he dismissed the charges on such a clearly laid out, open-and-shut case? There was something wrong that Webb just couldn't put his finger on. The more he thought about it, the more it bothered him. 'Maybe he's getting past his "best before" date … Naw!' Webb dismissed that thought immediately as he'd done a dozen times since leaving the courtroom yesterday.

July 20, 1330

A five-ton stake truck carrying thirty-two drums of hazardous waste pulled out of Mid-Con Waste Management's Toronto yard. Driving the truck was 'Mitch' Mitchell, one member of John Gant's three-man security team. He never told anyone his actual given name.

Riding shotgun with him in the cab was a second team member, Jay Morris. Both men were in their mid-twenties. Both were graduates of the provincial jail system. They had each served short terms for multiple assault convictions stemming from a gang fight outside a raunchy after-hours club in a seamier part of the city. And they were both well known to the police before that event too. At Gant's suggestion, Reiger had hired them to help manhandle the drums of illegal product the company needed to dispose of. If they could fight hard they could be taught to work hard, Gant had assured him. An eye for picking talent was one of Gant's few strong points — aside from his loyalty and his physical strength.

From the outset, Mitchell had demonstrated his gift as a

skilled driver. His vehicle handling was so smooth that regardless of its size, whatever he drove blended unobtrusively with everything else on the road. That was a definite asset in their business. Initially the two recruits had been considered expendable in the event that the law reclaimed them, but they had both quickly developed a loyalty to the organization that neither Reiger nor Gant could fault. They proved to be a solid link in Gant's part of the operation.

Within minutes of leaving the plant, Mitchell powered the truck out of the acceleration lane, onto northbound Highway 400. They were on their way to Mid-Con Waste Management's transshipping terminal at Britt on Georgian Bay. Situated on a major rail line, it was from this small port that legitimate liquid waste products were shipped. Ferried across Lake Huron by barge, they were bound for destruction in the high-temperature furnaces of a cement plant at Alpena, Michigan.

While most Michigan-bound product arrived in Britt by railroad from a variety of industries between Sudbury, Toronto and Montreal, Reiger always sent the unauthorized materials separately by truck. His thinking was that if any of it became confused with the legitimate cargo while being transferred from rail car to barge, it could accidentally end up in Alpena. If that were to happen, he feared that if discovered by U.S. authorities, he would be shut out of the United States permanently. He would no longer have a valid reason for using the barge, and the best illegal disposal site available to him would be forever out of reach.

On this particular trip, the load on Mitch's truck was made up entirely of PCBs, the final drums of the sixteen pallets that were discovered by Erin Franklin two days earlier. Mid-Con had legally shipped PCBs to Alpena for incineration for some time. However, recent regulatory changes had put a moratorium on PCB incineration. New research had shown that burning the product created small but measureable traces of furans and dioxin — bad stuff to be pumping into the atmosphere. So until the process could be perfected, there was a hold on that particular product stream for all waste managers.

And then of course there was the small matter of PCBs being among the products that Reiger's company had lost its licence to handle after the first round of court convictions. He had no desire to have any of these found in his possession in the event of an inspection, and snap inspections had increased following his first brushes with the law. As a result, he was 'liquidating' his stock at every possible opportunity. For now, this was the last of it.

July 20, 1405

Temporarily cooled off by his lake-water shower, Rick Webb made final checks of *Water Baby*'s mechanical and electrical systems. He was just about ready to cast off. Although the boat was equipped with an electronic fume detector, for his own peace of mind he always liked to sniff for gasoline fumes at the bilge blower discharge vent just to be sure. The presence of heavier-than-air gasoline fumes in the engine compartment could cause a deadly explosion at the invitation of a single stray spark. And on the sixty-year-old engine, an occasional spark from a loose ignition wire was not impossible. Smelling nothing abnormal, he was satisfied that he could start it up without undue risk to life and limb.

The four-cylinder Graymarine engine turned over slowly, but fired, caught and ran with its usual unfailing reliability. After easing the choke back in and setting the throttle to a medium idle, Webb looked over the transom to make sure that water was being pumped through the cooling system and out the exhaust. One more trip down into the cabin verified the battery charging rate was normal. At the same time, he settled at the navigating station to make a radio call.

"Thunder Bay Coast Guard Radio, Thunder Bay Coast Guard Radio, this is *Water Baby*, *Water Baby* on channel sixteen, over."

A brief pause, and then the reply, "*Water Baby this is Thunder Bay Coast Guard Radio, switch and answer on channel two-six please, over.*"

"Channel two-six, roger." Webb replied before switching channels.

"*Water Baby this is Thunder Bay Coast Guard Radio. How might we help you sir? Over.*" The radio operator's voice could have come right out of a BBC radio newscast — a clear, gentlemanly English accent. Rick smiled to himself. He'd spoken to this voice often before. No name or face came with it, but if you spent as much time on boats as Webb did, hearing a familiar marine radio operator's voice was like having a friend aboard.

"I'd like to file a sailing plan please. Are you ready to copy? Over," Webb replied. The Canadian Coast Guard had introduced sailing plans a number of years earlier, as much for its own benefit as for the boaters it serves. Searches for missing pleasure boats could be started in a timely manner and could be concentrated close to the route specified in the sailing plan, rather than waiting until a vessel was reported overdue days later. Although it was a voluntary program, Webb felt it would be foolhardy for anyone not to take advantage of it, particularly anyone sailing alone and at night.

"*Stand by one moment Water Baby while I pull up your file, over.*"

"Roger, standing by." Webb used the brief pause to

reach out into the cockpit and push the throttle lever down. The engine settled to a slow idle. Everything was running properly.

"*Water Baby this is Thunder Bay, over.*"

"Go ahead Thunder Bay."

"*Let's first confirm your vessel details Mr. Webb.*" From a computer monitor the operator began to read information previously provided by Webb. "*You are a thirty-seven-foot, steel-hulled sailing yawl, hull is middle blue with white cabin top. Decks and masts are natural wood finish, and you have a white dinghy aboard.*" These details could provide helpful identification information in the event of an aerial search and rescue operation.

The operator continued, "*If there are no changes to this information sir, could you please give me the details for the sailing plan you are filing at this time? Over.*"

"Roger Thunder Bay, there are no changes to the vessel description. There is one person aboard. I'm departing Parry Sound at this time and my destination is Killarney. Approximate ETA at Killarney is 0600 local time tomorrow. Over."

The coast guard operator confirmed the plan and wished him well. Webb signed off and returned the radio tuner to channel 16, the frequency used to contact other vessels and listen for emergency messages. He turned down the volume sufficiently to minimize the annoyance factor caused by the frequent chatter from the many pleasure boats on the water that hot summer afternoon.

July 20, 1420

From his place at the tiller, Rick Webb stepped down on the shift lever to engage reverse gear. *Water Baby* slowly began to ease back out of her slip. Once clear of the dock he tugged up on the lever to select forward gear, and the thrust created by the idling engine gradually checked the sternward motion of the yacht's eighteen thousand pounds. With the rudder turned hard to port, the eye-catching Dutch built yawl slowly turned away from the finger dock and gently gathered speed toward the harbour exit. The soft purr from her engine and the gentle burble of the small wave pushed aside by her graceful bow were the only sounds she made.

Once clear of the inner harbour, he increased the engine speed. *Water Baby* soon reached her normal engine-powered cruising speed of five knots, cutting a straight line across the glass-calm waters of Parry Sound.

Webb was a single man, but not by choice; he had been widowed eight years earlier. It had taken him until he was twenty-five to meet the right woman — someone who could willingly accept the unpredictable lifestyle of a conservation officer's wife. In her mid-twenties as well, Melanie had easily adapted to his frequent irregular shifts. And they weren't shifts with regular start and finish times like at a hospital, fire hall or police station. He could just as easily start work at three in the morning as any other time of day or night. It all depended on the time of the year, and who was poaching what, when and where.

Melanie had been an elementary school teacher, specializing in environmental studies. As well as having her own full-time grade three class, she was always in demand to make presentations to the other grades in the school. Whenever Webb brought home an orphaned wildlife critter he or a member of the public had rescued, Mel would fit him into the following day's lesson plan. The whole school would gather in the auditorium and the children always gave Webb their rapt attention when he showed up with snakes, turtles, herons or bear cubs. Even with the gymnasium packed with 300 children, you could have heard a pin drop.

He and Mel were nowhere near the end of their honeymoon period when she had been tragically killed in a highway crash just two winters after they married. She had been on her way back from the doctor's office with the wonderful news that she was expecting their first child.

The accident had left him devastated. It had taken him more than a year to recover from her loss and begin to resume anything near a normal lifestyle. And Webb knew that his life could never be truly normal again without Mel.

Though he was well past the mourning stage now eight years on, he still couldn't find it in himself to become attached to another woman — couldn't risk falling deeply in love; in love and always fearing that through some cruel twist of fate he could lose another sweetheart one day. He also felt that entering a new relationship would be a betrayal to Melanie's memory.

Rick now lived alone in an old Victorian frame home on a pleasant tree-lined street not far from the Parry Sound waterfront. He'd bought it as a distraction several years after Mel's death, and on his own he'd tackled a number of major renovations. At the same time, he threw himself vigorously back into his work, even outperforming his own high standards from before. Over time, he gradually restored his social ties, curling in the winters and playing pick-up softball during the summer months. But life was still empty without his sweetheart to share it with.

After Melanie's death Webb had owned a dog. Bought as another distraction, Jettie was a loveable, well-behaved female black Lab. But as faithful as only a dog can be, she was too dependent on the full-time attention that he just couldn't provide on his own.

It turned out that a cat, discovered quite by accident,

was a far more compatible pet for a single man in his line of work. Heywood, a big grey tabby, gained his name after Webb had found him as a kitten, cold, wet and abandoned, several years earlier. He had stopped for lunch on the island of the same name at the northwestern corner of Georgian Bay. When the bedraggled lost kitten wandered down the beach toward him, the officer took an immediate liking to the little orphan, and it adapted quickly to life as a sea cat.

Now, equipped with the latest in bulk feeding hoppers and feline water fountains — as well as a self-cleaning litter tray — the tomcat was perfectly content to be left at home, unattended for a few days at a time as Webb's work often demanded. And when they were together, the cat seemed to know when to be close and friendly, and when to remain aloof. That worked for Webb, as did the cat's love of catching the mice that plagued his old house and the nasty deer flies that invade most boats during the hot days of summer. At the moment though, Heywood was fast asleep, curled up on a cockpit seat cushion.

The breeze generated by the boat's progress through the hot afternoon air did little to ease the heat. But Webb held out hope that once he got out on the open waters of Georgian Bay, the lake would exert its normal cooling effect and conditions would become bearable at least. For the moment though, the pleasure of being in charge of his own ship again pushed physical discomfort to the back of his mind. Protected from the bright sun by a canvas awning over the cockpit, Webb was enjoying the sixteen-nautical-mile run down the sound toward the open shoal-free water past Red Rock light.

Working strictly from memory, he applied minor course corrections that kept *Water Baby* clear of a variety of navigational hazards, both visible and submerged. The eastern shore of Lake Huron's Georgian Bay was not only where he played, but it was also Rick Webb's workplace.

As an ECO, his duties included more than just the traditional activities of a conservation officer. Since the merger of the two government ministries, his workload now also included enforcement of a variety of environmental protection regulations. And while senior management had tacked the 'Environmental' tag in front of his traditional 'Conservation Officer' job title, they were still called COs, conservation officers or game wardens by almost everyone.

Webb and his fellow officers were trained to be proficient operators of a fleet of speedy, thirty-two-foot patrol vessels they used to cover vast stretches of the Great Lakes. These were sturdy, welded aluminum workboats with upgraded performance and enforcement packages. They were not pretty boats, but the officers wouldn't have traded them for anything else.

Webb's regular patrol routine during the past spring and much of the previous winter however, had been seriously curtailed by a number of investigations into major environmental contamination. Such cases required a great deal of time to investigate and prosecute. Yesterday's case against Mid-Con Waste was just one of several such labour-intensive projects. As he automatically guided his beloved craft out toward Georgian Bay, his mind strayed back once more to the unhappy demise of the Mid-Con case and all the hard work that had gone into his investigation.

'No, you're on vacation. You're not going to think about that,' he tried coaching himself. But it can be difficult to stop a person so entirely dedicated to their vocation from reflecting on the important issues of the workplace — even while on vacation.

July 20, 1500

The self-unloading bulk carrier *Blue Mountain* left the Straits of Mackinac passing under the guns of the historic fort on Mackinac Island, Michigan. She was sailing eastbound with minimal ballast, bound for the quarry dock on McGregor Bay in Lake Huron's North Channel. There she would take on a load of crushed stone for delivery to Midland, Ontario.

Six-hundred and forty feet long with a beam of seventy-two feet, the fifty-five-year-old lake freighter's ten thousand horsepower diesel was pushing her toward her destination at a steady fifteen knots. When loaded, she would require twenty-five feet of water depth, just to float free of the bottom.

July 20, 1605

Erin Franklin had been brought up from her storeroom prison to Reiger's office an hour ago. She was given a meal brought in from a fast food franchise, although judging from the fact that the chicken burger and soggy fries were as cold as Reiger's heart, it had obviously arrived some time before she was brought from the basement.

She wasn't alone. Gant had left Dwayne Goreham, self-proclaimed lady's man and the third member of his security team, to watch over her. And watch her he did. Having this goon ogling her the way he did made Erin feel violated. Although he was considerably smaller than Gant, he was still built like a brick wall and she didn't relish the thought of having to defend herself against him, if he became 'amorous.'

She was saved from that indignity by the commencement of another. Gant came back into the office and proceeded to bind her ankles and wrists with duct tape. Then he flung her over his shoulder in something resembling a fireman's carry and walked down the back hallway into the large warehouse area.

Without so much as an explanation, he placed her into the trunk of a full-sized car, giving her no chance to glance at a licence plate or even identify the make of the vehicle. The only intelligence she could gather was that it was so large it had to be from the 1980s or earlier, and the trunk compartment was very dusty. Before closing the trunk lid, Gant taped her mouth with the single comment, "I wouldn't want you drawing any attention to us."

4. LADY M

When Erin was pulled out of the trunk of the car, she was on the verge of heat exhaustion. She had been bound and immobile in the sauna-like temperatures of the old car's trunk during the entire three-hour drive north from Toronto. Only by a supreme effort of willpower, and only by the slimmest of margins at that, had she been able to keep herself from vomiting in the stifling heat. That would have been a guaranteed death sentence with the duct tape gag still firmly over her mouth. She was shaking badly and couldn't even stand. It was not out of compassion that Gant carried her quickly into the small office building; he simply didn't want the rest of the world to see her out in the open, not that there was anyone nearby but his own people. After removing her bindings, he helped her into a single-stall washroom where she was allowed to freshen up — in a manner of speaking.

The dingy little room had no window from which she could make a break — not that she had the strength at that point. While gingerly peeling the duct tape from her mouth, she ran the tap water to let it cool, and hopefully clear a little. The water was heavily tinted the orangey-red colour of iron, however she couldn't taste the iron for the overpowering sulphurous stench, and even that went largely unnoticed as she raced to quench her raging thirst. Before she considered herself anywhere near ready, Gant ordered her back out into the main office area. Willard Reiger was in the room with him, and it appeared that the two of them had just finished discussing something related to her imprisonment, for the conversation tailed off immediately. Reiger gave her the briefest of glances before turning and walking out the door, the gesture, an unspoken call to action.

Escorted by Gant and Goreham, Erin was led on a brief, forced march across several sets of railroad tracks in a weed covered rail yard. The place was most notable for its towering mountains of empty steel drums. Leaving the tracks behind, they marched her out onto a sturdy old timber dock. Barely able to walk without assistance, she was hurried across a flat-decked barge, which was heavily loaded with pallets of more drums. She guessed that some of these would be the same ones she'd been drawing samples from when she'd been grabbed two days earlier.

A big step down from the high side of the barge put her on the deck of a tired-looking black and white tugboat. A shabby orange life-ring was hanging on the side of the rust-streaked deckhouse. Faded black lettering on the life-ring read 'Lady M.'

No time was given to touring the ship. Instead, Erin was hastily ushered into what she initially thought was a darkened cabin. It was a rather rude awakening, though not a surprise, to discover that it was just another windowless storeroom, known in nautical terms as a locker. It was even hotter in there than it had been out in the sun, though not quite as bad as in the trunk of the car. Mounted in the deckhead was a pair of ventilators, no more than six inches diameter. But with the tug tied motionless to the dock on that hot summer evening, she could feel absolutely no air flowing through them. At least this time she'd not been bound and gagged — yet. With the noise of the tug's generator and the main engine, which had begun to throb just as she was ushered aboard, she assumed that Reiger's people weren't worried about her being heard by any passers-by.

In the pitch-darkness caused by the hastily closed door-like hatch, she felt her way along the bulkhead to find something she had glimpsed just before the hatch had slammed shut. In a moment, her searching hands came to an unfamiliar box on the wall about the size of a household light switch box, but it didn't feel like any light switch that she had ever seen before. What she didn't realize was that it was a shielded switch, used in locations where a spark might cause explosive fumes to ignite. Historically this had been the ship's paint storage locker — not that either the tug or the locker had seen any paint for quite some time. After a moment of trial and error, she found that pushing upward on a plunger at the bottom of the box turned on a light — of sorts.

The caged bulb, which Noah may well have used on the Ark at one time, was coated in grime. Nonetheless it lit up the locker well enough to see that there wasn't much there but a dirty old tarpaulin heaped on the deck. Too exhausted to care about anything at that point, Erin didn't continue to explore the small compartment, but instead lay down on the tarp and drifted into a troubled and uncomfortable sleep.

July 20, 1930

The tug *Lady M* slowly manoeuvred the heavily loaded barge away from the tar-coated timbers of the wooden pier. As the initial sternward momentum carried the two vessels out into the channel, two of the crewmembers cast off the lines securing the barge along the tug's starboard side. The eighty-five-foot tug turned to move to its towing position a short distance ahead. After idling slowly downstream to take up the slack in the towing hawser, the tug's old diesel responded easily to the call for ahead-one-third and the bulky 100-foot barge sluggishly turned to follow. As with many tugs still currently in service, *Lady M* was built in the early twentieth century — 1912 in her case — and had been given a major refit in the 1960s. Part of that rebuild had included replacing her original steam engine with a brand new 600 horsepower diesel. Though not as powerful as a modern tug, she was built to work hard, not fast.

In the wheelhouse, Mike Small (his surname belying his grossly overweight six-foot frame) was not a happy man. It had been a long day. The crew was dog-tired, having worked at loading the barge through the worst of the afternoon's sweltering heat. Due to a foul-up in the rail delivery schedule, the arrival of more than half of their cargo had been delayed. The tug was sailing six hours later than originally planned and Reiger himself had driven up from Toronto to go along on this crossing. It was going to be a bad trip.

Now well into his sixties, Small was originally from Flint, Michigan. He had spent most of his childhood playing between the banks of the Flint River where it flowed near his family home. There he had captained various watercraft ranging from a log raft — every kid's first ship — to canoes and rowboats, and eventually a variety of powered runabouts, each bigger and more powerful than the last. During the Vietnam conflict, while still in his early twenties, Small given command of a US Navy Swift Boat. On one patrol on the Mekong River, he had pulled a wounded and very frightened marine private, named Willard Reiger, out of a bloody firefight. He was the lone survivor of an entire platoon. Years later, Reiger had returned the favour when he eventually tracked down Small, working a dead-end job managing a rundown motel on the outskirts of Detroit. The offer of a position as tugboat captain couldn't have been a better reward as far as Small was concerned.

At first it was a dream job. The pay was decent — really good when you considered the modest benefits package it came with — and life in Canada seemed to have more promise than anything he'd tried on the other side of the friendly border. Spring, summer and fall were spent out on the lake; then with the tug decommissioned for the winter months he was free to do whatever he wanted until the ice left Georgian Bay the following spring.

For most of the past thirteen years, the *Lady M* had been towing legitimate cargos of hazardous waste to Alpena, Michigan, on the western shores of Lake Huron. Everything had always been on the up and up until two years ago when these special runs of Reiger's had started. Since then, everything had changed. The friendship between Small and Reiger was wearing thin — very thin indeed. Small had seen Reiger, who had always been a type 'A' personality at the best of times, become increasingly obsessed with moving more product and cutting more corners; always looking to increase his company's profit margin. Despite insisting on stringent standards of upkeep for Mid-Con's road-vehicle fleet, the maintenance budget for Small's beloved tug had been slashed. He had given up the annual spring repainting job just to cover the cost of subsistence level mechanical maintenance.

As for the 'special runs,' Small was now in it up to his ears along with the rest of them. It really galled him that rather than walking away from trouble at the outset, he'd allowed himself to be bullied into taking that first illegal load as a favour to his old friend — on the belief that it was a one-time deal.

Now, this was the sixth time that Reiger had assigned him the same disagreeable task. After the first run, Small had argued at length that they would all be in big trouble if it was discovered that Mid-Con Waste had handled and transported hazardous waste materials not listed on its licence. And that would be nothing compared to the potential penalties for the illegal dumping.

Reiger had taken the fight out of him early on by reminding him that his own involvement might be of great interest to the authorities, tainting his application for Canadian citizenship. So here he was, thoroughly stuck between the proverbial rock and the hard place.

The company's security chief and his three goons, who Reiger preferred to call loaders, had always accompanied the additional cargos of unlicensed toxins. The boss claimed that they were trained to handle and dispose of hazardous waste and were therefore a necessary addition to the crew. But Small knew that they were really there to make sure that he and his crew followed orders. The same quartet was along on this trip of course.

However, all of that paled in comparison to the new complications regarding tonight's run — situations that really raised red flags in the tug skipper's conscience. For starters, Reiger had brought aboard a young woman who didn't look at all pleased about the prospect of a lake crossing this evening. Small was most unhappy that she was being accommodated in the aft storage locker, as opposed to staying in a cabin. In addition to that was his observation that Reiger's goons had brought along some firepower this time. They'd never done that before; at least not that he was aware of.

Finally, to top it all off, there was Reiger's instruction to lie over an extra day in an anchorage at one of the small islands southeast of Manitoulin. They would be meeting someone out there on a business matter. He wouldn't elaborate beyond that, but as far as Mike Small was concerned, with the summer pleasure boat traffic running at its peak, it amounted to hanging out a sign saying, *There's Something Fishy Going on Here.*'

'Some friend Reiger turned out to be,' Small thought to himself. 'I save his skinny marine ass in 'Nam and he turns me into a bloody lootenant in his fuckin' band of outlaws. This run has all the makin's of a cruise up Shit Creek, and tugs don't carry no paddles.'

The tug skipper's attention returned to the present as young Billy Manion, the stocky, blond helmsman, was cautiously guiding the tug with her tow into a narrow stretch of the channel. Manion and Small were the only ones in the tug's wheelhouse at the moment. Two cabin cruisers, travelling side by side, were lazily idling upstream toward them. They were occupying most of the centre of the river.

"Keep your place in the channel Manion," Small growled as he pulled down on the air horn lanyard, giving one loud blast. Even if the pleasure boat skippers didn't know that the horn signalled 'I'm keeping to my right,' its sheer volume, plus the steady advance of the tug and its forty-foot-wide barge promptly convinced the two cruiser skippers to take shelter close to the granite walls that formed the banks of the Magnetawan River — one on each side of the river! Obviously at least one of them didn't know the meaning of the single blast.

"Boneheads," muttered Small.

"This old lady don't take shit from no one," Billy grinned, giving the cruiser captains a one-fingered salute as the *Lady M* squeezed impolitely between them.

Billy was from Byng Inlet, just across the river from Britt. As a teenager he had been one of those boys who was always seeking new adventures and usually running close to the edge of the law. He wasn't a bad kid — he was just filled with that sense of youthful immortality typical of his age. He had hired on with *Lady M* as crew just before he turned twenty, and Small had immediately noticed in him a real aptitude for handling the tug — another river rat like himself. As a result, Manion had spent most of his on-duty watches at the wheel since joining three years before. Mike was approaching retirement in a few years and had been grooming the boy for eventual promotion to mate — not that the future was very clear for any of them anymore.

July 20, 2100

 Lady M moved out of the Magnetawan River onto the calm waters of Georgian Bay, where along the coast, permanently wind-bent pine trees cling to low granite islands worn smooth by glaciation. As if painted by a famous Group of Seven artist, the whole scene was bathed in a warm orange glow from the hazy evening sun. The air carried a mixture of nostalgic summertime fragrances — pine, balsam and sun-baked moss — plus, of course, the tug's own pungent contribution of fuel oil and diesel exhaust.

 'All this beauty,' thought Small despairingly, 'and everything I'm doing here could destroy it.' Despite the heat, he felt cold inside. He prayed that the drums wouldn't be eaten through by corrosion before he could figure a way to undo his misdeeds, preferably without getting caught in the process.

 "Let out the tow now skipper?" Billy could see his boss's mind was distracted from the job at hand. It was an increasingly frequent occurrence of late.

 "Uh, yeah sure," Small nodded, then leaning toward the intercom box, he keyed the mic. "Mate to the wheelhouse."

 Ray Ethier entered the wheelhouse just as the tow dropped back 200 yards behind the tug. The diesel was working up to the revolutions needed to drag the barge through the water at six knots.

"Those goons done eating yet Ray?" Small asked. Reiger's loaders had taken over the crew's dining area to wolf down a big dinner.

"Charlie's 'bout to t'row dem out now," Ethier responded with a decidedly northern Ontario French accent.

The short wiry French Canadian from Timmins had worked for years on tugs during the short shipping seasons up on James and Hudson Bays before joining *Lady M*. He had arrived on *Lady M* the same year that Small had come aboard. He knew the business inside out, and was an avid amateur radio operator as well — a by-product of his years in the lonely sub-arctic region.

"Well, get our guys chowed down, and grab a bite yourself. You go now too Billy. Oh, where's the boss?"

"Ee's moved into your cabin. Charlie moved your stuff in wit' us guys in de h'admiralty suite." Ethier was referring to a dog-eared cabin occupied, under normal circumstances, by everyone except the skipper, who by rights, had a private and slightly less dog-eared cabin to himself.

Cat's paw ripples scuffed the calm water ahead as a breeze began to sweep over the bay. In the few minutes it took Mike Small to tune in and digest the marine weather forecast, the breeze had already picked up from the southwest to around eight of the twenty knots anticipated by midnight. It was predicted to veer to northwest after the passage of a series of rain squalls. That would make the planned off-loading of the illicit portion of their cargo either difficult or impossible when they arrived at the drop zone. The tug would have to be pointed into the northwest wind in order to hold the barge over the site. Unfortunately, there would be a substantial beam sea still running, the residual effect of an evening's worth of strong southwest wind.

Despite its width, the heavily loaded barge would roll badly, making it impossible to use the small forklift to unload the pallets. And if the forklift couldn't handle the job, Reiger's loading goons would be even worse off — that at least was a warming thought. However, their loss could neither be guaranteed, nor legally helpful in the long run.

If he informed Reiger of the changing weather before it was necessary, Small knew that the boss would order the stuff over the side into deep water long before they got to his dumping site. That would not do.

Small had picked a trench in the shoal waters over Dawson Rock specifically because at thirty-five feet, it was shallow enough to be able to easily retrieve the barrels once he figured out the salvage details. Of equal importance was the fact that there was pretty well no chance of being discovered by commercial fishermen there. Centred ten miles east of Lonely Island, the four-mile-wide, boulder-strewn shoal made it virtually impossible to set or haul a gill net without getting it snagged — it was one area of Georgian Bay that the commercial fish tugs never worked. It was also too exposed and too far offshore to be of much interest to the sport fishing fleet, and there were no known shipwrecks to attract the attention of recreational divers.

So telling Reiger of the impending weather would have to wait. How long he could delay, Small could only guess. Combined with the chop raised by the headwind as well as the force of wind itself, the drag on the barge had increased enough to drop their speed by almost a third of a knot already.

July 20, 2130

Rick Webb woke to the exhilarating sound of water rushing

past *Water Baby*'s hull as she surged forward under a freshening breeze. It was nearly dark, and he could feel the warm night air that entered the forward hatch blowing across his face. He lay half-asleep in the pilot berth on the starboard side of the salon, revelling in the comforting sound of the Georgian Bay water hissing along the waterline of the steel hull. It brought back happy memories of the naps he would grab when he and Melanie would take alternating watches so they could get up to the North Channel in one passage. That way they had more time to idle away in the waters around the Benjamin Islands.

Suddenly he sat bolt upright, alarmed. He hurriedly checked the time on the antique clock mounted on the cabin's forward bulkhead.

"Shit, I've been asleep! Damn, over two hours."

Webb flew up the companionway steps and tumbled into the cockpit, painfully banging a knee in his rush to check on the whereabouts of his boat. If the wind direction had significantly changed in that time, at the six knots *Water Baby* was now making, his pride and joy could be headed for disaster at any moment on the rocky shoals of Georgian Bay's eastern shore.

A quick look at the depth sounder showed eighty feet and peering forward, then to starboard and to port, he saw no above water obstacles in the half-mile of visibility that the hazy twilight provided. Even before reading the compass, Webb was relieved to note, by the relative position of the newly risen moon, that *Water Baby* was still headed roughly northwest, steering herself in the direction that he wanted to go, solely by the balanced trim of her sails.

He was disturbed that he could have slept so soundly. A couple of hours before sunset he'd simply gone below to escape the sun's glare for a few minutes. Normally a master of the ten-minute power nap, Webb figured that the final release from his recent work-related stresses must have overridden his internal nap timer. His mistake had been lying down to relax on the pilot berth.

"Good old ship," he muttered to himself, patting the cabin top affectionately as he began completing the chores neglected during his unscheduled absence from command. After turning on the running lights, he put on a pot of coffee to brew, and since he was unable to see any shore lights or navigation aids, he switched on the GPS receiver to establish a position fix. He normally preferred to navigate the traditional way by dead reckoning — taking bearings on known features and plotting the results onto his paper charts. But the GPS was truly an asset at a moment like this.

While waiting for the unit to locate enough satellites to determine its position, Webb gazed nostalgically at the navigating station. Set into nooks and shelves around the chart table, was an array of old, but theoretically functional receivers. *Water Baby* had been fully equipped with the oldest possible pieces of the 'latest technology' when he had bought her in 2001, but since it all worked and now contributed to the museum-like appearance of the boat, he didn't want to remove any of it. The radio direction finder, a relic from the 1950s, had been made obsolete back in the '90s when the last navigational radio beacons had been discontinued, though one could still get a rough position fix by tuning in to AM broadcast stations. The Loran-C had become obsolete a few years later when that land-based navigation system was shut down for good. And the GPS receiver that came with the boat was from an earlier generation too. It hadn't the electronic mapping capabilities of the modern units, but it still functioned just fine.

He regularly used the latest versions of GPS equipment, complete with radar interlink, on his government patrol boat and he really enjoyed the touch-screen charting capabilities of the upgrade models. But as long as this basic unit continued to work, he felt that replacing it would be a betrayal of his minimalist principles of pleasure boat sailing. Besides, owning a boat was costly enough as it was without buying more gadgets before they were needed.

The final pieces of marine electronics were two VHF marine frequency radio transceivers. The yawl's previous owner, an airline pilot, believed in redundant systems for that extra measure of safety. To the navigator's right, mounted on the aft bulkhead of the compartment, were all the ship's electric power switches and circuit breakers as well as several analog meters for reading battery state and charging rates. The visual effect of so much antiquated electronic gear in the confined space of the cabin made the navigating station resemble the control room of a World War II submarine — at least it did in his mind. However, a U-boat's interior wouldn't have been lined, like *Water Baby*'s, with cream-coloured panelling, framed in varnished mahogany.

Heywood, the ship's cat, was settled comfortably on the chart table as was his custom when the yawl was under way at night. "Hey there cat, if you're going to occupy the space, you could at least assume some of the responsibilities. Now get off there and let me see where the GPS places us." Figuring it was better to talk to an animal than to himself, he set the big tom on top of the companionway step.

"Okay, latitude 45° 33.0' north, longitude 80° 47.5' west puts … us … about … there," he said, transposing the receiver's readout onto the large Georgian Bay chart. "In layman's terms Heywood, we're about twelve miles off of Pointe au Baril." The wind had moved them nine miles while he had slept; about four and a half knots average speed. They had been making that speed before he slept, so Webb reasoned that it must have been the wind picking up and the resulting increase of the ship's speed to six knots that had so recently brought him back from his dreams. He recorded the new position in the logbook, right after the entry noting that he had finally been able to set the sails in a light wind after clearing South Limestone Island. That welcome change came only after motoring twenty miles out from the marina in Parry Sound in total calm.

Webb poured himself a coffee, black, and then retrieved his safety harness from the wet-gear hanging locker just forward of the chart table. He made his way back up to the cockpit, buckling on the harness as he went and snapping the other end of its lanyard to a heavy padeye bolted to the cabin top. He was now tethered to the boat with enough line to move about the cockpit and forward to the main mast, but not quite enough to fall over the lifelines on either side if he lost his balance on the shifting deck.

Preparing to rig the boat for night sailing, Webb started the engine and used it to power into the wind. In less than five minutes he had reefed the mainsail down to a smaller, more prudent size. Back at the tiller, he shut down the engine and allowed *Water Baby*'s bow to fall back on her original tack to the northwest. Now on the right heading, he cranked in some of the big genoa with the roller-reefing winch and played with the trim of the sail until the tiller pulled neither to one side nor the other. With occasional tweaking to the set of the small mizzen sail behind him, the old yawl would steer itself once more.

Satisfied that all was in order, Webb perched himself on his homemade helmsman's stool on the port side cockpit coaming. From there he could keep watch in all directions for any approaching vessels. Facing a long night on watch, he drained his mug and poured himself another coffee. Killarney was still at least eight hours away.

July 20, 2150

Ray Ethier had just arrived to take the next two-hour watch in the wheelhouse of *Lady M* as the tug's skipper turned up the volume on the VHF radio to catch a sécurité call being broadcast from the far limits of the radio's receiving range.

"... *the bulk carrier Blue Mountain is eastbound, entering Main Channel off of Cove Island in fifteen min ... (static) ... winds southwest twenty, gusting much higher during rain squalls ... (static) ...ountain out.*"

"Not good Ray," Small groaned. "We're down to barely five knots. We'll never be able to do the drop over Dawson Rock if the wind veers northwest. What's Reiger up to?"

"Dey moved de woman to your cabin h'after we pass h'out of de river, so 'ees in watching h'over 'er. Doesn't know dat de wind, she might shift." Ethier knew the score, and though he was worried about Reiger's plans for their female passenger, he was equally concerned that the toxins be delivered to the right place. While he was no fan of excessive government regulations, he knew that they had been absolutely wrong to start using the lake as a waste dump. "What do you t'ink you do Mike?"

"Best I can think of for now is we see what the conditions are like when we get over the shoal... maybe it won't be as bad as we think. At least once the wind has shifted, conditions will be the same everywhere out here, so we won't be able to drop the stuff anywhere. And if it's a no go, we'll have to put in at Club Island for the night. That plays into his hand, so it may not be hard to sell him on going straight there without dumping. Whoever it is he's meeting, it's supposed to happen out in one of these coves. And I've got a sick feeling that this so-called meeting has everything to do with that girl. Have you or any of the crew had a chance to speak to her?"

"No. Reiger and 'is goons keep 'er away from h'us. I h'ask de guys to keep h'an eye for 'er, but wit'out de guns der's not'ing we can do."

"Yeah, this whole pile of shit we're in really stinks. Anyhow, if we don't drop the product off tonight, we'll have to wait and see what the next night brings. If you have any other ideas, I'm all ears. And whatever he's got planned for that young woman, it's sure not looking good. This whole situation could go south for all of us in an instant."

A pause, then Ethier replied, "I h'agree. I'll t'ink on it while I do my watch. Got to be somet'ing we can do to 'elp de woman."

July 20, 2155

Having picked up the sécurité call made by *Blue Mountain* just moments before, Rick Webb took a second reef in the mainsail and further shortened the genoa as well. With the wind likely to pick up to twenty knots in the next hour or so, it would be much easier to do now than after the wind speed increased.

His caution caused *Water Baby*'s speed to drop to just under five knots. But that didn't concern Webb. He knew that when the wind speed increased, he'd have his six knots of boat speed back, and then some. *Water Baby* had been designed to sail in the North Sea where pleasure sailors considered a twenty-knot wind to be an everyday sailing breeze.

Knowing that rainsqualls often herald a shift in wind direction, Webb switched the VHF radio over to the marine weather channel. The forecast was just as he had suspected. The wind shift would mean that on his present course, he would end up either tacking close hauled, or motoring straight into the wind to get to Killarney.

Reminding himself of his promise to go wherever the

wind comfortably took him, he began to plot his strategy for the rest of the night. Seeing that he was presently cruising easily on a beam reach, which was the yawl's fastest and most comfortable point of sail, he would hold his present course until the wind actually shifted. Then, depending on how far up the bay he was able to advance before the wind started blowing out of the northwest, he would turn either northeast toward the Bustard Islands, or southwest toward Club Island. He knew Georgian Bay well enough that he could visualize either route in his mind and didn't need to plot it on the chart until the time came to make a decision.

July 20, 2210

The southwest wind, which had been building over northern Lake Huron all evening, was now averaging twenty knots as the bulk carrier *Blue Mountain* approached Main Channel, the largest of several shipping lanes between Lake Huron and Georgian Bay. Several minor rainsqualls had already overtaken the ship in the past half hour.

Captain Lorne Henry arrived on the bridge in time to observe his new second officer, Don Latham, handle the high-riding ship through the passage.

"Captain on the bridge!" barked the helmsman.

"Spent way too long in the navy, Thompson," said Henry, smiling at the man's simulated act of naval procedure. The likeable crewman had to be the most irrepressible character on the old laker. "Just steer the damned boat," he chuckled as he turned to address the second mate.

"How is it going Mr. Latham?"

"I hope you don't mind sir, but during the heavy rain showers I couldn't get a real good picture of some of the low-lying islands on the radar. So with the poor visibility and the wind getting up, I decided not to go through Yeo Channel as you had originally planned. We're on a heading for Main Channel sir. We just passed West Sister light buoy five minutes ago and we're on a heading of 090°."

"Hmm… you should have called me," the captain grumbled. "But your re-routing decision was wise all the same. We wouldn't want to crab sideways in that narrow passage if a sudden squall hit us just then. Ship's owners probably wouldn't approve if we came to grief on a rock in there."

As the captain was speaking, another brief squall lashed a deluge of rain hard against the starboard side of the wheelhouse. Visibility ahead of the lake freighter fell to little more than a few yards. The high-riding ship actually heeled over a few degrees, shuddering momentarily in the gusty onslaught and it yawed off course slightly before the auto-helm brought it back again.

"The 'possible showers' predicted in the evening forecast appear to have become a reality, Mr. Latham. Perhaps we should announce ourselves," the captain suggested.

"Already made the sécurité call sir, about twenty minutes ago. Actually, the last outbound ferry to South Baymouth immediately responded that he'd just cleared the channel. Caught him on the radar but we couldn't see him for the rain."

"Very well then, carry on." Henry casually hoisted himself up into the captain's chair to the left of the helmsman's position. Having an extra set of experienced eyes on the bridge was the prudent thing to do in these conditions.

July 20, 2315

Water Baby had just emerged from a brief rainsquall. Rick Webb was pleased he had the mainsail double-reefed well before the weather front had arrived. As predicted, the wind had increased to twenty knots, if not more. He'd rolled the genoa into what he liked to call a handkerchief sized foresail. *Water Baby* was still surging along on her northwesterly course, making an easy six and a half knots with the wind still on her port beam.

He watched as several miles off his starboard bow, light loomed on the horizon through the departing squall. It soon became apparent that the light was from a westbound ship. It was headed across *Water Baby*'s path. Over the next five minutes the ship's lights lay along the same relative bearing but were getting perceptibly brighter. The two vessels were on a collision course, and because the larger one had the right-of-way, Webb prepared to turn and pass behind it.

Easing the mainsheet, he let the wind swing the yawl's head to starboard, a little bit downwind. He steered his new course intending to pass close astern of the ship, which he now estimated to be approximately a mile away.

As the distance between the two vessels closed, two things became readily apparent. In fact, aided by a series of short loud blasts from the ship's horn, they became alarmingly apparent. The first was that although the ship was much smaller than Webb had originally anticipated, it was now very close indeed. In fact, it was less than fifty yards away. The second and of even greater concern, this ship was a tug, and only just at that moment, the barge it was towing heaved into view. It was made visible more by the white foaming wave pushed ahead of its blunt bow than by the feeble running lights it displayed. *Water Baby* was headed toward certain destruction under the bow of the barge if he didn't act fast.

Rather than turning hard to port into the wind and going about, Webb opted for a downwind jibe to starboard. Although at his present speed the manoeuvre would initially carry him still closer to the oncoming barge, this option was decidedly better than risking the genoa being back winded and the boat going into irons — stalling — in the path of the approaching steel wall.

Webb's quick manoeuvre was rewarded with success, though it wasn't pretty. The genoa momentarily hung up on the forestay almost refusing to change sides. But with the mainsail and mizzen free to change sides unaided by the skipper, *Water Baby* finished the jibe and pulled clear, out of the path of the towed barge with almost ten yards to spare. The tug was still angrily hooting its horn even after the danger was past.

In the glow of *Water Baby*'s running lights, Webb recognized the faded corporate logo on the barge as it passed — Mid-Con Waste.

"Those bastards," he muttered, mad at himself for not interpreting the situation correctly in the first place — and at Mid-Con for — well, just for being who they were.

July 20, 2318

Ray Ethier had been alone in the wheelhouse of the tug and had just finished unwrapping a fresh pack of smokes. He was lighting a new cigarette when he first noticed the running lights of a sailboat less than a mile off the port bow. He watched with some amusement at first as the approaching yacht appeared to take its time reacting to the fact that the tug was the stand on vessel — had the right of way.

But the humour had quickly evaporated as the first mate watched the sailboat, a ghostly outline in the darkness, alter its course to take it just astern of the tug. It would definitely not clear the tow if it continued on that course.

A sickening feeling came over him as he grasped the

lanyard and gave a series of urgent short blasts on the tug's horn. He held his breath and hauled back on the throttle as the imperilled yacht turned toward the tow in a desperate bid to escape. Just when it looked as if the barge was going to plow right over the small boat, she pulled clear and quickly passed down its port side, disappearing back into the night.

The tug was just coming back up to speed and the mate was still muttering his thoughts about how pleasure boaters should stick to day sailing when Small burst into the wheelhouse, followed closely by Willard Reiger and Billy Manion.

"What the hell's goin' on Ray?" demanded the skipper.

"I h'am jus' giving seamanship lessons to a weekend warrior, Mike," he said, filling in the highlights of the close encounter.

"Where are we now?" The terse inquiry from Reiger made the mammoth-sized skipper uncomfortable. He was now going to have to sell his boss on his version of where they had been dumping their deadly cargos for the past couple of years — minus the plans for eventual salvage.

5. CLUB ISLAND

July 21, 0025 hrs

The fourth rainsquall of the night swept over *Water Baby* while Webb was below pouring a coffee from the Thermos he'd filled earlier in the evening. When he went back up into the cockpit, he immediately noticed a drop in the air temperature from just a few minutes before.

The cold front was passing, and he could expect the wind to start blowing from the northwest any time now. He had pretty well made the decision to turn southwest and sail on a beam reach to Club Island after the wind settled in its new direction. It would mean sailing straight into the waves left over from the evening's southwest blow, but he felt more comfortable about entering that cove in the dark, than taking the downwind ride toward the rock-infested waters around the Bustard Islands.

Even while he finalized this plan in his mind, the wind was starting to veer. Webb kept sheeting in the sails until the yawl was sailing close-hauled. Then the continuing wind shift forced him to incrementally alter his course until he was sailing almost northeast. Finally, with the wind blowing steadily from the northwest he brought the boat about, and set his new course, steering 245°, bound for Club Island.

At first it was a slow bouncy ride, with the yawl hobbyhorsing head-on into the four- and five-foot waves, but he knew they'd soon lose the worst of their punch with the wind no longer pushing them in that direction. Once he was confident that the boat was holding its course, he dropped below and radioed his revised destination to the coast guard.

July 21, 0230

During the past two hours, the wind had eased to between twelve and fifteen knots from the northwest. The old waves from the southwest had rounded out and become longer between their crests. Although *Water Baby*'s speed was under five knots, the ride was more comfortable, and Webb was pleased with the progress he was making. The air had cleared, and the moon lit a silvery path ahead as the old yawl slid on through the night.

His attention was drawn to the lights of a boat off *Water Baby*'s port bow. This time he made sure he was paying attention. It appeared that he was gradually catching up with the Mid-Con Waste tug. For some reason it appeared to be farther north than it should if it were on one of its regular delivery crossings bound for Alpena. He guessed that they were possibly trying to tuck into the lee of the Manitoulin Island coastline in search of calmer waters. Webb was aware that towed barges were notorious for limiting a tug's speed when any substantial sea was running. 'And then again,' he reasoned to himself, 'knowing the age of the tug, it's just as likely they've had a breakdown.' He continued on his present course, passing within two miles of the tug and as time went by it gradually disappeared astern of *Water Baby*.

July 21, 0245

Lady M was pointing northwest with her engine idled down to keep the small ship and her barge stationary but still pointed into the wind. The tug was wallowing uncomfortably, lying broadside to the swell that still rolled in from the southwest. Erin Franklin had been returned to the storage locker because Gant's loaders were all waiting for orders from Reiger, and the custody of the woman was not trusted to the crew of the tug. In fact, if Reiger decided that he was going to issue the order to off-load, the tug crew was going to be every bit as occupied as Reiger's goon squad — the men he called 'loaders'.

Mike Small was engaged in another heated discussion with his boss in the captain's cabin. At issue was the decision on whether they should board the barge and commence unloading the barrels of waste in the present sea conditions, or proceed to find shelter and wait for the next night. Small argued that they needed to wait, claiming that their little forklift truck would be dangerously unstable on the rolling barge. Reiger had no practical experience working in such conditions, but his stubborn nature and his need to be in charge led him to disagree.

However, the decision was made for them by the brief appearance of Billy Manion, who announced that he and Ethier just heard on the VHF that *Cove Isle*, a Canadian Coast Guard light tending vessel, was being dispatched to the area to repair a navigational aid with an extinguished light. And *Cove Isle* was only twenty miles north of them right now.

It would not be smart to be caught by the coast guard dumping hazardous waste into Lake Huron. The drop would have to wait until the next night.

July 21, 0250

Under bright sodium dockside lights, the bulk carrier *Blue Mountain,* using her bow and stern warping winches, inched into position alongside the limestone loading facility at McGregor Bay. If all went well, it would take about eight hours to complete loading the ship.

Gordon Anderson, the first mate, was in charge of the ship's role in the loading process, so Captain Henry left the helmsman in charge of the bridge and headed to his cabin for some much-needed sleep.

July 21, 0500

Just as dawn began to emerge on the first full day of his vacation cruise, Rick Webb guided *Water Baby* into the calm waters of the harbour at Club Island. Carved into the eastern side of the three-kilometre-long island, this cove was a fairly shallow, roughly circular anchorage. It was approximately 400 yards in diameter, offering decent shelter from heavy weather originating from any direction but the east. The bottom, consisting of flat limestone shelves strewn with rocks and boulders, did not provide the best anchoring conditions, but *Water Baby*'s thirty-five-pound, Northill folding anchor was ideally suited to the job.

The surrounding land was limestone alvar — flat terrain with only the skimpiest covering of soil over the bedrock and completely bare in patches. Vegetation varied from scatterings of mosses and lichens on the bare rock, to sparse dry land grasses, wildflowers and sedges where there was a thin layer of soil, giving it the appearance of open grazing land. In areas where the soil was slightly deeper, generally along clefts and ledges in the bedrock, thickets of stunted white cedar and spruce formed natural hedges.

The only apparent evidence of human activities on the island were a dilapidated shed, the remnant of a long-abandoned commercial fishery station, and a thirty-foot high pile of broken limestone sitting beside water-filled excavations of a quarrying venture that never really got off the ground. The stone pile stood sentry over the fishery shed near the southern side of the harbour entrance. Several semi-submerged dock cribs lay near the southern shore, just inside the entry passage.

This morning, *Water Baby* was the only boat present. Webb dropped anchor on the south side of the lagoon, about halfway to the far end. Exhausted by his long night crossing, he climbed down the companionway steps, switching off the yacht's running lights on his way past the navigating station. He had climbed out of his clothes and was just getting comfortable in the V-berth when he realized he'd almost forgotten to close his sailing plan with the coast guard.

If he didn't report in and woke up later in the day to find the coast guard in the midst of an unneeded search, that would be embarrassing for him and annoying for them. Returning to his berth after making the call, he didn't dwell on it for long. Sleep came almost at once.

July 21, 0610

Captain Lorne Henry woke to the insistent ringing of the phone beside his berth aboard *Blue Mountain.*

"Henry here," he sighed as he put on his glasses to glance at the clock.

"Wiggins, sir. The first mate asked me to tell you that the quarry's loading belt broke down. The shore contractor is working on it now, but they'll probably have to get some new parts brought down from Sudbury."

73

"Well hell. There goes our quick turnaround ..." Henry paused. "Are you in the radio shack Wiggins?"

"Yes sir."

"Phone the broker's office will you, and leave a message for him to call me as soon as he gets his fat ass into work this morning. Every time we snake our way up to this God forsaken port, we seem to run into one bloody delay or another. The bastards can call someone else next time they want a load picked up here."

"You want me to tell them that sir?"

"Ah ... no Wiggins ... just have him give me a call, would you?"

"Yes sir."

By this time, Captain Henry was too worked up to sleep anymore, so he got up, decided not to shave and went for breakfast instead.

July 21, 0820

To the limited extent that a tug could hurry, it had taken Mike Small until dawn to hustle *Lady M* far enough south to evade untimely detection by the approaching coast guard vessel. They probably picked them up on radar, but at least they weren't caught with their pants down.

Their detour had taken them back out onto the normal track one would expect them to take en route from Britt to Alpena. From that position, if the coast guard crew observed them making for Club Island, they would have aroused little suspicion. It would have simply be seen as a tug and barge making the prudent decision to wait for lighter winds before making an open-water crossing. Small had taken shelter there a number of times in the years that he had been on the Alpena run.

Now, as they idled slowly into the quiet waters of Club Island cove, the crew rafted the tug and barge together, side by side, so that they could be handled as one vessel during the anchoring process. The only other boat in the harbour was a blue yawl. Ethier claimed it was the same one that almost tangled with their tow during the night.

July 21, 1330

Webb awakened to the gentle motion of his boat swinging on its anchor. He'd slept well, but with the boat still closed up following his night crossing, he was getting uncomfortably warm. Rising and stretching, he opened the forward hatch over his head. A gentle breeze immediately swept down and began to refresh the air in the cabin.

Looking out through the cabin ports, Webb was surprised to see the Mid-Con Waste tug *Lady M* and its barge lying at anchor near the middle of the cove, though closer to the north side. The anger beginning to boil inside him once again was for Reiger and Mid-Con, not the tug, and last night's close call — that was a risk one took when venturing out on the big lake at night, and more his own damned fault than anything. Nor had he any anger for the tug's skipper.

Having met Mike Small once out on the bay three or four years back, Webb was under the impression that he was a pretty decent guy — he was certainly pleasant enough. He was big and jowlsy with a ruddy complexion and no distinguishable neck. But what had really struck Webb about the man was that despite being terribly overweight, Small moved about the rolling tug with the grace of a ballroom dancer. On that particular occasion, the tug was hove to, rolling gently in the middle of Georgian Bay while the engineer repaired a steering problem. And when Webb had pulled his patrol boat alongside to see if the tug was in trouble, the skipper had offered him a Pepsi and they had sat and conversed on a variety of subjects of mutual interest to them both — mainly boats. In reference to his trips to Alpena, Small had explained why the company was shipping materials across the lake by barge rather than the long way around by truck or by train. That had appeared legitimate enough — a pretty sensible business decision, really.

No, it wasn't Small who was the source of his grievance. It was the dismissal of the court case against Small's employer that was still galling him. Every time he thought about it, he still felt something really smelled odd about that deal.

And now it seemed strange that with the wind having subsided to a light breeze, the tug wouldn't be under way on its delivery run to Michigan. Conditions for such a transit should be ideal for the rest of the day. Maybe, he pondered, with the barge as heavily loaded as it appeared to be, they wanted to make the crossing in the flat calm of the night. This possibility became even more likely when Webb turned on the VHF to listen to the marine forecast as he went to the galley to prepare something to eat.

"*Winds over northern Lake Huron easing later today, becoming calm tonight,*" the recording said, while on Georgian Bay winds were predicted to be light and variable all day. He'd seen it often enough; although the two bodies of water were adjacent parts of the same lake, conditions could vary considerably from one to the other.

July 21, 1430

James Franklin parked his Cadillac down by the harbour on First Avenue East as he had been instructed. If it hadn't been for the car's air conditioning on that hot Friday afternoon it would have been a miserable drive to Owen Sound. Even so, he'd had to fight his way through increasingly heavy cottage-bound traffic as Toronto area residents began to pour north out of the city for another summer weekend.

The judge took his overnight bag and an old fishing tackle box from the trunk and made his way down to a dock bearing a weathered sign reading, 'Sound Water Taxi'. It was less than a hundred yards from where he had parked his car.

Despite the stifling heat, a chill ran through him as Franklin recalled the telephoned instructions he'd received early in the morning. The caller was as brief and as threatening as he'd been during the first calls forty-eight hours earlier. The only difference was a rumbling noise that muffled the voice a little, but not so much as to hide the fact that it *was* the same voice. Reiger had the judge right where he wanted him. The real frustration was, despite knowing who was behind it, for Erin's sake he couldn't risk asking for help. As he'd reminded himself frequently since this horror began, desperate men regularly make poor choices, and when pushed, a bad situation can go all to hell, really fast.

He had already feared that the worst had happened when, after dismissing the charges against Reiger and his company, he hadn't heard back from them until just this morning. That delay had been the longest, most agonizing two days in his entire life. In his desperation, he had been on the verge of calling the police just as the phone had started ringing.

Now he was twenty minutes early for his ride, and there was no one at the dock, so Franklin eased his big frame onto a dilapidated wooden bench by the water's edge. Despite his sixty-four years, he was still a towering facsimile of the 230 pound university football player he'd been so many years before. Only his snow-white hair and his life-experienced face suggested his age.

About five minutes before the appointed time, a short,

skinny red-headed man, perhaps in his mid-thirties, stepped down onto the dock.

"You Kingfisher?" he asked Franklin.

"Oh ... ah ... well, yes." For a moment he almost forgot that he was supposed to answer to that nickname. "I'm hoping for a chance to catch a big one," he finished, sticking to the silly script he'd been given by Reiger's spokesman. Amateurs!

"Just call me Red," said the man as he led Franklin down the dock. "I'm to take you out to meet your buddies at the boat."

They walked past the weathered twenty-one-foot runabout that Franklin had assumed would be the water taxi and headed instead for a dazzling black cigarette boat, sporting four shiny chrome exhaust pipes. The name *Flash* was artfully painted down the sides of the sleek low-riding boat in gaudy yellow lightning bolt characters.

"This isn't your average water taxi, Red," ventured Franklin, doing his best to sound casual.

"I borrow it from my brother-in-law for long distance runs like this. Helps him with his payments, eh? Besides, we'd be after midnight getting there in my old barge," he nodded up the dock indicating the old runabout. Stepping aboard the big muscle boat, he unlocked the louvered teak companionway doors.

Franklin was puzzled by the reference to a long-distance run. Just where was this so-called meeting going to take place?

Ducking down into the cabin, Red took a pair of buoyant key fobs off the dinette table and flipped some switches on the cabin's main breaker panel. Back in the cockpit, more switches brought bilge blower fans to life. Finally, the water taxi driver inserted and turned each of the two ignition keys in succession. The resulting deep snarling roar left no doubt that the engines had started. Franklin helped bring the dock lines aboard and the two high-performance V8 engines smartly barked out an idling rhythm in time with each other as the boat slipped out of the harbour.

Not knowing what involvement his driver had in the unfolding drama and concerned about the idea of a long trip, the judge dared to ask, "Where are we meeting them?"

"Dunno. They told me to radio when we got up the bay and they'd give me a rendezvous point … depends on the fishin' they said." Now clear of the inner harbour, Red smoothly advanced the throttles and the boat was immediately up and planing. It quickly reached a cruising speed of forty knots over the calm waters of Owen Sound as it headed northeast toward Georgian Bay. There was little point in attempting further conversation over the howl of the tuned engine exhausts, so for the time being Franklin settled down for a lengthy ride to where, he knew not.

July 21, 1450

Having tidied up after a relaxing brunch of coffee, orange juice, a western omelette and a small salad, Webb resolved to salvage what was left of the day. He released the straps that held the little six-foot dinghy to the cabin top and used the mainsail halyard winch to lift it free of its chocks, then flipped it upright and launched it over *Water Baby*'s port side. He had always promised himself that he'd do some fishing around the shoal waters off some of the islands surrounding Manitoulin. The light, variable breeze created ideal conditions for his preferred fishing methods.

Webb was soon rowing his way around the outer shoreline of the island. Even before arriving at the spot he had figured would provide the best fishing, he had managed to hook several decent smallmouth bass. When he finally arrived at the wide shoal area on the west coast of the island, he let his boat drift about like a leaf in the breeze, lazily pushed this way and that without really going anywhere. As time wore on, he caught and released over a dozen bass, several weighing in at over three pounds. Contrary to what some of his clients at work thought, the CO spent very little time fishing, so this afternoon's outing was a real treat.

July 21, 1530

George Ridley, his golf bag slung from his shoulder, took the short cut across the lawn as he always did. He expected to see Jim Franklin, already sitting in the Cadillac in his own driveway, waiting patiently for his next-door neighbour — as *he* always did. But Jim wasn't there. Leaning his clubs against the front porch railing, the retired schoolteacher mounted the steps and tried the door. It was locked. He rang the doorbell. There was no answer.

Ridley was puzzled. He and the judge played golf every Friday afternoon, without fail, spring, summer and fall. And the few times Jim hadn't been able to make it, there'd always been either a text or a voicemail message to say so — along with his apologies.

He dug out his key ring and selected the one for Jim's door. The two of them, both being widowers, had exchanged keys several years earlier. In making the suggestion, Franklin had said, "Old guys have a way of falling downstairs and dying … or falling down dead, without using the stairs … just to save a few steps. I'd rather you found me when I was dead for a day than have poor Erin finding me after a week."

Both had just turned sixty at about the same time. The conversation had been lighthearted and made in the spirit of their age. But right now, it sent a chill up Ridley's spine. He opened the door and called out for his golfing buddy. No response. A quick tour of every room on the main floor brought no results. There was no sign of his good friend at the bottom of the basement stairs either and the rest of the tidy basement was clear too. Out through the kitchen door and into the garage, he found no Jim — and no Caddy.

'Well, that's weird,' the neighbour thought. He pulled out his smart phone and tried Jim's number. He got an annoying message: *'The customer you have dialled is currently not available.'*

Back in the kitchen, George went to the phone on the end of the counter. No incoming messages were indicated. He picked up and dialled Jim's housekeeper from memory. She was also George's housekeeper. They shared her services, and on Tuesdays and Fridays, they'd each get half a day of house cleaning from her. She had just left George's place for home as he was heading out the door with his golf clubs.

"Hello, Mary. It's George speaking … Yes, I know, but he isn't here. Did he say anything about going away while you were here this morning?" But Mary's answer left him even more puzzled. His bed had been slept in, but other than that there'd been no sign of the judge when she arrived after breakfast. And he'd left no indication of where he'd gone.

"I never thought to mention it to you this afternoon George. I just assumed that maybe he had court somewhere else. Do you think he's missing?"

"No, I just don't know where he is, that's all." He didn't want to upset the poor woman — she was just recently widowed herself. "Don't worry Mary. I'll track him down somewhere," he said with somewhat renewed confidence. She had at least pointed him in the direction of the next call he needed to make.

Checking the phone for Jim's pre-programmed numbers, he speed-dialled the court office. "Oh hi, Betty. It's George Ridley here ... Yes, I'm at his place." It appeared everyone had call display now-a-days. "Betty, we're supposed to go golfing together this afternoon. Is he there? ... Oh ... Did he get called to sit court somewhere else today? His car is gone and he didn't leave me any messages ... No? Yes, that's totally unlike him. Tell him to give me a call if you hear from him would you please? Thanks."

"Mysteriouser and mysteriouser," Ridley said to himself as he pondered his next move. He was hesitant about calling Erin. He didn't want to alarm her just because her dad was missing for a few hours. But she was the only other person he could think of who might know of Jim's whereabouts. So he hit the speed dial and waited.

Just the voicemail on her home-office phone, and he didn't quite know how to phrase a recorded message to her without causing her undue concern. So without leaving a message, he moved on to her cell phone number. But like Jim's, her cell was either switched off or out of range. 'Well, she's a busy girl. I'll have to try later.'

Still, it was unsettling that Jim would just disappear without leaving a message. He always told someone. He was meticulous about that. That's why they'd exchanged keys — so they could keep track of each other.

As Ridley let his mind ponder the situation, he grew more and more concerned. He carried his golf bag back home, got into his own car and drove down to the local police detachment. Something like this required a personal appearance. He figured that missing persons don't normally qualify as missing after just half a day, so it might take some forceful face-to-face persuasion to get them interested.

July 21, 1610

Just abeam of Cabot Head at the northeastern-most tip of the Bruce Peninsula, the powerboat *Flash* settled down into the glassy surface of Georgian Bay as her engines were brought to an idle. Much to the relief of James Franklin, Red shut off the throbbing engines so that he could clearly hear the directions he was about to receive from Willard Reiger's people.

"The Big One, the Big One, the Big One, this is Red, Red, over," the water taxi operator spoke into the microphone. Aside to Franklin, he shook his head sadly, commenting, "You fishermen are all alike … the guy says to me 'you don't need to know the boat's real name' … you're all paranoid someone will find your favourite fishing spot, eh?"

Franklin shrugged an acknowledgement, "what can I say?" All the time he was wondering what indeed he *could* say. Was this Red fellow part of the Reiger operation? Or was he just a contractor hired to do a job? His gut feeling, from what little conversation he'd managed with the man over the past hour and a half, led him to believe that the driver was probably not involved, but the experience of years on the bench kept him from taking the man immediately into his confidence. However, an idea was forming in the judge's mind.

The VHF squawked as someone in Reiger's party responded, telling Red to proceed to the cove at Club Island and deliver his passenger to the largest boat there.

"Red," Franklin asked, "is there a toilet aboard this rocket?"

"Yup, down below. Just duck as you go forward. When they advertise standing headroom in these things, they don't really mean for tall guys like you."

As Franklin stooped down into the low companionway,

Red restarted the engines and accelerated gently, so as not to upset the balance of the older man moving forward through the cabin. With the destination now known, the throttles were advanced until the big craft was skimming easily over the flat water at forty knots again. They'd arrive at Club Island in about half an hour, and then Red could head home with a healthy fare in his pocket.

In the cramped quarters of the speeding boat's head, the judge formulated a brief distress message, which he printed on a sticky note pad he had found on the galley counter when he first descended the short companionway steps. When he was done, he made his way back out to the cockpit, sticking his urgent note on the dinette table as he passed. Although he was pretty well satisfied that Red was not part of Reiger's crew, Franklin did not want the water taxi driver accidentally tipping his hand while they were alongside Reiger's boat. Hopefully Red *would* see the note though, when he replaced the cruiser's keys after returning to Owen Sound.

July 21, 1610

The sergeant in charge of the evening shift at the Parry Sound police detachment settled at her desk and opened her laptop. Her shift was just ten minutes old. She was about to make a couple of requested changes to the duty roster, when an older gentleman came to the front counter. It took her only an instant to search her memory, connecting the face to a name.

"Mr. Ridley! It's been years," she said smiling and got up to approach the counter. Only as she spoke did the retired teacher realize who he was facing.

"My goodness, Sandra Wilmot. My shy little grade ten history student. You have certainly morphed into an impressive — and if I might add, attractive — authority figure.

And a sergeant no less. Congratulations."

"Well thanks sir …"

"No, it's just George, now. I'm retired and you're grown up."

"Okay, thanks George. Being a late bloomer was the pits, and puberty was a real bitch, but I shot up about eight inches at the end of it and then adulthood taught me a bit of assertiveness. After some bumps in the road, I got my stripes and now I'm back in town.

"So, what can we do for you today?"

"I seem to have misplaced Jim Franklin, my golfing buddy."

"Judge Franklin is missing?" she asked, alarmed.

"Well, I don't know if I'm allowed to call him missing yet — it hasn't even been a full day."

"George, that's a myth. In Ontario and most other jurisdictions now, if you have reason to believe somebody is missing, then we start the process right away. The sooner, the better too. So, come on around the counter, have a seat here and tell me your concerns." And he did so, in detail. And her fingers flew over the keyboard as she entered his statement into a missing person's e-report.

"It's a Caddy he drives, isn't it?" she asked as she switched screens to pull up the motor vehicle registry database. Entering the judge's name and the street name quickly narrowed down the search.

"Black Cadillac, two years old," George specified.

"Yes, there it is in the system. Okay, now let's see where it is on the ground." And with that, she picked up the phone and hit a speed dial button that Ridley couldn't quite read from his side of the desk. "The folks at OnStar are very good about this sort of thing," she said to him and then quickly spoke to the answering party, giving her name, rank, a security code and the vehicle identification number. Just asking to locate the missing vehicle almost took longer than it did for the operator to track it down and give her the address. Adding that to the information on the screen in front of her, she gave the OnStar representative a case-file reference number, then thanked him and hung up.

"Do you know if he has any friends or family in Owen Sound?"

"Not that he's ever mentioned. As well as golfing, we usually play cribbage at least one night a week. And the way we play, we spend more time discussing the good old days, current events and the meaning of life than we do actually playing cards. Although to most people he's a private man — isolated from the masses because of his profession — he's never kept any secrets from me. In fact, considering some of the things he has told me privately, I'm certain of that."

"Well, that's where the car is now. And it's down by the harbour, not at a residence. Hmm. Does he have any girlfriends? Or other um ... intimate attachments?"

"After he lost his Mary-Jane fifteen years ago, he never had the heart to take up with anyone else, though there have been plenty of women who would gladly pair up with him. No, the one remaining woman in his life is his daughter, Erin. And he'd move heaven and earth for that girl. I'm the only candidate for 'other intimate attachment' but we just play cards and golf and drink ... a bit."

"Okay George. Thanks for coming in. The judge is a favourite of ours too. As soon as I push the send button, the rest of the world will know he's missing as well. And I'm immediately assigning a detective constable to work the case. When Owen Sound responds with a unit to check out his car, OnStar will remotely unlock it for them, and they can do a proper search over there. We'll call you if we need anything else and also as soon as we find anything out."

"Thanks Sandra. I sure hope he's alright."

"We'll do our best to find him, George." As much as she wanted to, Wilmot was not about to tell her old teacher not to worry. She'd seen too many missing persons cases end badly.

July 21, 1640

When *Flash* next idled down her thundering engines, the muscle boat was just entering the cove at Club Island. There were three sailboats at anchor and a commercial tugboat tied to a barge. Red was obviously somewhat confused. He had been expecting a big party yacht, decked out with downriggers and outriggers — all the garish paraphernalia of a large sport fisherman.

But James Franklin knew that the Mid-Con Waste tug would be the destination. Barely able to contain his anxiety and desperately hoping to find his daughter still unharmed, he pointed at the tug, and nodded at Red, "Yes, that one."

The fact that Red didn't know which boat he was looking for reassured Franklin that he'd definitely made the right decision in leaving him the note. He just hoped the man would find it later.

July 21, 1645

Reiger's loader, Goreham, stuck his head in the open doorway to the captain's cabin aboard *Lady M.* "There's a fancy speedboat headin' this way Mr. Reiger. That the one you were waitin' for?"

"Yes. Have Gant bring the passenger in here." Reiger looked out onto the portside deck of the tug just as the crew were taking lines aboard from the sleek cigarette boat.

Out on deck, John Gant had everything organized. The judge was helped aboard with a greeting, sufficiently cordial to appear normal to the other boaters in the harbour. Franklin instantly recognized the voice of the threatening caller.

As the water taxi driver handed Franklin's gear up to the tug's deck, Gant gave him the pre-arranged payment, in cash, and a parcel which he asked Red to mail for him. The driver set it on the cockpit floor, in front of the now vacant passenger seat.

Before the judge could ask any pointed questions out in the open, he was whisked directly into the captain's cabin. Sound travels remarkably clearly across calm water and Gant had no intention of letting anyone on the other boats in the anchorage get even a hint of trouble. Reiger's loaders and several of the tug's regular crew gathered on deck to take in the departure of the cigarette boat. Its testosterone-enriched exhaust note echoed in harmony off the dense wall of low cedar trees lining the nearby shoreline. They were all impressed.

July 21, 1710

Almost twenty minutes into his return trip to Owen Sound, Red eased the throttles of the speeding *Flash* back to an idle, then shut the engines off. Nature was calling. He couldn't put it off any longer. The sleek weekend racer rose and fell gently on the receding effects of its own wake as Red went below toward the head.

On the dinette table he noticed a sticky note that hadn't been there when he'd picked up the keys several hours earlier. He peeled the note off the table as he passed and entered the head.

TOXIC WATERS

July 21, 1712

Aboard *Lady M*, John Gant looked at his watch. Satisfied that the water taxi, *Flash*, would be far enough from their location, but still within radio range, he turned on a small transmitter and pushed the "test" button. Upon receiving a green light, he punched down on the detonator button.

"Flash," he muttered to himself. "Assignment complete, Red. Job well done."

July 21, 1713

With his ears still ringing after the big bang, the first thing Red became aware of was that water was rushing in under the door of the head. It was already up around his knees and rising fast. Dazed and winded by whatever had exploded, it took him precious seconds to realize that his brother-in-law's boat was sinking — fast. "Man, is he going to be some pissed!"

Though it was jammed by the force of the explosion, pulling the head door inward to open it was easy. He had lots of help from the pressure of the chest deep water that was already flooding the main cabin. As Red worked his way aft, he discovered that the once speedy yacht now ended at the companionway. The aft portion of the boat had vanished — cockpit, engines, everything — gone! And the raging fire that comes with every boat explosion in the movies hadn't materialized. The boat's fuel tanks sank quickly, more or less intact, still attached to the aft portion of the hull that was weighed down by the big engines.

As he swam out into the area where the cockpit had once been, the entire bow section settled low in the water behind him, and then disappeared. The galley kettle, some chunks of Styrofoam and a couple of life jackets bobbed up to join him. Other than that, the boat completely vanished. And then Red looked at the little wet scrap of paper he still had clasped in his hand; and then he began to realize the full urgency of the message written on it.

July 21, 1713

Fishing in the shoal waters off the northwest corner of Club Island, Rick Webb was just about to cast his lure toward a promising rock formation when a distant peel of thunder rolled across the water. Direction was a bit hard to pin down as the sound faintly echoed off the other islands in the vicinity. Somewhat distracted by the noise, his cast fell short of his target, and as he reeled the line back in to try again, his mind replayed the odd-sounding rumble.

Almost a thunderclap he thought, but with no ominous storm clouds visible in the sky, he was inclined to put it down to someone blasting — except blasting is often a deeper sound, partially muted by the rock it is breaking up. 'Strange. Ah, there. A perfect cast ....' except no fish went for the lure.

July 21, 1715

After dogpaddling for several minutes around the patch of water that had swallowed his brother-in-law's boat, Red grabbed the nearest life jacket. He was not a strong swimmer, and he knew that if he wasn't rescued, or able to make it ashore pretty quickly, the cold Georgian Bay water would claim another victim before the day was out. He'd taken the required boating courses to get his captain's licence and he knew his odds of survival — right now they were not great.

Halfmoon Island, a low, crescent-shaped limestone and gravel sliver of land, was the nearest dry ground to him. It was located just a couple of miles back toward Club Island. He headed off in that direction, guessing that if racing swimmers could do a little over four miles per hour, back and forth in an Olympic pool, he could dogpaddle and backstroke, with a bulky life jacket on, somewhere between one and two. All he had going in his favour was the life jacket, and despite being a smoker, he considered himself to be in pretty decent condition.

July 21, 1805

Well into his long, cold swim toward the safety of Halfmoon Island, Red felt a wave of relief wash over him as he observed a big motor cruiser approaching his position from the south. It was a forty-five-foot sport fisherman with twin diesels, loping along well below planing speed. At seven or eight knots, it would pass within yards of him shortly. Anyone affluent enough to have a boat like that would probably have not just cell phones on board, but also a satellite phone to boot! 'Thank goodness for small mercies,' he thought to himself, 'now I'll be able to call the cops.'

July 21, 1817

As the big sport fisherman drew closer, Red waited to spot whoever was at the helm so he could wave them down. Yet the closer it came, and even as it passed within twenty feet of him, he could see no one at the controls on the flybridge. Red began hollering to attract someone's attention and just as he took a deep breath to yell once more, the high wake from the big motor yacht slapped him full in the face. By the time he'd stopped choking and sputtering, the boat had passed far enough beyond him that even his shrill whistles drew no attention from any of the occupants aboard.

Truth be told, the owner was one of those arrogant fellows who had implicit trust in his GPS-guided auto-helm with its interfaced anti-collision radar warning system. He was down below in the air-conditioned cabin serving cocktails and canapés to his guests — potential clients for his thriving import business. And of course, in the modern way of such things, the sound system was cranked, belting out heavy metal tunes. Those on board could barely hear the boat's diesels let alone the swimmer they'd just passed.

July 21, 1845

Red was dog-tired, still furious at the absentee cruiser captain and rapidly getting closer to hypothermia. He'd been alternating between a dog paddle and his version of a backstroke for what seemed an eternity, but each time he rolled onto his front to resume his slightly speedier dogpaddle, Halfmoon Island seemed no closer. Mind you, a sliver of land standing only five feet above the lake surface always seems farther away than it really is. He held on to that one faintly optimistic thought as he struggled slowly onward.

Just at the point where he thought he could go no farther, Red was tearfully relieved to hear the sweetest sound he thought he'd ever heard. The wake from a distant and unseen passing boat made a clearly audible splash as it washed over the rocks at the south end of the island. He still had over a hundred yards left to cover, but he knew now that he'd make it somehow.

6. DISTRESS

Webb rowed the dinghy back into Club Island's cove, satisfied with his afternoon of poking around its rocky shores. It was the best day of fishing he'd had in years. Of all the bass he'd caught, he was happy just keeping a one pounder for his dinner. The rest had been caught and released.

Some folks wouldn't thank you for a feed of bass, but as a kid, Webb had spent his summers on a lake where bass and pan fish were the predominant species. He figured that either bass *was* an acquired taste that he'd simply grown up with, or its detractors knew nothing about cooking it properly.

Two American sailboats had arrived in the cove since he had left earlier. They were rafted together and tied off close to shore in the southeast corner of the anchorage. There were children and dogs playing ashore on the stony beach near the boats and the adults appeared to be enjoying after-dinner drinks in the cockpit of the larger boat. Typical of friendly sailors, they waved and exchanged brief greetings with Webb as he rowed past on his way to *Water Baby*. The Mid-Con Waste tug was still anchored near the middle of the cove.

July 21, 1910

When he first crawled ashore on Halfmoon Island, Red was chilled through. He'd stopped shivering shortly before his landfall, so he knew that he was truly hypothermic — dangerously so. Your shivering mechanism stops when your core temperature drops below a certain level. Fortunately, he had the presence of mind to get out of his cold wet clothes, and as he was laying them out to dry, he realized that there was a good deal of residual heat in the rocks from the long day's sunshine. Lying down on a flat limestone shelf with his back tucked up tight against the warm ledge of a slightly higher shelf, Red began the slow process of re-warming himself. After a time, he got back up to shivering temperature, and then exhausted, he eventually slept.

July 21, 1925

James and Erin Franklin had been allowed to remain in the captain's cabin aboard the tug *Lady M* following a tearful reunion several hours earlier. However, they were being continuously guarded either by Gant or one of his security team.

In the privacy of the captain's head, Erin had finally been given an opportunity to take a shower. That had been refreshing, but without clean clothes to change into, she felt she had just taken one step forward and two steps back. However, lack of cleanliness aside, her mind remained keenly attuned to the much greater predicament of their captivity. She had come to the full realization that it was entirely possible the only reason she and her dad were still alive was that Reiger hadn't yet decided how, or maybe when or where to get rid of them. And the fact that he was extending a small degree of comfort — the shower and the tug captain's cabin — was just to minimize the risk of their getting panicky and causing a commotion. Had she known the truth, it was a brewing mutiny on the part of the tug's skipper and crew that Reiger was trying to avoid.

While she was relieved that her father had come to find her, and she had known he would if he could, Erin was angry with herself that she had sealed his fate too. She had to figure a way for them both to escape — before Reiger made his move.

When she stepped quietly from the tiny combination head and shower room out into the office area of the captain's cabin, she could hear her father talking heatedly with Reiger on the other side of the louvered door to the skipper's sleeping berth. Although the noisy air conditioner mounted in the cabin's overhead made it impossible to hear exactly what was being said, she knew her dad was attempting to negotiate their release — to persuade Reiger that he was rapidly painting himself into a corner. But judging from what little she could hear of Reiger's responses, she knew that the man just wasn't getting it.

While she stood there, fear welling up inside her, she suddenly realized that there was a two-way marine radio mounted on a corner of the captain's desk. This was the opportunity she'd been waiting for. She knew she had to take advantage of the distraction created by her father talking to Reiger and the overriding noise of the air conditioner. Without hesitating she leaned over the desk and quickly grabbed the microphone.

"Mayday, Mayday. We are being held hostage on a boat somewhere on Georgian Bay," she spoke urgently into the mic in a hoarse whisper. Releasing the transmit button, she waited. There was no response. She started again, watching the radio as she spoke. Realizing that the unit was not turned on, she was furious with herself for wasting precious time. Desperately aware that she could be discovered at any moment, she reached over and turned on the power switch, hoping that the radio did not need to warm up before it worked. Once more she began to repeat her distress call.

July 21, 1930

It was a lovely warm summer evening. Webb sat in *Water Baby*'s cockpit tending his fish which was simmering in a foil pan on the barbeque. The aroma of the fish, cooking in a dill seed, onion and butter marinade, mingled agreeably with the summertime smell of the cedar trees growing between the cracks in the limestone bedrock along the shoreline. Heywood, the cat, was frolicking about the deck, stalking the seagulls that were swimming nearby and hunting deer flies with his usual great success. There was the pleasant murmur of lighthearted conversation and laughter drifting over the cove from the two American sailboats. And although it spoiled the ambiance somewhat, he had by now become accustomed to the continuous muted rumble of the diesel generator buried in the bowels of the tug anchored across the cove.

Taking a sip of scotch from his glass, he thought to himself, 'if my Mel was still with me, she would have loved this.' Her memory was still lingering when his nostalgic frame of mind was shattered. The VHF down in the cabin suddenly came to life.

"Mayday, Mayday. Please help us. We're being kept on a boat …"

"Bitch! How'd you …" Click. Silence.

The first had been a female voice, obviously distraught, followed immediately and partly overlapped by an angry male voice.

Although Webb had adjusted his VHF down to a low volume, the incoming signal had been strong and clear. But after several minutes of dead air, he began to wonder why the coast guard hadn't responded in an attempt to reach the vessel calling Mayday. Those Canadian Coast Guard radio operators were always on their toes when there was even a hint of urgency to a call. They knew that during the panicked moments of an emergency, even folks trained in proper radio procedure were known to blurt out the most disjointed messages. Thinking it through, he deduced that the call had to have been transmitted, probably accidentally, on the one-watt power setting designed for local calling, not for widespread broadcast.

In that event, he quickly concluded, the radio transmission had originated nearby. Only another boat in the same cove, or one passing very close to the island could have registered such a clear low-power transmission. And since boats didn't pass close to the west side of the island — way too many shoal areas out there — then he should be able to see something going by the entrance to the cove. And it would have to happen within minutes. But nothing did.

July 21, 1930

Aboard the tug *Lady M*, an enraged John Gant slammed a giant fist down on the VHF in mid-sentence as he vented his anger at Erin Franklin. The radio's plastic housing became instant garbage. Its working parts immediately stopped working. As the security chief dragged her around the corner into the sleeping area of the captain's cabin, Reiger raised the obvious question. "Did she get through? Did anyone hear her?"

"I don't know," he fired back, exasperated. "You said you'd watch them both while I went for a bite. She was fiddlin'

97

with the controls and talkin' into the damned thing when I came through the door. I don't think she had it figured out yet, but we won't know now ... the radio's toast," Gant finished uncomfortably.

"Well, send Jay in here and you get up to the radio in the wheelhouse and listen there for any sign of trouble. While you're up there, you watch the other boats around us to see if they behave like they've heard anything." As Reiger indicated, putting one VHF radio out of commission did not leave the tug without communications to the outside world. There was still the ship's primary VHF in the wheelhouse.

July 21, 1935

Webb's thoughts had already switched out of vacation mode and the detective mind of the conservation officer was back on the job. He desperately wanted to contact the police, or even one of his fellow COs, but using his cell phone was out of the question.

When the phone company had stopped providing analogue cell service years earlier, he lost the great coverage provided by his bulky two-watt bag phone. With only 0.6 watts of transmitting power, the silly little smart phone they sold him as a replacement, simply didn't have the range from this far offshore. And placing a radio call of his own, requesting outside help, was a non-starter too — whether the action was taking place aboard the tug or some other nearby vessel, his call would no doubt be monitored. In fact, there was likely someone listening at that very moment, just waiting for somebody to transmit a message.

In reality this was a police matter, but being the only peace officer of any sort in the immediate vicinity, he was morally obligated to get an investigation started. Like it or not,

Webb was now the lead investigator on the case. As such, he immediately began to focus on the problem at hand, mentally assessing what little evidence he had been given.

First step: eliminate unlikely parties from the list of suspects — the two American sailboats in the cove. There was a continuous procession of children, adults and dogs passing freely in and out of their cabins and back and forth by dinghy to the nearby gravel beach. Their relaxed behaviour appeared totally spontaneous and uninhibited. Furthermore, there was no evidence that they'd even heard the transmission. Their radios were probably shut off while at anchor. They were clearly not holding any hostages.

No other vessels had yet passed the entrance to the cove, so none were near enough to be heard so clearly on a one-watt transmission. And that quickly narrowed his list of likely suspects down to one vessel — the tug, *Lady M.*

Second step: establish what is known about the remaining suspect on the list. Knowing what he already did of Willard Reiger's outfit and their apparent disregard for the law, Webb figured that the odds were strongly in favour of the call for help originating on board the tug. Had he detected a hint of generator rumble in that brief transmission? Replaying it again in his mind he couldn't be sure — but maybe he had.

The voice had been female — a woman's, or a girl's. Sounded like a younger woman, late teens maybe but definitely not a child's voice. The message said 'we'. How many girls does it take to make a compliment of 'we'? Two or more. More? That sinister connotation left Webb cold. "Is that jerk into human trafficking too?" he asked himself aloud. Ontario had been in the news recently as being a growing centre of that activity. 'Sex slaves, terrorists, or just illegal migrants heading for the States?' he wondered. And in the same moment he realized that the latter two categories wouldn't be calling for help. They would want to get across the lake undetected.

That led to his next line of inquiry — sex slaves? Or just someone who has pissed off old Reiger? Sex slaves would tend to be younger. Piss-offs would include who? Business competition? Not too likely. It's usually men who dominate Reiger's field. Environmental activists? Knowing Reiger's track record, Webb was willing to bet all his chips on the last group. If only he had satellite internet access here like he did on his patrol boat — there he would have been able to check the ministry's list of pain-in-the-ass people who were every bit as eager to get rid of Reiger's ilk as he and his fellow officers were — but always seemed to want to make the ministry look bad at the same time.

Standing to move down into the cabin, Webb changed his mind. If the radio call had been made from the tug, Reiger's crew might be watching him right now, anticipating a reaction. He smoothly turned his motion into the act of leaning over the barbeque to check the progress of his fish dinner, but his thoughts were racing forward as he began to plan his next move. The fish was cooked, so he turned the heat to low just to keep it warm. Too bad — even on low, it would still end up over-cooked.

As for the distress call, he figured he would have to play it cool. Any sudden activity aboard his boat could betray the fact that he had heard the Mayday. His years of experience dealing with criminal minds made him reasonably confident that if he didn't act immediately, any watchers on the tug would assume he hadn't heard anything. And in reality, there was little he could do right away anyhow.

July 21, 1943

Turning toward the Franklins who were now sitting side by

side on the captain's bunk, Reiger angrily addressed Erin. "I cut you some slack so you could get freshened up, and you tried to put a knife in my back. Well that was really *stupid.*

"Jay," he turned, speaking to the newest arrival in the cabin, "we're putting the Franklins back in the locker where she spent last night. They've worn out their welcome in here. Get Mitch and Goreham and bring some duct tape. I don't want to hear another sound out of either of them from now on."

July 21, 1950

Aboard *Water Baby,* Webb made a show of nonchalance, eating his fish dinner on the folding cockpit table. It wasn't too badly overcooked, but it was drier than he liked. Although he occasionally had to go below to make coffee and bring out dessert, he took his time finishing his meal. And then he read, or at least pretended to read a paperback novel after he was done.

However, as much as he liked to lose himself in a good action story, his mind could not have focussed on the book even if he had tried. Instead, while periodically turning the pages in his unread book, strictly for effect, he was busy trying to figure out how to approach the problem of responding to the brief distress call. The call had come from the tug. Of that he was now completely convinced.

He would just have to wait for dark and then get over to the tug unnoticed. Only then could he determine if he could board her and skulk about in search of a damsel, or more, in distress. Maybe it was a trap. Maybe they knew that *Water Baby* was Officer Webb's boat and wanted to get even with him. No, they'd gotten well enough even by winning their case in court just a couple of days ago.

What if he was discovered snooping around the tug? He'd have to talk his way out of it ... maybe something like, 'I just came over to visit Mike Small'... pretty lame, but short of coming right out and asking if they had hostages aboard, it was all he could think of on the spur of the moment.

An additional complication was that he didn't have a gun with him. He never carried his service pistol with him on vacation — that ran counter to government policy — and although he usually brought his shotgun along on fall cruises to hunt waterfowl or grouse, he never bothered with it during the summer.

As various scenarios ran through his mind, it kept coming down to the same bottom line — Webb knew he would have to investigate the call for help. The final draft of his rough plan then, was to get aboard the tug and attempt to determine if anyone was being held against their will. If so, he'd try to free them. If for some reason they couldn't be extracted without drawing attention to himself, he would have to return to *Water Baby*, slip out of the cove and head toward Tobermory.

From eight or ten miles south of the island he'd be able to get a cell signal and phone the police. But seeing he didn't want to lose visual contact with the tug that was "Plan B". The bottom line was that he just had to make a success of boarding the tug.

And then another thought suddenly occurred to him — something that could throw still one more snag into the already complicated situation — and it should have been the first thought to leap into his mind. It was evening and the winds were calm now. The tug could simply up anchor and take off for Alpena before dark — any time now — before he could act. Again, he couldn't risk making a radio call to the coast guard in the open for the same reason he'd already ruled out that option — it would most certainly put any hostages in immediate jeopardy.

'Shit, my options here are really limited,' he thought as he mulled over a few remaining possibilities — none of which was very promising. If the tug left before he got to try boarding it, he'd just have to slip out of the cove right after it and race south toward Tobermory until he could get a cell phone signal. He'd call the police and point out the direction the tug was last seen heading. They would just have to take over from there.

July 21, 1955

Aboard *Lady M* the Franklins had been gagged with duct tape and their wrists bound behind their backs with the same material. After verifying that the tug hadn't swung on its anchor, and that the starboard-side deck was still facing away from the other boats in the cove, *and* there was no one out taking a casual stroll on the island's open grasslands, Goreham and Morris led their prisoners, one at a time, out of the cabin and aft to the paint storage locker. Once each prisoner was seated on the deck in the small compartment, Morris bound their legs together at the ankles. The bulkhead hatch was closed and locked with frightening finality.

July 21, 2030

Detective Constable Tina Stambury pushed the keyboard tray back into its slot under the desktop and rubbed her eyes. Ever since George Ridley had filed his missing persons report in the afternoon, she'd been on the phone and sitting in front of the computer full time. She was looking for possible clues in the case of Judge Franklin's apparent disappearance.

She had an indirect personal interest in the case too. After moving to Parry Sound with her family from Exeter in southern England, Tina had spent her final two years in high school in the same class as Erin Franklin. They hadn't struck up a friendship as such — Erin had been a very quiet, withdrawn student — but they had been on the same team for a couple of complex science projects, and Tina had appreciated the extra effort that Erin had put into those group activities.

The detective recalled hearing through the local grapevine that after Erin had graduated from university in the sciences, she had gone on to become an environmental activist — a thorn in the flesh of corporate polluters, particularly in the Toronto area. It was just too bad that her mother had died so young. Now, with her father gone missing, that could be especially tough on her if things went badly, she thought.

Bearing the family background in mind, Stambury's investigation had started in that dark area that must be considered in every missing persons case — at least in the case of persons adolescent and older — and that was suicide. That was not impossible in the case of the judge, considering the loss of his wife and now living alone since Erin had moved on. But after a follow-up conversation with Ridley, she felt suicide became less likely a possibility. One thing in particular did not fit as far as the detective was concerned.

She felt that a suicidal person would probably not drive almost three hours to a place he'd not come from, had never lived, nor had any known connection to, in order to do — what — jump off the dock? Google Earth showed her that the Owen Sound waterfront was the nearest feature with any obvious suicide potential near to where his car was parked. The location just didn't fit, particularly when considering he lived within a kilometre of any number of docks from which he could have leapt in Parry Sound. Besides, he was known to be a strong swimmer. Would a swimmer choose death by drowning? A quick look at several reference studies on suicide suggested that drowning would be a less likely choice for a swimmer. And finally, Ridley said he just never saw his friend as depressed or suicidal.

The next category she had investigated was that the man might have simply wandered off lost, due to dementia. Again, it was an unlikely scenario from what she personally knew of the judge and no one she spoke to had seen any evidence of diminished capacity in Franklin's behaviour, recent or otherwise. That avenue was quickly shelved as highly improbable.

DC Stambury had then moved on to the possibility of foul play, and that led to a search through old court records of cases tried by Judge Franklin. She was trying to find someone with enough of a grudge to want to disappear the man. That was going to be a big category to cover. Franklin had tried a great many cases in his twenty-three years on the bench.

Recent cases he'd dismissed weren't considered. People whose cases are dismissed might be pissed off at the crown attorney for prosecuting them, but not at the judge for letting them off. 'What about someone else pissed off that the judge had let someone off,' she wondered before abandoning that train of thought. 'No', she decided, 'that's stretching it too far … at least for now.'

The largest group she was targeting were convicts recently released from custody and likely to bear a grudge. Though the list was growing, she had the sinking feeling she was missing something — something on a different track entirely. But neither she nor Sergeant Wilmot, who agreed with her, could put a finger on it. Well, she'd grab a coffee and go outside for a smoke and maybe something would fall together for her.

July 21, 2150

Night had eventually fallen, but with a nearly full moon, Webb could easily see anything he wished to observe in the cove. With the moon being that bright, he was not at all happy about his chances of sneaking aboard the *Lady M* undetected. After considering the dirty white background of the old tug he was about to sneak around on, he decided his white T-shirt and tan cargo pants would provide the best camouflage he could come up with. It was a totally counterintuitive concept for night-time operations, but the bright moonlight pretty well negated normal night-ops black garb.

He rowed ashore close to where *Water Baby* was anchored, being careful to position himself so that the yawl was between the tug and his dinghy, blocking the bad guys' line of sight as much as possible. The little white boat would be an obvious give-away if the Mid-Con people saw it going ashore at that time of night. They would have already figured out that he didn't have a dog that needed to go ashore — the primary reason that most recreational boaters row to the beach late in the evening.

As soon as he landed, he pulled the dinghy up into the bushes and out of sight, then he hiked inland about a hundred yards from the water's edge. Working his way to the right, he began a careful clockwise circuit around the cove. Over the first quarter mile or so, he was fully concealed by the dense evergreens. It was easy walking on the generally flat limestone surface, and even areas that were strewn with broken rock were well enough illuminated by the moon that he was able to maintain a brisk pace. As he began to come even with the west end of the harbour though, he started to encounter more and more open patches where he could possibly be seen from the tug. Picking a new route still farther away from the cove usually gave him renewed cover, although at one point he had to backtrack for ten minutes to avoid crossing an open area in full view of the 'enemy'. On another occasion, when the cover completely ran out, he resorted to crawling on his hands and knees to keep a low ridge in the terrain between him and any observers aboard *Lady M*.

After reaching the north side of the cove, he began working his way through several particularly dense cedar thickets back toward the shore. Finally, he looked out on the tug through a cluster of brush close to the water's edge. Staying motionless for a full five minutes, he watched for signs of activity aboard the suspect vessel anchored 100 yards offshore. Between him and the tug lay the barge, its port side snugly moored along *Lady M*'s starboard rail. As a result, his view of the tug itself was almost completely obscured by the barge and its tarp covered cargo of steel drums. The muted rumble of the diesel generator running in the bowels of the tug made it impossible to listen for voices. The situation was certainly not leaning in his favour.

Though basically unarmed, he did carry his heavy-duty pocketknife in case he had to cut someone's bindings to set them free. Anxious to avoid detection, Webb eased himself carefully over the slippery limestone rocks, into the water at the edge of the cove. To slip at this point, splashing clumsily into the water would be a good recipe for discovery.

Soon he was swimming a quiet breaststroke toward the barge. Upon reaching the high vertical side of the vessel, Webb worked his way to its stern where he came to a set of steel ladder rungs recessed into the transom. He eased himself upward very slowly in order to avoid causing the water to cascade noisily off him back into the cove. Although there was little chance that anyone inside the deckhouse would hear his approach over the rumbling generator, Webb knew that anyone out on the afterdeck, just yards away now, would not be so handicapped.

Slowly, using the cargo of chemical drums for cover, he made his way across the stern of the barge. After another cautious pause, he crept forward along its portside walkway, eyeing the deck of the tug the whole time. When he came to where the hulls of the two vessels came together, the CO made his way undetected down onto the deck of the tug. Using all the stealth mastered in his years of experience stalking poachers, Webb tiptoed silently to the aft portion of the tug's deckhouse where he climbed a permanent ladder to the deckhouse roof. He didn't want to leave any more of a trail of water drops on the tug's decks than absolutely necessary. Furthermore, on the cabin top, he figured there was less chance of being seen by anyone on board, as long as they all stayed inside.

Working his way quietly forward, Webb stopped beside an old sixteen-foot aluminum boat that was lashed to the cabin top. At each place he saw light coming from an opening, he eased himself out over the side of the deckhouse. Peering in through the open ports, he began to put together a mental list of those he could see on board.

In what passed for a wardroom or dining lounge, four men were playing a noisy game of poker. One rather overweight, grey-haired man wearing a dirty white apron would be the cook. And judging from their sun-browned hides, two men wearing faded blue jeans and T-shirts, could be deckhands. The fourth, wearing overalls so blackened with grease that one would never know their original colour, had to be from the engine room. It was possible that these could all be regular tug crew. Friend or foe? He couldn't begin to guess.

He moved forward to the next porthole, the light there was dim, but of the four sleeping berths he could see, two were occupied. However, with no corresponding porthole on the opposite side of the cabin he couldn't know how many berths there might be in there. Furthermore, Webb didn't know how many it would normally take to crew any tug, let alone this specific one. It hadn't come up in his conversation with Small the one time they had chatted. The absence of intelligence was made worse by the fact that he hadn't dared to watch them with his binoculars all evening for fear of arousing their suspicions.

The next space forward proved to be a moderately tidy cabin containing at least one berth. Two men were in there and he recognized them both. The first one was the rotund form of Mike Small. The second man, standing opposite him and looking his usual arrogant self, was none other than Willard Reiger. The two men were obviously involved in a heated discussion which Webb would never get to hear. The porthole glass was closed and an RV type of air conditioner whirring away on the deckhouse roof drowned out their voices.

After creeping all the way forward to the aft end of the raised wheelhouse, his stealthy efforts were suddenly blown. He was in the process of edging himself into a standing position to look in the rear window when a light flared inside. He was illuminated like a framed picture on an art gallery wall, lit up for anyone in that compartment to see. Webb froze in position — hoping — knowing that in nature a prey in motion was far easier for a predator to detect than one frozen still.

The lone man in the wheelhouse had been looking right through Webb as his lighter flared to light up a smoke. In the end though, all he had apparently seen was the glare of the lighter flame and his own face reflected in the glass. And fortunately for Webb, the man turned away just before killing the flame. The guy must have been looking in another direction right up until the instant he thumbed his Bic, otherwise the officer's moonlit approach along the deckhouse roof would have been observed in full detail. Webb silently cursed himself for not expecting the opposition to have a watch posted in the darkened wheelhouse. 'Dumb, dumb, dumb, *dumb*,' he cursed himself. His heart was pounding as he sat down on the roof and pressed himself tight against the aft side of the wheelhouse bulkhead. He needed to regain his composure and think out his next move.

He had covered all the normal living spaces and found no one in apparent distress. He wondered if it was possible to access the below decks area without going through the deckhouse. Perhaps there was a hatch near the winching gear on the tug's aft deck. No, the more logical place to house hostages would be in the fo'c'sle, though it was highly unlikely that either compartment would be equipped with a VHF radio for a hostage to access. He'd probably have to check out both places — if he wasn't stuck here for the rest of the night.

July 21, 2210

In the captain's cabin, Reiger had just cut off the final argument with Mike Small, bluntly stating that if he didn't like the work, there were other tug drivers looking for a job. With Gant's armed goons aboard, the threat implied more than just a loss of employment.

"Now, let's get this show on the road. We've got a load to deliver and other business to take care of before another day is wasted. Gant, wake up your guys; tell them we're moving. If they're hungry, grab something before we start dumping. And shake out the tug's crew too.

"Small, get this boat going now. I want that product dealt with tonight."

July 21, 2212

The man on lookout duty in the wheelhouse took a deep drag on his cigarette and sat once again. Webb could feel the soft thump as the man pushed his back against the aft bulkhead — the other side of the same steel surface that he, himself was leaning against. It was finally safe to move.

As he cautiously worked his way back toward the tug's stern, he passed a pair of small dorade vents mounted on top of the aft end of the deckhouse. He'd passed them on the way forward and paid them no attention. They were mounted over a compartment that appeared to have been added as an afterthought. The ventilators were miniatures of the type of vent seen on the decks of older ships — the ones that look like the loud end of a tuba. He thought for a moment that he'd heard voices coming from one of them. He stopped to listen and was about to dismiss the sound as having come from the card game one cabin forward when he heard a voice — a female voice.

July 21, 2214

Pleased to be on the verge of action again, Gant walked through the crew berthing area and the wardroom rousing his own people and telling the tug crew that they were needed for action immediately. As the poker game folded, Gant stepped out on deck. He thought he detected a brief movement, a shadow passing through the light cast by the moon. He stood quietly, turning his gaze in the direction of the moon. Yes, there it was again.

July 21, 2215

Edging cautiously toward the nearest vent, Webb put his ear next to it. Judging from the warm musty air rising through the ventilator, it was hot and stuffy in the space below. He could hear two people talking. Straining to hear what was being said over the steady throbbing of the diesel generator, Webb never heard the approaching footsteps. But he heard very clearly the hammer being cocked on the pistol in John Gant's hand.

Having no choice but to follow the big security guard's directions, Webb found himself bound tight, gagged with duct tape, and locked in the very compartment he'd been trying to listen into when he was caught. And he was now without his knife; Reiger's man was very efficient.

Within less than a minute of the CO's imprisonment, the tug's main engine started up and he could hear the anchor chain rattling into the chain locker far forward in the vessel's bow. Things weren't going quite the way he had planned.

July 21, 2225

While Rick Webb was trying to get his bearings within the dark locker, a man's voice spoke out. It was actually more of a hoarse whisper. "Turn on the light for a second."

After half a minute of listening to something that sounded like coarse cloth scratching against a rough surface, a dirty old light bulb on the locker's overhead came to life. Webb squinted briefly while his eyes adjusted to the light, though it was scarcely blinding. An old man in casual-dress clothes was sitting and looking very uncomfortable in one corner. Between the old man and Webb, a young woman, looking even more the worse for wear, was just sitting down to lean back against the bulkhead. Both appeared, like Webb, to be bound and gagged by duct tape.

Puzzled as to who had done the talking, he was surprised when the old man spoke — through a narrow slit in the tape that covered his mouth.

"Webb?" As soon as the old man spoke, Rick Webb recognized the voice, and then immediately, the man.

A muffled, "Yudff Frachliff!" was all that Webb could enunciate through his nose, doing his best to acknowledge the judge's surprised greeting.

"Quick Erin, here's the blade," and with that, the two sprang into action, no longer held by the bindings of the tape still attached to their limbs. "Webb, this is my daughter, Erin," the judge made the brief introduction. "Officer Webb here is the one who brought the last round of charges against Reiger and his company. Webb, we're leaving the tape on to look as if we are still tied up. Just leave it stuck to one ankle and rewrap it again around the other if anyone comes to check on us."

Erin, giving Webb a stony stare, used the sharp edge of an ugly old paint scraper to cut through the tape binding his wrists. "You can cut open the mouth hole on your own. If they come back in, just purse your lips and the tape will look untouched." Even as she demonstrated the technique, she didn't hide the fact that she was not kindly disposed toward the clumsy lout who'd just botched what could be their only chance at an outside rescue. She wondered if he was another one of those ham-fisted, arrogant officers who just cruised through their careers, high-grading the easy charges and skating around anything that looked like real work. 'Well, at least Dad seems okay with him,' she thought, but she wasn't at all confident in his opinion on this particular matter. Environmental COs didn't rank very high on her scale of human intelligence.

In that same brief moment, Webb came to the

realization that this was the 'Iron Maiden of Enviro … something-or-other' that the Toronto guys spoke so disparagingly of. At least he'd won the bet with himself when he 'put all the chips' on the hostage being an environmental activist.

'Yeah, she does seem a bit of a cold fish,' he thought, 'and she sure doesn't look too pleased to see me.' He didn't miss the flash of determination in her dark eyes. Determination, seasoned with a strong dose of disdain. 'Then again,' he concluded to himself, 'I probably wouldn't be all that excited about entertaining guests either if I'd been made a prisoner in a place like this … as I guess I actually am.' He decided he had better try to keep things civil, even if just for the judge's sake.

"Better turn off the light again and open those vents before we run out of air in here," the senior Franklin said as Webb finished creating a speaking slit in his gag. "It's hot enough in this stuffy cabinet as it is. We shoved bits of this old tarp into the vents to keep the light from showing on deck."

Helped by the forward motion of the tug through the warm night air, the worst of the stagnant air slowly began to dissipate as Franklin explained how his daughter had been taken hostage. He went on to describe how one of Reiger's men — the big security guy he was sure — had demanded a court acquittal on the pollution charges in exchange for Erin's life. After the Franklins had filled in the details of their misadventure, Webb regretted his recent thoughts concerning the judge's mental faculties.

"Oh God, I'm really sorry Your Honour —"

"Just call me Jim … we're not in a courtroom here, Webb," interrupted James Franklin.

"And I'm just Rick. But after I confess all the names I've been calling you the last few days you may wish to reconsider. I have to tell you, except for the fact your verdict left us totally speechless, Bill Samson and I were just about ready to spit bullets when you dismissed the case. But while we were thinking maybe you needed to have your head examined, here it turns out that you were doing the only thing any sane father would do. I am truly sorry we thought ill of you."

"Webb … um, I'm sorry, your surname just seems to flow more naturally." Rick smiled his acceptance of the judge's preference, though in the pitch-black darkness of the locker, he was the only one to know it.

"Anyhow," Franklin continued, "there's no need to apologise. Even knowing that the legal system would eventually repair the damage I was about to do to your case — and a well-prepared case it was, I must add — *and* knowing that Erin was in grave danger, it still twisted my guts to have to make that dismissal. It just goes against the grain, you know?"

Webb detailed for them how, merely by chance and the changeability of the weather, he happened to be in this particular part of the lake, and he finished with the experience of his failed rescue attempt.

With the background filled in, the three of them went on to discuss their apparently limited options for rescuing themselves. And even then, sitting there in the darkness, any time Webb offered an opinion on something, he continued to detect a chill in the judge's daughter's comments.

Outlining his observations on the size and mixed allegiances of the opposition, Judge Franklin noted an obvious disaffection on the part of the tug's crew for Reiger and his thugs.

"The way I see it," said the judge, "if the water taxi operator had found and acted on my sticky note, then we should have seen police activity before now. That being the case, I think our only hope now is that Small has a streak of decency in him and somehow helps us to escape. Unfortunately though, Reiger seems to run the operation with an iron hand."

"And *that* being the case," said Webb, "I'm thinking we're going to have to 'MacGyver' our own way out of this." And at his request, they stuffed the rags back into the ventilators and turned on the light once again.

'MacGyverisms,' thought Erin as she worked. 'Those Rube Goldberg inventions only work on old TV shows. Surely this guy can't be serious. The three of us against man-mountain Gant, wicked Willard Reiger and their three fighting-fit thugs — not to mention their guns. That's just great.' She was not encouraged by the officer's line of thinking — not one bit.

Only after Webb carefully searched the locker for concealed exits — there were none — and for items they could use as weapons in a fight, did he turn off the light. A rubber mallet, presumably for closing paint can lids, was all he could add to their inventory of ready-made weapons. It had been caught in a bulky fold in the old tarp and had not been noticed by the Franklins.

Before the light went off, he had torn three long narrow strips of canvas from the tarp. When it was dark once again, Webb asked 'the Iron Maiden', not by that name of course, if she would hold the ends of the torn tarpaulin strips together while he, guided by feel alone, began to braid them together. Neither of the Franklins interrupted Webb's concentration. While the judge was curious as to the nature of weapon the man was blindly fashioning, Erin was incurious and unimpressed.

"There, a paint scraper, a rubber hammer and a canvas mace … sort of," Webb said when he was finally done. What he had fashioned was a crude two-foot length of 'rope' with a softball-sized knot at one end. "Actually, it's more like a poor imitation of a monkey's fist. Not great … it's lighter than I'd hoped it would be … but its victim won't know that until after it hits him. I'm counting on the element of surprise. The main thing is that we are all armed now, in a manner of speaking.

"Erin, you take the scraper, and you get the 'gavel' sir. My guess is that when they come to get us out of here, we may be facing a very limited future. I'll assume that the big fellow…"

"Gant," filled in Erin.

"Knowing my occupation and guessing at my training, Gant'll likely rate me as the greatest risk of causing problems, and I hope he'll stick closest to me. If I get a chance to move on him, I won't likely be able to give you two any advanced warning. And I won't be following Queensbury rules. When I do go after him though, strike out quickly with your weapon at the nearest enemy, and then beat it for anywhere on the boat that looks safe. I'm hoping that will be in the midst the tug's regular crew, but we'll have to see how it plays out.

"If your victim grabs your weapon and won't let go, don't hang around. Let it go and move out of range. Once we're out on deck, there may be other potential weapons — use anything you can pick up on the fly to swing or throw. Just strike hard once and move on." At least Webb was reasonably confident that Erin would not be the type to faint when the first bad guy yelled 'Boo!'

July 21, 2250

When the water taxi skipper awoke, he was stiff and sore, both from his marathon swim and from sleeping on the bare rock. The night was warm and very muggy, and he was relieved to discover that the same warm rocks that had brought him back from hypothermia had also done a decent job of drying his clothes. As he dressed, he pondered his next move. Build a fire. Actually, three fires — the universal distress signal. Good thing he was a smoker. Although his cigarettes were now just soggy mush, he still had his lighter. He tested it. It worked. His next thought was, 'God, I sure could use a smoke.'

Combing along the beach and amongst the few low patches of scrub bush on the island, Red found lots of small, dry wood for kindling, but little of the body wood needed to sustain one, let alone three fires. In any event, he set out three piles of brush, each about twenty yards apart on the high — well, not so high — beach ridge on the centre spine of the small island. Only when a boat passed near enough to recognize three fires as a distress signal, not a beach party, would he touch off the fires.

'Mind you,' he thought, 'in this day and age of the 'me first' generation, the appearance of party activity might draw more boaters than any distress signal ever could.'

7. DEPOSIT

July 21, 2345 hrs

Mike Small was alone in the wheelhouse of the tug *Lady M*. His orders from Reiger were to sail out to the dumping grounds he had been using and get rid of the unauthorized toxins they were carrying. The boss had at least accepted the tug skipper's rationale for dumping over Dawson Rock — that is, the 'unused by anyone' part.

After dumping their illicit product, Reiger's plan was to return to Club Island and wait for the American sailboats to leave in the morning. As soon as the cove was clear of witnesses, they would take the game warden's boat in tow and get rid of any evidence of their involvement with the warden, the judge and his daughter.

Small had lost his final argument with the man. Each of his points had been stubbornly rebuffed. The worst he had *hoped* would happen was that they would drop the hostages back at Club Island, or one of several uninhabited islands in the area. After that they'd land at the nearest quiet beach on the mainland, abandon ship and quickly make their way into hiding, or out of the country — each to his-own devices. After all, he'd argued, they were already in enough trouble as it was. Did Reiger think he could just carry on doing business as usual after this? What about the offshore accounts he'd been transferring money into over the last few years? Didn't he realize it was time to fold his tent and disappear into the night?

Reiger had been furious at the suggestion that he should just walk away from his own company, his life's most significant accomplishment. The offshore funds were for a rainy day, he emphasized.

"*Rainy day!*" Small had blown his stack at Reiger's under-estimation of the situation. "*Jesus* man, with a game warden, a judge, and his daughter missing, it will be rainin' cops and detector dogs before the weekend is over!" But Reiger had remained unmoved.

Standing at the wheel of *Lady M,* Small now knew that Reiger and Gant had moved far beyond the point of no return. They'd lost all concept of reality and they were dragging him and his crew down with them.

The tug skipper had finally come to the end of his tether. He had wanted to take a stand ever since Reiger had brought the judge's daughter aboard, but those guys were armed, and he just hadn't had the nerve to follow through. But now that there was absolutely no doubt what was planned for the captives, he couldn't put it off any longer.

Any further delay put not only the lives of the hostages in serious jeopardy but also the lives and the futures of his entire crew. He was truly sorry he had waited so long to act. Although he felt sick about having to leave his adopted country, he knew that his application for Canadian citizenship would be automatically rejected because of his involvement in this whole rotten fiasco. After getting out of prison, he'd be sent packing, out of the country and back home to another anonymous dead-end job. So now there was nothing to be gained by his further inaction.

The principles of honesty and decency drummed into him so long ago by his parents and his teachers, told him that this was the time to act. Regardless of the personal consequences he had to try to undo some of the damage he'd taken part in. He had to put the interests of others ahead of his own welfare for once. Maybe with their help, he and his crew could turn the tables on Reiger. With that in mind, he engaged the tug's auto-helm and went to brief his men.

July 22, 0040

The water was calm over the shoal known as Dawson Rock. Mike Small deftly manoeuvred *Lady M* alongside the barge. While his own crew secured the two vessels side by side, Reiger's loaders boarded the barge and immediately began removing tarpaulins and untying the lashings that held the illegal toxins firmly to its deck. All of the lights on the tug and barge were extinguished.

Working only by the light of the moon, and when needed, small, hooded flashlights, they made their final preparations. The loader named Mitch guided the forks of the lift truck under the first pallet of illicit drums. Very slowly he inched the load close to the edge of the deck setting it down when it was overhanging the water by just under half of the pallet's length.

After backing the truck's forks clear of the load, Morris and Goreham both pushed on it and the pallet tilted over the side. The positive buoyancy of the wooden pallet and the small amount of residual air trapped in the drums had been overcome by wiring scrap metal weights to the pallet frames before they left the barge. Still lashed to the pallet by steel packing bands, the drums slowly sank to join several hundred others left on earlier trips. Sixty-four more drums of PCBs were now on the lakebed.

They had not weighed down the pallets until they were

ready to drop. Scrap metal wired to their cargo would look awfully suspicious in the event of a surprise inspection.

It took time to do it by feel and by the light of the moon alone. Each pallet had to be moved out from the others and set in a small open space on the crowded deck of the barge. There was only room to work on one pallet at a time. So it had taken an hour and forty minutes to uncover the load, attach the weights and off-load the sixteen illegal pallets. Another twenty minutes were taken up re-securing the remaining cargo to the deck of the barge. Finally, the tug and tow were under way once more.

July 22, 0245

The atmosphere in the wheelhouse and crew spaces aboard *Lady M* was tense. The tug was heading southwest once more; the barge now carrying only a legitimate cargo of industrial waste bound for destruction at the cement plant in Alpena. As soon as they had finished dumping the last of the drums at Dawson Rock, Reiger left instructions with Gant to wake him before they arrived back at Club Island. Then he went to the captain's cabin to get some sleep. Gant sat alone in the wardroom drinking coffee and devouring most of an apple pie while his three loaders and the tug's cook retired to their berths. Small and Ethier were in the wheelhouse. Billy Manion was down in the engine room with the engineer making some final preparations for what was to follow.

The coffee was bitter, but Gant was disinclined to go to the trouble to brew a new pot. As a result, he unknowingly proceeded to drink most of the ground up Gravol pills dissolved in the pot by Charlie the cook, who'd been acting on the skipper's instructions. Most oral medications taken for motion sickness come with warnings against driving or operating machinery after taking. A normal dose can make one drowsy. The dose consumed by Gant was enough to put down a horse.

July 22, 0310

Mike Small placed the vessel under the control of the auto-helm once more and signalled that it was time for him and Ethier to leave the wheelhouse. Descending quickly to the main deck, Small hurried to the starboard access hatch of the storage locker containing Reiger's three prisoners. Above him on the deckhouse roof, Ray Ethier and the crew were working as quietly as they could, rigging the tug's mast-mounted derrick to sling the old outboard-powered tender over the side.

After several failed attempts to unlock the padlock securing the paint locker, Small dared to briefly shine his pen light onto the stubborn lock. The key went in, but the lock wouldn't turn.

"Shit!" The lock was not one of the 'keyed alike' locks they always used aboard the tug. Although all shipboard lockers were normally left unlocked while under way, prudence dictated that all locks should be able to be opened by the same key. And each member of the crew was issued a copy of that key. This practice reduced the chances of someone not being able to open a crucial hatch in an emergency.

A quick trip around to the port side hatch revealed the same situation there. He could have used any of several heavy tools on deck to twist the lock off the hasp, but the noise would most certainly bring even the sleeping Gant out of the adjacent crew quarters. Quickly climbing the ladder at the aft end of the deckhouse, Small joined his crew. They were lowering the old aluminum boat over the starboard side, stopping only when it hung level with the main deck, just a couple of feet above the water.

"Billy, they switched the locks on us. Hurry down to the engine room and get me the bolt cutters. But don't wake up any of those assholes whatever you do. Hank, you and Ray get the outboard motor primed and ready. I want it running when we hit the water." When he had finished passing orders to his crew, Small knelt down on the deckhouse roof and spoke into the dorade vent.

"Judge, it's Mike Small speaking. I'm real sorry about what they've done to you three. We're trying to get you out but Reiger changed the locks. One of my crewmen is going down to the engine room for bolt cutters. We'll have you out in a few minutes, and then we'll all get away in the tender."

July 22, 0315

A simultaneous sigh of relief was audible from the three captives in the storage locker as they listened to the hurried footsteps on the compartment's overhead. Judge Franklin was midway through telling the other two how he would pass along his recommendation for leniency in Small's case, when the voice sounded in the ventilator again.

"We've got problems up here. Reiger's awake and spittin' mad. We tried to slip a Mickey to Gant, but he's comin' 'round too. Young Billy couldn't get past them to get the bolt cutters, and we can't break you out of there without them discovering our getaway. They've got guns and we don't. Any minute now they'll find the crew are missing. The way I see it, we can only help you if the five of us bug out right now. We'll send help as soon as we can get to a radio or a phone … I'm real sorry. We've gotta go now!"

"Okay go … hurry," the three captives called up the ventilator in unison.

July 22, 0317

Just as Mike Small finished calling down his final message, Ray Ethier got the forty-horsepower Johnson Sea Horse started, then sat, his hand ready on the tiller handle. Because the boat was still held above the water in its sling, the roar of the outboard's exhaust was loud enough to be heard by every one of Reiger's gang aboard the tug.

Small slid down the ladder to the tug's aft deck like a submariner hurtling down into the control room during an emergency dive. Five running steps carried him across the deck to where the tender was hanging over the water in its sling.

"Cut 'er now," Small hollered at Billy Manion as he half-rolled his bulk into the getaway boat.

Even before Small's weight fully settled on the bottom of the big aluminum boat, Manion had cut the aft sling line through. The boat's stern dropped into the water and the forward motion of the tug dragged the remaining sling ahead, slipping it from underneath the bow.

As soon as the bow dropped free of its sling, the tender began to slide aft along the tug's chunky beam. But it was held close to the larger boat by the suction created as the two vessels moved through the water, side by side.

Hank, the engineer was sitting in the bow of the aluminum boat. He quickly grabbed an oar and pushed it hard against the side of the big tug. As soon as the bow began to swing away from it, Ray Ethier twisted the throttle wide open. The five men in the tender immediately felt the thrust of the boat accelerating forward.

Quickly steering to turn away from the tug and head back in the opposite direction, Ethier cut as close to the bow of the following barge as he could. He cleared it only by inches. That was just as well, for at the same instant as they began their pass down the side of the tow, shots rang out from the aft deck of the tug. Fortunately for Small and his crew, the shots either went wide or were intercepted by the blunt bow of the steel barge.

Sitting on the bench seat forward of the driver's position, Mike Small pulled a weathered old hand-held compass from his jacket pocket and sighted it ahead just to the right of the direction the old, battered Prince Craft boat was headed. After watching his skipper for a brief moment, Ethier turned the boat slightly, correcting his course until Small nodded his approval. Fixing his gaze on a particular star, the tug's mate would be able to hold that course until the skipper asked differently.

"What do you figure we're doin', twenty knots maybe?" Small called out, looking back at his mate for concurrence.

"When we first get dis rig," Ethier shouted forward toward Small over the roaring outboard, "I try her out alone between two buoys. She do t'irty-two knots dat day."

"Yeah, but the outboard and the gas alone weigh more than you do Ray," the skipper called back, sporting a grin that was clearly visible in the moonlight. "No, by the time you add in the rest of us four, she'll be doing real good to make twenty. Nothing more. Anyhow, at twenty knots we should reach the nearest phone at Britt in about an hour and forty-five minutes."

July 22, 0317

The three hostages were staggered by this latest setback, falling so soon after it had appeared that they might make their escape. Sitting, in the paint storage locker aboard *Lady M*, they were silent — stunned. Outside they could hear the roar of the outboard motor as Small and his crew hurried away. Their only consolation was hearing the outboard continue motoring into the distance after Reiger's gang stopped shooting.

"Well, despite the fact that Small is most likely a man of his word, until outside help actually arrives, I think we'll have to assume we are on our own now." It was Webb who spoke first, voicing the thought they all shared.

"Agreed," replied Franklin senior. "I'm guessing that that Red fellow never saw my note when he took *Flash* back to Owen Sound, so we'll have to carry on with your plan the instant any of Reiger's gang opens that door … but without the advantage of having any potential allies aboard."

A contemplative silence fell over the captives again, as the tug's diesel dragged its ungainly tow on into the night.

July 22, 0433

Rushing eastward over the calm surface of Georgian Bay, the open aluminum boat carrying Mike Small and the rest of the tug's crew had made good time for the first hour following their escape from the tug. But in the past fifteen minutes, everyone on board had begun to notice a slight rattling sound in the engine. Worse still, the noise intensified; gradually at first, but then suddenly, with a final clattering *bang*, the outboard stopped — dead.

"Merde! She's cassé," Ethier exclaimed. Everyone sat, dumfounded, nothing more said for a moment.

"If it weren't for bad luck, we wouldn't be having any luck at all," Billy Manion chirped up.

"Shut up Billy, this is serious," Small snapped. "Sounds like she tore herself up inside. Did you guys remember to mix any oil in the gas for this motor?"

"Sure. Hank even told me to put in a bit more than it calls for," replied Manion defensively.

"Ja," the old Dutch engineer elaborated, "I tell the boy, 'this motor is not run hard for a long time. You give it extra ounce of oil for each gallon.' But I think it is broken crankshaft maybe. Too little oil would make pistons get hot and expand and it would seize up, but not break up inside like we heard." Always prepared for an emergency, Hank picked up a small tool roll he'd brought with him and moved to the back of the boat, trading places with Ethier. Flashlights were produced and they prepared for exploratory surgery — but without any real optimism.

Removing the cover from the outboard, the engineer pulled on the starter cord, but it would not budge. Immediately beneath the recoil starter assembly was the flywheel. He tried turning it by hand, but it too, refused to move, and that was due to catastrophic damage within the power head, just as Hank had suspected.

"I am sorry, I cannot fix it," the engineer said, totally deflated. The surgery was cancelled before it even began.

"Not your fault Hank. The thing was over fifty years old and it was already well used when we bought it. God only knows how many hours it could have had on it." Small was temporarily at a loss for what to say beyond that, but he knew they couldn't just quit. They still had one mode of propulsion remaining aboard, so he began to rally his troops. "You ever rowed a big old Greek galley, Billy?"

"No Skipper, I never even seen one."

"Well, by the time we pull into the Britt Coast Guard station, rowing a galley will seem real easy, 'cause movin' this aluminum pig with its mismatched oars, both bein' too short for the job, is going to be pure hell. But we can't let Reiger get away with what he has planned for those people.

"So let's get at 'er. We'll all take short shifts to avoid burning ourselves out, and then we'll see who's got the biggest blisters when we get there. Fifteen minutes apiece. My turn first."

July 22, 0440

The tug *Lady M*, under the less than expert command of Willard Reiger, returned to the cove in Club Island. Anticipating that the visiting American sailboats would still be at anchor there, Gant and his men had rafted the barge alongside the tug before entering the anchorage. That was just as well, for in their ineptitude, it had taken several messy attempts to complete the task. Anyone watching would pretty quickly realize that these were not regular tug men, and although it was impossible for the tug to be inconspicuous, Reiger had no desire to draw any more attention to it than was absolutely necessary.

Anchoring the rafted together vessels in the cove had gone more smoothly. Since they'd be leaving the barge in the cove for the next part of the operation, they dropped its anchor, instead of the tug's. It mattered little that the anchor wasn't properly set on the rocky bottom. There wasn't a breath of wind, and the weight of the anchor and its chain would hold the two vessels stationary for the time being.

Reiger, waiting impatiently for the unwanted sailboats to leave, was rewarded by some early morning activity aboard both boats. Unbeknownst to him, the two-boat flotilla was in a hurry to get north to Covered Portage Cove before that favourite pleasure boat destination filled up for the night, and so preparations were under way for a really early departure.

For Reiger, the suspense was building. In fact, it was just about driving him mad — even at the best of times he did not handle inactivity well. And at that particular moment, he had no idea how much time he would have to cover his tracks if

Small and his crew had alerted the authorities. However, since the tug crew members were involved just as much as the rest of them, he figured it was most likely that they'd just go to ground, not wanting to draw any official attention to themselves either. In fact, Reiger was sure that would be the case — but still — there was always that nagging possibility.

July 22, 0455

Much to Reiger's relief, the two American sailboats winched up their anchors and motored out of the cove in single file, turning north as soon as they were clear of the offshore limestone shoal. Finally, he could take care of his remaining problems — the witnesses stowed in the tug's paint storage locker.

July 22, 0505

The temperature in the paint locker aboard *Lady M* had remained insufferably hot all that long muggy summer night. Worse still, the hostages had not been provided with any food or drink since Erin and her father had been fed the previous afternoon. Webb and the Franklins were beginning to feel the effects of dehydration. Their deprivation, they all agreed, was all the indication they needed that Reiger and his men had no plan other than disposing of them. All they could do was wait and hope for a chance to break out at the first opportunity that came along.

For the first while, Webb and the judge had done their best to pass the time by swapping fishing and hunting stories, so there was a sense of comradeship building between them that bolstered their spirits — a little.

Erin's spirit on the other hand, having been in captivity

much longer than either of the other two, was at an all-time low. Compounding her misery, she continued to blame herself over and over again, most particularly for her father's capture. And she was still steamed at Webb for botching his rescue attempt.

Sensing her ongoing distress, the two men let their conversation lapse. It was during that period of silence that they heard footsteps approaching down the deck of the anchored tug and then the rattling of the padlock securing the hatch as it was unlocked.

"Your weapons … get ready," Webb whispered hoarsely to the others. The new morning's light slipped through the widening gap as the hatch was pulled open.

Gant and his three men stood on deck in a semicircle just outside the locker entrance. At a nod from their leader, Dwayne Goreham stepped inside, opened a utility knife and began to cut the tape binding Webb's ankles. Just as the thug realized that the tape had already been cut through on the opposite side, Webb too, realized that their element of surprise had just expired. He knew that this would be their only chance to bolt. If Goreham raised the alarm first, there would not likely be any other chance of escape.

"Now!" he gave the rallying cry to the others — again, a hoarse whisper.

At the same instant, Webb sprang into action, his heat exhaustion momentarily cast aside. Surging up and out of his crouched position, he drove his head with all his remaining energy straight into the solar plexus of the man with the utility knife. Goreham grunted. Winded and immobilized he dropped the knife.

The CO kept moving forward, driving the man back out through the locker hatchway, and when his heels caught on the coaming across the bottom edge of the opening, Goreham fell backward, slammed to the deck. He was no longer a threat.

Gant, caught by surprise, was next in Webb's path. But with his momentum broken by the effort needed to push the stocky Goreham out of the way, his attack was limited to a fist delivered in a wicked upper cut to the big man's genitals. This coincided exactly with a giant fist, still clenching a pistol, landing a blow to the side of Webb's head. His lights went out instantly — there was no 'seeing stars' the way they say it happens — it was just over and out. He never got to test his canvas bludgeon.

Judge Franklin started his attack shakily. Stiffened after sitting in one position for most of the night, he stumbled over the same coaming that had felled Goreham, dropping the rubber mallet in the process. But he recovered faster than Mitch Mitchell who, still surprised by the sudden commotion, didn't anticipate being tackled by a white-haired former football player. Mitchell went overboard.

Hindsight would suggest that the judge should have moved in to finish off Gant, who was curled up in a fetal position and displaying definite signs of discomfort following Webb's attack. He probably should have taken control of Gant's gun, but strong parental instinct sent Franklin immediately to the aid of his daughter.

Erin had dashed out of the locker close on the heels of her dad. Now cornered at the bow of the tug, she was waving the utility knife Goreham had dropped. She was locked in a stalemate with Jay Morris, the only chivalrous member of Gant's gang. She had already tried to rake his face with the paint scraper, but her aim was low and Morris had deflected it down and away, bouncing the tool off the tug's rail and overboard. He was empty-handed, and although he could have picked up any number of blunt weapons within a few yards, he was hesitant about hitting a woman. Arriving at the bow undetected by Morris, the judge prepared to tackle him from behind. But at that same instant, Franklin felt the muzzle of a pistol pressed against the back of his neck.

"Freeze!" said Reiger, who had joined the party late. He brought the show to a sudden end.

July 22, 0615

As the sun steadily gained altitude above the eastern horizon, what had been a warm, muggy night was already developing into another hot, sultry day. Not a breath of air stirred over Halfmoon Island. Red was sitting propped up against a large boulder, ostensibly waiting for a boat to come by and rescue him, but for the moment he had dozed off, dog-tired after his long night on the uninhabited island.

He awakened to the familiar, though annoying whine of three personal watercraft — those aggravating single-seat boats that had morphed out of snowmobiles. They were buzzing their way northward and were just about to pass the island. Caught off guard, he didn't even have time to light one of his signal fires, let alone all three, so he grabbed his orange life jacket and began jumping up and down, waving it madly over his head. Relief swept over him the instant one of the operators happened to see him. The guy slowed down and gave him a big friendly wave — before opening the throttle full out to catch up with the other two machines.

"*Assholes!*" he shouted. Red's opinion of the damned noisy things was no higher than it had been a few minutes earlier.

8. ESCAPE

July 22, 0715 hrs

The first thing Rick Webb became aware of was a splitting headache. And his senses were transmitting either badly scrambled information to his brain or none at all. He had no idea how long he'd been like that, but gradually, he started to become aware of his surroundings.

He began to notice odours which were somehow vaguely familiar, but difficult to recognize in his disoriented state. Every boat has a distinctive smell, which is actually a combination of odours given off by various components aboard. Webb's olfactory senses were picking up and sorting through a collage of smells including hints of steel rust, recent varnish, old mahogany, moth balls, gasoline, coffee grounds, hand soap and ancient sponge-rubber seat cushions. And then he knew. He was aboard *Water Baby*.

With that knowledge, his survival instinct, an instinct bred into us all, kicked in and started reorienting his other senses. Although his vision was still blurred, Webb began to see his surroundings, though what he was seeing still confused him. Everything within view appeared upside down. Only gradually did the reason for that become apparent when he finally realized that his belt was caught on the heavy bronze hook he used to hang the garbage bag near the navigating table. He was partially suspended, upside down on the companionway steps. It took another few minutes before his mind worked out a solution to this problem. But after struggling to release his belt buckle, he went cascading down onto the cabin sole amidst the spilled garbage. That initiated a whole new wave of painful sensations.

As he lay on the cabin floor, he began to pick up other facts relating to his situation. The boat was sluicing through the water, fast. But it was rock steady and not heeled over. Nor was it the boat's own engine that was driving it forward. There were other people in the cabin. They were talking to him, urgently, but he couldn't understand what they were saying. It took another minute before the situation crystallized — they were sitting, tied back-to-back on the salon carpet, trying to talk through duct-tape gags.

"Jim," he whispered hoarsely, trying out his voice. It was dry and shaky but audible, and hearing it gave him the confidence he needed to begin taking action. It was slow going at first; he was stiff and in a whole lot of pain. But it was action all the same.

He unfolded himself up off the linoleum galley sole and moved into the salon to free Erin and her father. Despite their immobility, the mere presence of the judge and his daughter gave Webb a sudden sense of purpose and with the adrenalin now kicking in, a miraculous return to his normal practical self — although he still hurt like hell!

"I think this is where I'm supposed to welcome you aboard *Water Baby*," he winced at the effort of trying to force an impish smile. "I'd normally offer drinks at this stage, but I think we've got more urgent matters to attend to." His weak attempt at humour fell flat with his audience, but he'd done it as much to distract his own mind from the pains he suffered, as to give encouragement to the Franklins.

Franklin senior however, was relieved that Webb had recovered enough of his mental capacity to at least try for a witty comment while obviously being aware of their grave situation. Erin, on the other hand, dismissed it as an airheaded, cavalier attitude toward their dire circumstance, thinking that the guy was useless in an emergency — again.

Unsheathing a sharp knife he grabbed from the galley, he quickly cut the duct tape binding them together. A touch more delicately, for fear of nicking someone's flesh, he freed their tightly bound wrists. While Webb was working at releasing Erin, the judge ripped the tape from his mouth, grimacing, and greeted his rescuer.

"Webb, I thought you were dead. After they bound us together down here, they threw your body down the steps as if it were a bag of laundry, then slammed the hatch over and nailed it shut. Ever since then you just hung there, motionless."

"What's our present situation?" Webb asked.

"They're towing us somewhere with the tug."

"Are any of them still on board?" Webb tried without success to open the companionway hatch as he asked.

"The three that brought us down here got back on the tug from my side before we started moving," said Erin, who had been facing to starboard while bound to her father in the salon. "I didn't see any others on deck."

"None in view on my side either." Stepping aside to allow Webb to try opening the forward hatch, in vain, Jim Franklin added, "From what I've seen and heard while they were moving us down here from the tug, our time is short. Reiger's not going to want to keep us around much longer, and that pack of jackals with him is just as bad as he is. Our brief dirty fight with them didn't gain us any friends either."

"So, did we win?" Webb's questioning grin was again, a grimace.

"Well, you'll be pleased to know that when we parted company, Gant was still walking like a bow-legged cowboy, suffering from your quick jab between his legs," the judge responded, giving the highlights of the parts of the battle that Webb had missed. "On the negative side of the ledger, they made a lot of retaliatory noises down here before they brought us aboard."

"So I see." Webb said. A burning anger flared inside him as he looked around the cabin, listening at the same time to the judge's briefing. The VHF radios and most of the other electronics had been smashed and the wires cut; their primary communications links with the rest of the world were gone. Picking up his smashed phone he asked, "How about your cell phones?"

"Still on the tugboat I think," Erin spoke for the two of them.

Turning his mind to finding a solution to their predicament, Webb asked, "How long have we been moving?" He stared momentarily at the bulkhead compass inside the cabin.

"We started moving just after six o'clock according to that," Jim Franklin nodded toward the ship's clock.

"Did they tow us directly from Club Island?"

"Yes."

"Been going pretty much the same speed since we started moving?" Webb looked out through the galley ports trying to estimate their speed. The glassy lake surface made it difficult to judge, but the wake made by the tug as it hauled them through the water gave him the feeling that they could be doing as much as eight knots.

Erin Franklin responded, "Well, I think they started out towing us way too fast, because this boat began erratically yawing back and forth and rolling violently at the same time.

Almost immediately the tug's engine slowed down and since your boat stabilized, their engine hasn't changed its note."

Webb worked quickly on the local nautical chart with a set of dividers before speaking again.

"It's seven-thirty now. He's towing us southeast. We should be roughly four miles east of Halfmoon Island. If he has plans to ram and sink us, the deepest water in Georgian Bay, five hundred sixty-odd feet, is an hour and a half to the south. He won't want to wait that long. Besides which, that's less than a mile offshore from the National Park — someone would see the action for sure. But out here it's still over three hundred feet deep, and if there are no spectators around … well … he has no reason to delay if that's what he's got planned.

"That dark sky off to the southwest probably heralds one mean thunderstorm," Webb continued, looking out the starboard portholes. "No more than half an hour away I'd guess, but likely much sooner. If we are ready when it hits, it could be a real help to us. If we're not, then I imagine Reiger will put it to *his* good use instead."

Webb unlatched and swung the hinged companionway steps toward the navigating station, opening the engine compartment for inspection. He intended to engage the transmission into forward gear from inside the cabin to stop the propeller shaft which he could hear freewheeling at high speed. Prolonged continuous spinning of the shaft without the engine running could damage the transmission. If events unfolded as he hoped, they would need it in good running order shortly. Reaching in, he grasped the shift linkage on the far side of the engine and pulled hard. As the clutch shuddered momentarily before bringing the spinning shaft to a stop, he cursed aloud.

"Shit. The bastards have rigged aircraft cable around the

through hull valves back here! What the Christ are they planning?" But he knew the answer even as he asked. "Ramming is definitely not in their plans."

Two of the rigged valves in the hull were for the cockpit drains, one was the household water supply for the galley, one provided cooling water for the engine and the largest was the drain for the galley sink. All of the through hulls were located well below the water level. The five individual cables were connected to one single cable which Webb saw was led out through a ventilator to emerge on deck. There was no doubt in his mind that the single cable was attached either directly to the tug, or somehow rigged to the towing hawser.

It appeared that Reiger was planning to scuttle the yawl by using the tug to pull on the cable, tearing the valves from the inside of the hull. Each cable appeared to be a different length, so that the whole force of the main cable would come to bear on each fitting in succession, not all at once. It was a guarantee of certain success. Nothing short of cable cutters would remove the deadly yokes from the targeted valves.

"It's imperative we get out of this cabin immediately. If those through hulls are sheared off, the boat could go down in as little as twenty minutes," Webb said. "We need to get the cable cutters from the toolbox in the sail locker and we can only access that from the cockpit."

He reached his arm as far as it would go into the space aft of the chart table. He was hoping to get at the locker area under the starboard cockpit seat. "Damn, I can't reach." Looking quickly around the cabin, he opened the wet hanging locker next to the navigating station and pulled out a short, wooden-handled broom.

Once again he extended his arm into the space under the cockpit seat. Holding the broom handle out to maximize his reach, he angled the far end of it up against the underside of the starboard seat locker lid. With all the strength in his wrist he twisted upward and felt the lid move. Satisfied with the result, he looked at Erin.

"Claustrophobic?" he asked.

"Nnnno," she responded hesitantly — unsure of what was coming next. The guy was full of ideas but his initial rescue attempt and everything else she'd seen him turn his hand to, left her feeling that he was a little short on substance.

"This boat was built with a quarter berth option," he said as he raised the chart table top and started flinging a variety of hardware and spare parts from the sectioned off area underneath onto the galley countertop just behind him. "If we eliminate the ship's spare parts from this area, and remove the sectional divider," he grunted as he lifted the wooden frame up and out, "it becomes a quarter-berth that runs out under the cockpit seat.

"You are the slimmest and shortest of the three of us. I need you to worm your way into the berth headfirst, instead of feet-first. Then push the locker lid open, sit up and get out into the cockpit. It doesn't feel as if they secured the lid. Maybe we've finally caught a break.

"Find out what's jamming the companionway hatch. But for God's sake, keep your head down. We don't want you getting shot at, and we don't want to tip them off that we're back in the fight."

Erin sat up on the edge of the quarter berth, then leaned sideways and lowered herself into the space. Once lined up with the narrow berth, she rolled onto her back and started wriggling into the area beneath the cockpit seat. Just when she thought her knees, which were still bent, wouldn't allow her to go any farther, she found herself under the locker lid. Lifting up on the lid, she found that Webb was only partly correct — a rope fastened across the seat held the lid down so that she could only lift it an inch or two.

"Give me a knife," she said impatiently.

Webb grabbed the knife he'd used to free the Franklins, and reached into the cramped quarter berth space, passing it aft until he could feel her take it firmly from his grip.

After extending the blade through the narrow gap, she made quick work of the restricting line. Flipping up the seat lid, she worked her way out into the cockpit.

She could see right away what had jammed the companionway hatch closed.

"Have you got a hammer or some kind of pry bar," she called through the hatch. "They nailed a board under the hatch, jammed between its bottom lip and the top edge of the door."

"The toolbox is in the sail locker under the port cockpit seat. Be careful, it's heavy. The hammer and pry bar are both in the main compartment underneath the top trays. Take your pick," Webb called back and then looked at Franklin, standing beside him in the cabin. He was curious as to the source of the woman's apparent boat savvy. "You own a boat too?"

"No, but she spent several summers at a sailing camp as a youngster, and in recent years she has crewed regularly for friends who have a sailboat on Lake Ontario, as well as attending several boating courses over the last couple of winters," he smiled, a father's pride clearly showing through. "And she has always been handy with tools. She used to help me with most of the repairs around the house before she left home." Then, looking a little uncomfortable, he decided that it was time to broach a more delicate matter while he had a moment alone with Webb. Being a good judge of character — necessary in his profession — Franklin had easily picked up on the chill between his daughter and Webb right from the moment of their introduction.

"She's not always … umm … how should I put this … well, she's not always 'user friendly,' so to speak. Competing for recognition in a traditionally male-dominated field has toughened her hide … perhaps, a little too much. Also, I've heard it said that some of the folks she has to deal with in your organization have given her a less-than-complimentary nickname … and that hasn't helped either."

"Thanks for the background. I've heard the moniker," Webb confessed, quite embarrassed that the judge knew what was being said of his daughter by some of his fellow officers. "I'll admit that she did seem to fit the profile when we first met last night. But from what I've seen ever since then, I'll tell you, I'd rather have someone with her iron will along on this misadventure than some hysterical cry-baby, male or female. And if we can get free of these guys it'll sure help having an additional seasoned sailor along too." Webb paused and smiled, then flinched as he heard the sound of nails being pulled from the fine wood of the mahogany hatch. "Now, let's take back control of this ship."

Franklin was relieved that Webb had taken it the way he did. Having planted a seed of understanding in the officer's mind would hopefully encourage a little improved détente between the two of them — as long as Erin picked up on the new vibe. And women were supposed to be good at detecting that sort of thing. In any case, they'd all need to work as a team if they were to have any chance of getting out of this situation alive.

Webb was out into the cockpit as soon as Erin had removed the vertical hinged door portion of the hatch. Squatting low to avoid being seen from the tug, he quickly scanned the horizon for any sign of other vessels. A sailboat, motoring its way northward toward Killarney, was receding a mile or more to the north off their port quarter. Aside from that, there were no other boats were in sight. The sky to the southwest, on their starboard side, was looking blacker all the time. The storm was approaching quickly.

"As soon as that boat is out of sight, it'll just be us and Reiger, no witnesses to screw up his plans," Webb told the others. "We've got to act quickly, before he pulls the plug." He winced at his own unintentional reference to the Mid-Con man's scheme for sinking his boat. "At least now, if the boat goes down, we're no longer trapped inside the cabin."

Grabbing the cutter from the toolbox, Webb quickly set its jaws over a slack loop in the offending cable where it emerged from the vent on the poop deck. The extra loop of cable was obviously intended to allow the boat to drop back even farther after the hawser was released, guaranteeing that the wire rope would come taut with a really nasty jerk. That would thrust the entire force of the load onto the through hull fittings. He had to cut it now before Reiger had a chance to act first and he had just started to apply force to the cutter handles when Erin stopped him.

"Cut it farther forward," she said as she took in the situation. "If you cut it back there, assuming you are planning to feed it overboard afterwards, the cable could get wrapped around the propeller when you start the engine." And to herself she thought, 'It's amazing the guy ever learned to walk.' She allowed him no credit what-so-ever for the fact he'd just survived a significant brain concussion.

"Crap ... you're right. Thanks ... I wasn't thinking." Webb was both embarrassed and relieved that she had thought of what should have been obvious to him.

Staying in the cover of the cockpit, but reaching out onto the portside walkway, Webb placed the cutter's jaws over the cable there and put all the force he could muster into squeezing the handles together. It wasn't easy to apply the necessary pressure when he couldn't get out there on the walkway and lean his weight directly on the cutter's handles. The high-quality stainless-steel cable was tough. He prayed that it would not be now that the cable would suddenly tense, pulling the guts out of his lovely old ship. And with that thought and the sudden surge of adrenalin it produced, the cutter handles came together, and the cable lay severed on the deck.

"Here, take this Jim," said Webb, handing the cable cutter to the judge. "See if you can reach into the engine compartment and cut the inboard ends of those cables. Get them out of there. If it can't be done, tie them off somehow so there's no slack. The last thing we need is to get them tangled around the propeller shaft in there when we start her up.

"Erin, as soon as your dad gets them secured, start the engine, but leave it idling and in forward gear. Give me a wave as soon as you have it started." He showed her the controls as he pulled life jackets out of the lazaret locker. "Put these on and hang on when the wind hits. Keep one hand for the ship and one hand for yourself. If the squall that comes with this storm is typical for the lake, it'll look really ugly. But don't worry; it'll blow itself out five or ten minutes after it starts. I've had this boat through two big squalls before this. She'll take good care of us.

"I'm going to crawl forward, and when the squall is in full stride, I'll cut the hawser, if they don't do it first. As soon as you feel the boat break free from the tug, turn hard to port. Take us straight downwind and go to full throttle at the same time. Then we'll figure out what to do next."

July 22, 0740

Willard Reiger was in the wheelhouse of the tug. He had been watching the sky blackening in the southwest. He was no sailor, but he knew that it would probably rain in the next little while. He had also been watching one other boat, a sailboat, motoring off into the distance behind them. It was almost out of sight now. They would soon be alone with their prey. Then they would sink the game warden's sailboat, away from the prying eyes of the rest of the world.

With him in the stifling confines of the small wheelhouse were the four members of his gang, John Gant, Jay Morris, Mitch Mitchell and Dwayne Goreham — his only supporters. Goreham was at the wheel.

"Get ready to undo that tow rope," Reiger glanced briefly at Gant and the others as he started giving last-minute instructions. "Remember, just undo the one end of the rope. The other end has to stay attached to the tug so it can pull on that cable back there."

Gant nodded at Jay who left the wheelhouse, descended to the main deck and headed for the stern. Mitch climbed out onto the deckhouse roof as planned and headed back to where he could relay signals between the wheelhouse and the winch deck. They weren't going to use radio instructions to do this job — they didn't want witnesses of any kind.

July 22, 0742

Crawling forward on *Water Baby*'s portside deck, Webb realized that he was still well hidden from view to anyone watching from the tug. Because she was being towed through the water considerably faster than her theoretical hull speed, his boat's bow was raised high and her stern squatted low as she tried to climb up over her own bow wave. Exceeding the yawl's hull speed was also applying thousands of extra pounds of tension to the towing hawser, so he was surprised to see that the

Reiger's gang had used a one-inch-diameter twisted nylon line instead of the regular big two-inch hawser that was used to tow the barge. It was stretched tight under the load. However, with both ends of the hawser secured aboard the tug after being passed through the two sturdy hawseholes in *Water Baby*'s bow, the line was in effect, doubled. It was still below its breaking strength even though it was stretched well beyond its rated safe working load.

'Pretty stretchy stuff,' thought Webb. 'I could get badly thrashed by the loose end if they let it go first.'

When he had rigged the cable to shear off the through hull fittings in the yawl's engine space, Reiger had shackled the forward end of it to some kind of landlubber's knot in the hawser just inches in front of the yawl. Releasing the other end of the towing line from the tug would allow the end that stayed with the tug to jerk hard on the cable. And the way he had it rigged, while the guts were being pulled out of the yawl by the aircraft cable, the return loop of the hawser would simply be pulled back through the yawl's hawseholes, leaving the line free to be retrieved aboard the tug. What Webb didn't know, was that Reiger had tried to use the tug's proper tow rope, but its large diameter made for such a tight fit in *Water Baby*'s hawseholes that he feared it might bind and not do what he had intended. He wasn't a sailor, but he'd built his business with his own two hands. He had a strong grasp of all things mechanical.

The storm was approaching quickly and the sailboat to the northwest, the only other possible witness, was almost out of sight now. Lying low behind the raised bulwarks at the bow of his yawl and out of sight of the tug, Webb quickly fed the thirty feet of loose aircraft cable out through the hawsehole to let it trail in the water. He didn't want that wicked thing attacking him from behind as it whipped overboard to follow the stretched hawser recoiling toward the tug. And now, thanks to the stern reminder from "Iron" Erin, it was short enough not to get wound around the yawl's propeller shaft.

Taking a careful peek over the bow, Webb observed one of Reiger's men walking down the deck toward the stern of the tug no more than sixty yards ahead.

Webb took out a razor-sharp fish-filleting knife from his belt sheath. He wished he'd brought a second one as a backup, but it was probably too late to go back now. Not knowing how difficult the tow hawser would be to sever, he began to draw the blade firmly across the place he planned to make his cut. The straining line appeared as though it would part within several firm strokes of the knife. Another glance over the bow showed Reiger's man standing near the stern bitts onto which the line was cleated. He was looking up at a second man who was standing on the after end of the deckhouse above the paint storage locker.

The wind in advance of the storm was stirring up ugly ripples on the water less than a hundred yards off to the starboard side now.

July 22, 0744

Aboard *Lady M,* Willard Reiger was beginning to think that the rain shower they were about to encounter was going to be more aggressive than he had first thought. A warm, satisfied glow spread through his gut as he realized with a rare but demonic smile, that the sky off to the right side of the tug was now blacker than he could ever recall seeing it in daytime. This unexpected development was going to work in his favour. It would be perfect cover for what he was about to do to the game warden's boat.

"Make a quick right turn here," he barked at Goreham.

"Head straight for the blackest part of the cloud. In a rainstorm like that, no one but us is going to be able to see this happen."

Just as the tug began to respond to the helm, a wind more ferocious than any of the men in the wheelhouse had ever experienced, began to shake the superstructure of the small ship.

"Jesus," gasped Goreham, and Gant's jaw dropped in awe, as a solid wall of wind-driven rain slashed hard against the wheelhouse windows. In an instant, the tug's bow was totally obscured from view. The wind speed indicator read ninety-eight knots. This was what the lake sailors called a white squall.

Amazed by the terrifying force of the wind, Reiger knew that it was time. He waved urgently at Mitchell who, blown off balance by the sudden gust, had just barely managed to save himself from going overboard by grabbing a dorade vent on the storage locker roof. Straining to hang on, while watching for the signal before his view of the wheelhouse was obliterated, Mitch managed to relay the message to Morris.

July 22, 0744

As the tug began a slow turn to starboard, Webb's heart sank. He figured that Reiger suddenly had some other scheme in mind now.

Just then, the squall he had been hoping for slammed into the starboard side of *Water Baby,* laying her over to thirty degrees or more of heel. Webb was ecstatic; it was even stronger than he had dared to hope for. At almost the same moment, the yawl turned into the wind, still in tow, still following the tug.

He had no idea if the Franklins were in any position yet to carry out their plan and now the clock was ticking. Any time now, Reiger would make his play. The minutes dragged by as he waited for a signal from the cockpit. Webb began toying with the idea of going astern to check on them when he suddenly felt the engine vibrating through the deck. It was a most reassuring sensation.

Relieved, he peeked over the bow again. The tug had become completely hidden behind a wall of driving rain and sea spray. The waves, in less than four minutes, had built to over three feet, and were short and steep. Each successive wave was even higher than the last.

The bow plunged into a trough, thoroughly soaking him with solid green water, not just spray. Webb got to his knees and began to work his knife into the tow line. One stroke took him a third of the way through and a second took the cut past the halfway point. As the bow started to pitch up to climb the crest of the next oncoming wave, the hawser stretched tight as an iron bar. He sliced hard, pulling the knife toward himself as he drew it through the remainder of the distressed line.

The instant that *Water Baby*'s bow rose to the top of the wave, the forces of the wind, waves and the brute horsepower of the tug stretched the hawser to its limit. The straining line parted with an explosive snap. The steel shackle took off in the direction of the tug like a missile.

July 22, 0748

"I don't think he saw me John," Reiger said to Gant as he nervously looked out into the squall that had swallowed them up. "Get out there and make sure they drop that tow."

Not about to look like a wimp in front of his boss, Gant quickly left the dry security of the wheelhouse to make sure his crew had done the job.

But Morris had already received the relayed signal and

was fighting to release the end of the taut towing hawser. The first three figure-eight wraps around the bitts had come off easily, but the fourth one had a small loop pinched under the wrap below. As strong as he was, he just couldn't make it budge. Even if at that moment he had taken his eyes off what he was doing, he wouldn't have been able to see more than ten yards in any direction. And Jay Morris never saw the pound-and-a-half steel shackle as it accelerated toward him. He died instantly, never knowing what smashed into his skull.

9. THE CHASE

July 22, 0750 hrs

The instant she sensed the hawser breaking, Erin had the tiller hard over and the throttle wide open. With the wind pushing hard on the mainmast and rigging, *Water Baby* pivoted almost before the next wave crested beneath the hull amidships, and within seconds the yawl was flying downwind, almost surfing down the short steep waves.

Webb made his way aft toward the cockpit, holding tight to the lifelines and grab rails on the coach roof all the way. The first squall he'd ever encountered had heeled the boat over to twenty degrees and he had no sails up on that occasion either. He had learned later that the wind that day had topped eighty knots. If indeed she had heeled to thirty degrees just now, then this blow had to have been close to a record. Over the years, the lake had seen squalls of one hundred knots or more.

The wind was still screaming through the rigging, still blowing at hurricane force. In all his experience on the lake, the big squalls were normally afternoon events. For it to happen this early in the day meant that there was one hell of a cold front coming through. If it was one of the mythical gods of the sea or the wind who had arranged for the squall to arrive at such an opportune moment, he was delighted with both the timing and the result.

When he climbed into the cockpit, Webb found that the judge had closed the companionway hatch to keep the worst of the torrential rain out of the cabin. Now Franklin was sitting on the port side of the cockpit, looking somewhat apprehensive and very wet.

Erin, sitting up on the tillerman's stool with her back to the shrieking wind, was intent on keeping the yawl running straight downwind to avoid broaching. They were heading pretty much northeast as Webb had wanted. The expression on her face was gradually changing from one of sheer terror to a sort of cautious elation. She decided that it was the same feeling an Olympic athlete would get when, before actually seeing the scoreboard, was pretty sure she'd had a winning run. And in that wind-blown, rain-soaked face, Webb could almost detect a hint of warmth that he'd not noticed before in the Iron Maiden of Envirobusters.

Refocusing his attention on the situation at hand, he was pleased to note that their speed was steady at almost seven knots as they continued forward, pushed by the engine and the following wind on the bare spars and rigging. However, in order to 'spare the horses,' he reached down and throttled the engine back to a point where it was still pushing hard, but running smoothly and no longer shaking the boat. The speed remained unchanged, still almost half a knot over the boat's theoretical hull speed. Satisfied, he sat down on the cockpit seat opposite the two Franklins, giving them a relieved smile and an exaggerated thumbs-up.

"Nice job Erin, thanks. We got away and we're still afloat." He looked back in the direction from which they had come, expecting to see the tug in hot pursuit. Though the rain obliterated the visibility anything more than a couple of boat lengths behind them, he knew what they were still up against.

But just as he was thinking of tempering his victory statement with a comment like, 'Of course, we're certainly not out of the woods yet,' Erin spoke up.

"You know this isn't anywhere near to being over, Webb," she said, "Reiger's not about to give up that easily."

"I know that ... only too well."

July 22, 0800

It took several minutes before Mitch could get Reiger and Gant to understand that the line had separated at the sailboat, rather than being released by their man on the tug. And that Morris was either badly hurt, or dead. It was therefore possible that the cables rigged to sink the yacht had not done their job.

"Turn this tug around and find that boat! We'll have to go and sink it ourselves." Reiger, never even thinking of his downed crewman, was in a rage. He sneered at Gant, "They must have gotten free somehow. You were *supposed* to have put them out of commission.

"Follow that goddamned boat, and if you see it, ram the Jesus thing," he spat at Goreham, who by then was thoroughly disoriented by the zero visibility of the storm. Having no idea how to steer a compass course, even if he'd been given one, he was having a tough time just controlling the *Lady M*. By then the waves were six feet high and there was just the right distance between their crests that when the tug was broadside to them, as it happened to be at that moment, the vessel rolled drunkenly — sickeningly for those not accustomed to stormy seas.

Seeking to head off in a new direction Goreham spun the ship's wheel as one might spin a wheel of fortune. He didn't care which way the boat was headed, just as long as it would stop rolling like that. But in doing so, he managed to complete a tight circle. The tug crossed over the two trailing ends of the severed hawser.

Within less than half a minute of snagging the loose lines, the propeller, acting as a fast winch, hauled the body of Jay Morris overboard. His corpse had become entangled in a loop that had enveloped him at the instant of his demise. Gant's former loader ended up bound tightly to the propeller by the hawser, like a fly bundled into a spider's web. Furthermore, the propeller and its shaft quickly wound in all of the slack line. As powerful as the tug's diesel was, it stalled abruptly when the hawser came up tight. It was still cleated to the towing bitts, and still below its breaking strength.

All conversation in the wheelhouse stopped the instant the engine died. The screaming of the wind, which was actually beginning to subside, suddenly sounded much louder. The tug, lying broadside to the waves once more, wallowed just as drunkenly as before.

Reiger was the first to react and immediately demanded that someone restart the diesel. Gant and Mitchell, both in a hurry to avoid their boss's continuing tirade, rushed down the companionway steps toward the tug's engine room. After several failed attempts, it was Mitch who, with a greater mechanical aptitude than the giant, figured out that the propeller shaft would not turn due to outside forces.

A quick trip to the tug's aft deck revealed two startling details. The first was the puzzling absence of Morris's corpse. The second, and more germane to their mechanical problems, was the fact that the trailing ends of the towing hawser were pulled tight over the stern where they angled down under the hull toward the propeller.

After cutting the inboard ends of the line free from the bitts, Mitch suggested that Gant should hold on to them while he, Mitch, ran the engine slowly in reverse to unwind them off the propeller shaft. But as soon as reverse gear engaged, Gant watched helplessly as the thick line pulled through his giant hands, the big diesel pulling them easily from his vice-like grip. The lines were so tightly jammed onto the shaft there was no way they could be backed off by hand.

Gant made a quick trip back down to the engine room. A brief conference with Mitch revealed that since the line had been cut loose, they could at least proceed forward again. However, with a 120-yard wad of heavy towing line, a corpse, and the tail end of the aircraft cable wrapped around it, the propeller was not able to push as much water it was designed to. As a result, when they returned to the bridge, they discovered that the tug at full power was making just over seven of its normal ten knots and was vibrating badly at that. Unbeknownst to them, the force of the diesel, trying to winch the line onto the propeller shaft, had bent the shaft enough to induce even more vibration than Morris's body alone was responsible for. And that had further reduced the propeller's efficiency.

In the meantime, during the unwanted shutdown, Reiger had been fiddling with signal gain settings on the radar set in the wheelhouse. He was finally able to get a vague image of what he believed could be *Water Baby,* retreating to the northeast.

July 22, 0815

The squall's fury had passed and the rain had slackened somewhat, though it was still driven by a fresh, twenty-five-knot wind, now blowing from the northwest. And it was a chilly wind. The clouds were beginning to break up. The rain would stop soon, and their position would once again be exposed to Reiger aboard the tug.

Rick Webb, Jim Franklin and his daughter, Erin were sitting in *Water Baby*'s cockpit looking like drowned rats, victims of the deluge of rain. Relieved to be at least temporarily free from Reiger, none of them had immediately noticed that they were growing colder by the minute.

As they waited and watched for the tug to come racing out of the rain toward them, Webb finally broke the silence. "I don't know what they're up to back there, but we're all going to catch a bout of hypothermia if we don't get dried off and into some warm clothes. Erin, they'll be a bit big on you, but help yourself to whatever you need of my things in the three drawers under the settee on the starboard side of the salon. Long-johns are under the jeans … I hadn't expected needing them this summer, but I never leave home without them. And there are some sweaters and jackets in the hanging locker in the passageway across from the head. Oh yeah, dry towels are in the small locker behind the stained-glass door above the hanging locker." He looked toward the judge with obvious concern, before continuing. "I'm afraid I don't have anything anywhere near your size Jim. You can wrap yourself in a blanket from the 'V' berth though."

"Not to worry," the big man responded. "Reiger's thugs threw my overnight bag into your forward cabin when they brought us aboard … he wanted all evidence of us off the tug. I've got a small selection of dry things, even a windbreaker."

"Okay, you two go and change now while I stand watch. We'll have to wait and see what their next move is going to be," Webb said, nodding in the direction from which they all expected the tug to appear. He didn't voice his opinion that they wouldn't have long to wait.

With the wind now on the port beam, *Water Baby*'s speed under engine power alone had fallen to just barely over six knots. As the visibility began to improve, there was still no sign of *Lady M*, but Webb knew that when it came to a chase, his yawl could never outrun the big diesel tug. He needed to put as much distance as he could between the two boats during the tug's unexpected absence. With that in mind he lashed the tiller in place and began to remove the covers from the main and mizzen sails in preparation for adding wind power to his small ship.

July 22, 0815

"There! ... *there*, now follow that damned dot!" Reiger implored Goreham none too kindly, as he pointed aggressively at the radar screen.

Goreham spun the wheel once again and waited for the outer dot, presently on the bottom of the radar screen, to swing around to the top. Then he centred the wheel and made several small adjustments until the target dot held steady ahead of them. While he had little understanding of manoeuvring a tug, an image on an electronic display was something he could relate to.

"All those video games you waste your time on might come in handy after all," Gant offered from the sidelines, as he watched Goreham accurately follow the blip on the radar screen.

"Lot fuckin' easier than that compass shit I tried to do earlier." The reply was made with a bit of a grin, his confidence beginning to return.

The wind had slackened considerably, but was still brisk, and now blowing from the northwest. The four men in the tug's wheelhouse went silent for a time as they watched the image on the radar screen. Were they getting any closer to it? Opinions were offered both ways, but eventually Goreham pointed out to the rest of them that the blip had been just outside of the three-mile ring on the screen ten minutes earlier and now it was fully on the ring. *Lady M* was gaining slowly.

July 22, 0820

Rick Webb was cold and shivering hard by the time Erin came back up on deck, but he insisted on staying there until they had rounded up into the wind and winched the big mainsail up to the masthead.

"Okay… le..let's…g.. get the… genoa… set." He could hardly get the words through his chattering teeth.

"Go on Webb," Erin's voice registered her obvious annoyance. "Get below and get warmed up. Dad can help me with that when he gets up here. It's a head sail, not a space shuttle. We can manage."

He wanted to tell her that he could do it, but by then the wind had chilled him so completely he couldn't fully form the thought, let alone the words. He let himself unsteadily down the companionway steps into the relative warmth of the cabin and began to strip off his wet clothes in the main salon. He was even too cold to realize that he was changing in full view of the judge's daughter. Not that she had much time to watch while she steered the yawl — but she did notice, with a degree of amusement.

'Yeah, he must be really cold, if all that talk about shrinkage is true,' she thought. At the same time, she was beginning to admit to herself that he'd pretty well aced their escape. He'd finally succeeded in one attempt out of three. 'Wouldn't have been a passing grade in school, but we *are* still alive … for now. So I guess I'll give him a conditional pass.' And having seen the man stripped down to his most vulnerable self, she felt something stir inside her own self that she didn't recognize. But with the situation as tenuous as it was, she didn't pursue it. And just as quickly, the feeling passed.

July 22, 0825

Willard Reiger was not at all happy about the recent downturn in his fortunes. But he was confident at least, that they would regain the upper hand over his escapees in the next while. However, if he had known a few basic mathematical formulae used in navigation he would have seen that at their present rate of closing, it was going to take at least another two hours to catch up to the sailboat — and the situation on either vessel could easily change in that time.

A check of the engine gauges suggested to the men in the wheelhouse that despite its handicap and the annoying vibrations in the drive train, the tug was running acceptably. And while Goreham steered, Reiger instructed Gant to make sure his men and their firearms were prepared for action. The hard-earned lessons from his Vietnam years came back easily in the stress of the moment.

"Hey boss, isn't that them up ahead?" Goreham's eyes, tiring of squinting at the radar screen, had chanced a glance out ahead of the tug.

"Boy if it is then you've got better eyes than mine," Reiger replied, peering ahead. "I don't see anything."

"It's gone now, but I swear I saw white sails for a minute … Yeah, there it is again."

This time Reiger saw it too as the top half of the yawl's mainsail poked above the lake-level mist, drizzle and windblown spray, and then another veil of rain faded the image once more. "It's still a long way off, but…" he glanced up at the radar screen that Goreham had already returned to, "it is inside that three-mile ring now."

July 22, 0840

"Any sign of the tug yet?" Webb asked as he arrived back in the cockpit. He was bundled in all the remaining warm clothing he could put his hands on.

Both Franklins answered to the negative. Erin was again at the tiller, and the boat was moving quickly toward the northeast, the water sucking and hissing along the hull as the speed log read just over 6.5 knots. He announced that he had put the kettle on to boil. There would be instant coffee, tea or hot chocolate available in a few minutes — whichever they preferred. And he'd put out the makings for sandwiches, but it was self serve only. None of them had eaten anything since the previous day; Webb's overcooked bass dinner being the most recent.

Before he had rejoined them in the cockpit, he'd made a hasty job of returning the spare parts to the quarter-berth area under the chart table. It was bugging him that every time the boat rolled, items of hardware banged and rattled annoyingly back and forth across the stainless-steel galley countertop. And despite the fact they had bigger issues to worry about, it had looked just plain un-seamanlike. Now it looked like a galley once more.

"Look, I'm sorry," he said to Erin as he sat down. "I shouldn't have suggested you wouldn't be able to set the genoa without me. It's just that as a single-handed sailor, I've been used to doing everything on the boat myself. With the stress of our situation, and the cold of the moment, my mind was starting to get as numb as the rest of me."

"You men are all alike," she quipped, and there was a slight change at the corners of her mouth, though not quite a smile. "You think you're immortal … that you can do it all by yourselves."

"Well, if *that* isn't a case of the pot calling the kettle black," injected the judge with a smile. He was thinking of the circumstances that had started the ball rolling on this whole misadventure.

Erin's eyes first shot daggers at her father, then a small smile escaped from her. Again, Webb thought he could detect a slight softening of her attitude toward him — part of her smile had been clearly directed at him. And he smiled along with the two of them. Then he froze up inside as he realized that he was beginning to like her. He quickly tried to shy away from the thought. A new relationship under normal circumstances troubled him enough after losing Mel so long ago. But to take a liking to a woman who was already imperiled by their present circumstances — well that was just inviting another heartbreaking conclusion. Sure, it was a conclusion they were desperately trying to avoid, but the odds just were not in their favour at this point.

For several lingering moments, Rick worked to shake the thought of any lasting friendship with the woman from his mind. If by any chance they survived this nightmare, Franklin would resume being a judge, Webb would resume bringing customers to the judge and Iron Erin would resume annoying the COs in the Toronto office. Their separate lives would pick up right where they had left off before all this happened.

"Why are we heading in this particular direction, Webb?" The judge brought the topic back to the business of surviving.

"Umm, three reasons, actually," he replied after a brief pause. "None of them great, but given the circumstances, they're the best chance I can see for us. First, with the wind abeam, this is our fastest point of sail; second, this is the direction the cold front is headed, and while it won't be long before it races ahead and leaves us in clear weather again, I figure every minute they can't see us is another minute to our advantage; and finally, although we would be on an equally fast tack on the opposite course, and a whole lot closer to head for Tobermory to get help, we'd have to double back and sail right past those guys. I don't think they would willingly let us do that. So unless we see positive evidence that they've either sunk or quit, we'll aim for the coast guard station near Britt.

"Oh yes, one more thing. I know it's about a five-hour sail from here, but if we can manage to get close to Britt, that's part of my patrol area; I know those waters well. There are several shoals up there I know we can sail this boat between, at speed. But the gap will be too narrow underwater for the tug … where they won't be able to see the rocks in time. It's a long shot, but if we can beat them off until then, we might just be able to entice them to run aground there."

"Okay," Judge Franklin said, carefully weighing the evidence, "but how are we going to stay ahead of that tug for five hours?"

"Ah, well now Your Honour, I know that in your profession you've dealt with some of the lowest forms of human scum that exist in this fine land. And I'm betting you've learned a few things from them in the process. I just happen to have an opening in the ship's dirty tricks department." After a pause, and a sly look at the judge, Webb stood and headed down into the cabin. "Are you interested?"

"How could I possibly refuse?" Franklin got up to follow him. "Do you have any firearms on board?"

"Come now Jim, this is Canada the Good. Sunny ways and all that stuff," Webb responded cynically. "The great leaders in their almighty seats of power tell us that other than for sport hunting and biathlon shooting, there is no need for us citizens to bear arms; not even legally armed peace officers when they go on vacation.

"However," he continued with a mischievous grin, "I do happen to have a 12-gauge flare gun … although it's amazing when you think of it, that the federal government hasn't declared that to be a restricted weapon too."

"Hey you guys," Erin called down the companionway, "I think the tug is following us. The rain quit, and there it was. I'm *pretty* sure it's the tug."

The two men came back to the companionway and looked astern. They could see a small shape on the horizon, perhaps as much as three miles away, Webb thought. The most noticeable feature of the tiny image was the black smudge of diesel exhaust dirtying the sky right above it. Just to be sure, he turned briefly to the navigating station and picked up a pair of binoculars before heading back up to the cockpit. He briefly studied the sooty smudge astern, then handed Erin the glasses.

"They must have that diesel running at emergency speed ahead," he ventured as a sinking feeling crept into his gut. "And at full speed, it'll take him less than half an hour to catch up with us. Damn. We'd better hurry with whatever weapons we can invent … PDQ! You okay up here for now Erin?"

The younger Franklin nodded, putting on as brave a face as she could. She had already experienced ruthless treatment by Reiger and his goons — she wasn't encouraged about their chances.

After directing a brief look of concern at her, Webb went back below and turned his attention to showing the judge an inventory of on-board materials that had the potential to be made into weapons. As desperate as the situation appeared, he refused to turn his scotch bottles into Molotov cocktails until they'd saved the revered whisky in a couple of empty thermoses. Only then was gasoline, intended for the portable generator, substituted — and that operation was carried out on the poop deck, for safety sake.

His wine, he wasn't nearly as fussy about, and they quickly poured the contents overboard. It was homemade wine that only cost about a dollar a bottle to make, and after emptying the generator's gas jug to fill them, they had a total of five such weapons recapped or corked and ready to throw. With no wicks, these simply provided a flammable fuel delivery system — much safer than holding and throwing actual flaming projectiles from aboard a lively floating platform.

Next, the judge busied himself sorting through *Water Baby*'s supply of emergency flares.

"A lot of these are expired. You know that, Rick?" Franklin commented with a straight face.

"Fine time to worry about the legal niceties Jim," Webb shot back with an accompanying grin. It was reassuring to know that even in a tight spot, the judge could do some leg pulling too. And the switch from surname to his given name was appreciated.

"In that box, they're all past their pull dates. I kind of like to save them in case of an emergency, you know? My complement of approved up-to-date flares is in the other box I gave you. But most of the old ones will burn too, so this might be as good a time as any to try them out."

"Oh they'll burn all right. I'm going to tape five or six of these out-dated handheld ones around a new one. The heat from that one will ensure the others will burn, and they'll be hell to put out too." As the judge began taping together a bundle of flares, he called up to the cockpit, "How close is the tug now, Erin?"

She looked, paused, and then responded slowly, not wanting to get their hopes up only to be dashed once more. "It *looks* as if it's closer than when I first saw it, but not by much. From the exhaust smoke it sure looks as if it's working hard, so why is it still way back there?"

Puzzled, Webb put aside his work and returned to the cockpit. "You're right. Maybe they've got some kind of mechanical problem. Without Small's crew aboard there's a chance those city boys might have screwed something up … we can only hope."

Taking a long thoughtful look back at the labouring tug, he offered, "That's got me thinking, and this is a bit of a gamble, but if I *can* coax another half knot or more speed from this old ship, we might just be able to outrun those bastards. The downside is that I have no idea how long my old engine will last at full throttle. If I open it up all the way, something could fly apart in short order, or it could do just fine. Of course, the main drawback is that if the engine fails, we'll quickly be 'up the creek,' only it'll be out here in the middle of the lake with nowhere to hide. Then we'd have to fight it out somehow, if we could.

"The other option is to carry on just as we are. I know it will motor on indefinitely running like it is now. What do you two think?"

"If we carry on at our present speed," the judge replied without hesitation, "it appears certain that we will be overtaken, as much as they seem to be dragging out the process back there." He had already weighed the possibilities before the subject had come up. After only the briefest pause, he continued, "We'll have to launch a defence at that time anyhow. If we can stall for more time, maybe we'll see another boat, or a coast guard chopper … whatever … before Reiger overtakes us. Rick, if we wreck that old iron beast of yours, running flat out to save my daughter, I'll buy you a new engine."

"I agree," said Erin, nodding in agreement. "I mean the part about going full throttle. I can't afford my car payments, so you'll have to take an IOU if the engine saves my dad."

Again, as brief as it was, another smile was shared by all three of them. And Webb really liked Erin's smile — as brief as it was. And again, he had to caution himself against the attraction he was beginning to feel toward her.

July 22, 0855

Detective Constable Tina Stambury had stayed all night, trying in vain to find missing pieces to the puzzle of the missing judge. She was just about to pour another coffee and head out for still another smoke when her desk phone warbled. A detective from the Owen Sound city police department was the caller. He apologized profusely for not getting back to her sooner with the results of the search of the judge's car last evening but extended a peace offering to her — he might have another piece for her puzzle.

No, nothing about the car suggested foul play, he said. Only one set of prints was found, and the same prints were on his golf clubs in the trunk. While there were no prints for his honour on file anywhere, by deduction, those on the car were obviously his.

The new piece to the puzzle came when he went on to explain about a missing boat, borrowed by a local water taxi operator named 'Red' O'Reilly. The water taxi operator worked from a dock located within eighty metres of the judge's car. The boat had been legitimately borrowed during the early afternoon, but had not been returned when it was expected in the evening. And neither O'Reilly nor the boat had shown up by this morning.

'One more piece, yes,' Tina pondered. But if it belonged to her puzzle, she had no idea just how it fit in — other than the missing boat possibly being the next stage in Franklin's journey. A journey to where? Huron is a very big lake. Tina assumed that someone in Owen Sound had notified the coast guard. And the Owen Sound detective had assumed the same thing. The missing boat report had been made during the previous shift, but somehow it had fallen through the cracks, the victim of a communications failure during the shift change. That would not become evident for some hours yet.

July 22, 0910

Aboard the old aluminum skiff, progress for Mike Small and his crew had come to a standstill when one of their two mismatched oars broke. They had managed several hours of discouragingly slow progress before then. Small estimated that they might have been making about two knots, but the boat was, as he had originally predicted, a pig to row. Nor could any of the oarsmen keep the beast moving on anything resembling a straight course. And so, when trying for the thousandth time to turn the bow back toward their destination, a frustrated Ray Ethier pulled just a bit too hard with his right hand and the oar snapped at the oarlock. Although they were able to retrieve the blade before it floated away, they had absolutely no means of splicing it back together.

Sculling with the single remaining oar had turned out to be a waste of time. The technique moved the boat, but it took over twenty seconds to travel one boat length. As a result, they had been becalmed for hours off the coast and were still miles from Britt and Byng Inlet.

They could only watch helplessly as the black clouds of a squall line swept toward them from the southwest. For the five men aboard, life quickly changed from frustratingly boring to somewhat unnerving — experienced tug men don't go as high up the fright scale as 'terrified.'

"When this hits, everyone sit down on the bottom of

the boat," Mike Small said as he began to organize his crew for the storm's onslaught. "And make sure your life jackets are done up proper." He'd been on the lake through numerous squalls since taking the job with Mid-Con Waste, but he had always had the luxury of turning the heavy tug into the screaming wind and waiting for the five-minute fury to exhaust itself before resuming course and moving on. But out here in this open boat, he was concerned that the wind could pick it up like a paper plate from a picnic table and throw them all into the water far from either the shipping lanes or the pleasure craft routes.

The men lowered the dead outboard motor on a rope over the bow. Tethered there it would act as a drogue or sea anchor and keep the boat pointed into the wind. They had not ditched the outboard when it died because Small said he was sick of throwing stuff into the lake — that was what had gotten them into this mess in the first place. After tying any other items of useful gear to the seats — there weren't many — the tug's tender was as ready as they could make it.

This was the same weather system that had given *Water Baby* her chance to escape over an hour earlier and twenty-five miles to the southwest. In fact, it had actually lost some of its punch by then, but it hit the small boat hard just the same. The sea anchor idea worked, more or less, but as an eighty-knot wind whipped up the waves, it was soon evident that they had too much weight forward. They were taking water over the bow. Small, who sat amidships between the two centre-most seats, had to tap Billy Manion on the shoulder to get his attention.

"Move to the back," Small's shout was carried off by the wind, but his hand gestures were understood. And after moving one more man farther astern, the boat had achieved a reasonable degree of trim. Only the top couple of inches of the worst waves came aboard after that. The crew used everything that would hold water, from hats to the top of the outboard's discarded cowling, to keep the boat bailed out. In less than ten minutes the wind subsided to a brisk twenty-five knots. At the same time, it veered until it was coming pretty well out of the northwest.

"Hot-damn that was fun," exclaimed Manion as he dumped overboard the last of the water he could scoop up with a battered old coffee can. He was still on an adrenalin high. "Scared the shit out of me when it hit, but when the water started covering the bottom, I didn't have time to think about it anymore."

The comic relief sparked by their youngest crewmember broke the tension and ignited smiles on the other four faces. They had survived the squall without any problems. And even as they chatted about the experience, the wind continued to ease until it steadied at around fifteen knots.

July 22, 1030

Webb's efforts to coax more power from *Water Baby*'s engine had shown positive results. The four-cylinder antique, pounding and shaking as it was, had added enough power that along with the wind in the sails, the yawl kept surging forward at almost seven knots. Unfortunately, it was becoming obvious that the increase in the boat's speed was still not quite enough to pull away from the tug *Lady M,* and Webb judged that they weren't much more than a mile ahead of their pursuers.

Acknowledging that some time in the next couple of hours a confrontation with the criminals on the tug was inevitable, Webb insisted that the Franklins each grab a berth below and try to catch a few winks before the opening of the next act. Though they hadn't realized it until their skipper made the suggestion, they were both beat. Neither of them had slept much at all since the whole ordeal had started several days earlier.

Lying in her berth thinking that trying to take a nap would be an exercise in futility, Erin drifted into a sound sleep. Her second last fading thought was to wonder if Webb was just trying to get her out of the way again. And her last thought was the acceptance that her initial anger at him was pretty much in the past. She knew deep inside that she had him to thank for their reprieve from an immediate end — temporary though that might still be.

Her dad, who just about lived on power naps, woke up a short while after hitting the rack. But he took advantage of the comfortable bed, lying there just resting until he too fell into a proper sound sleep.

July 22, 1100

"Where the hell have you been?" Reiger demanded harshly as Dwayne Goreham slipped back behind *Lady M'*s big wheel.

"Went for a piss. Is that alright?" The evidence on the front of his jeans indicated that he had done so from the windward side of the tug.

"What if the boat had turned while you were out? We can't afford to lose any more time. Why haven't we caught up to them yet?" While he was pretty confident that Small and his crew had simply run, and not alerted the authorities — there were no police choppers beating down on them yet — Reiger still had to run the sailboat to ground and eliminate all three of the witnesses aboard. It would be the certain end of him if any of them survived.

"Look, *I* don't know. They must have speeded up. We're going as fast as we were when we first took off after them. And I turned on the auto-pilot when I left." Normally insulated from Reiger's blunt manner by his immediate boss, Goreham wished that the giant security chief would return to the wheelhouse. The hands-on supervisory style of the company's owner was beginning to wear on his patience, and he hadn't had any sleep since Small's crew had jumped ship.

July 22, 1115

Running from the belt-driven water pump to *Water Baby*'s engine was a rubber hose, three-quarters of an inch inside diameter. It was double clamped to the hose fittings at both ends, a standard marine safety practice. Through this hose, the pump fed lake water into a series of passages in the engine block to keep the engine running at the proper temperature. Webb had inspected the hose when he launched the boat in May. Although the rubber had hardened with age, the hose was still sound then and he'd felt that there was no need to replace it. Nevertheless, the anxious skipper checked conditions in the engine compartment frequently now because of the unusually harsh treatment being forced on the straining machinery. Each quick inspection had revealed no problems. Everything was running as it should.

But, shortly after his most recent inspection, a small drip of water, originating where the hose joined the water pump, began falling harmlessly into the yawl's bilge. After a short time the drip became a dribble, then a small stream. The hardened rubber hose would have lasted all season if it had not been for the excessive vibrations of their full throttle dash for safety.

Suddenly, unable to hold together any longer, the brittle rubber cracked completely through and broke off at the water pump connection. A sudden jet of water spewed from the pump, straight at the carburetor intake. The vacuum created by the hard-working little power plant sucked sufficient water into the updraft carburetor to literally flood it out. The engine gasped to a sudden stop.

Webb leapt immediately down the companionway steps into the cabin. Opening the engine compartment, he quickly determined the cause of the sudden failure. Reaching into the now silent machinery space he shut off the cooling-water seacock, although with the engine no longer turning the water pump, there was just a dribble entering the boat. With the tug *Lady M* continuing to gain on the yawl, there was no time to try to affect repairs, nor was there any guarantee that the engine could even be restarted without a major overhaul. He didn't know what kind of internal damage the sudden intake of cold water might have done.

Awakened by the sudden silence, both Erin and her father joined Webb who had already returned to the cockpit. With only the sails pushing her along now, *Water Baby*'s speed soon fell to 5.8 knots — no longer enough to stay ahead of the tug.

In the ominous silence that grew between the three of them, each awkwardly avoided eye contact with the others, and none of them shared their thoughts on their chances of surviving Reiger's final attack.

Gazing forward, Erin noticed something quite large floating on the water, perhaps half a mile away on the port side. "What's that?" she asked, not daring to sound hopeful.

The others followed her gaze, squinting to get a clearer picture. Webb, not trusting his own vision, picked up the binoculars.

"Rub-a-dub-dub ... five men in a tub ..." A slow smile spread across his face as he announced the arrival of, or at least their arrival *at*, the reinforcements.

"It's Small and his crew … broken down probably … oh shit, their motor's completely gone! Quick, sheet in the main and the genoa a little and we'll sail up alongside of them. They won't have any weapons either, but if they're willing to join our side, they'll sure help to even the odds." The Franklins shared Webb's enthusiasm readily, as he nudged the yawl a little closer to the wind, aiming for a rendezvous with the men in the open boat.

July 22, 1120

The outlaws in the wheelhouse of *Lady M* were still too far away to see the latest developments aboard *Water Baby*, but Gant, who was now taking a turn at the wheel, noticed both the slight course change, and the definite drop in her speed.

"They're up to somethin' on the sailboat," he announced, looking over at Reiger who was sitting impatiently on the captain's high seat.

Ten miles ahead, the rocky islets near Georgian Bay's eastern shore were just beginning to come into view. From previous conversations with Small — back before their relationship had chilled — Reiger knew that the coast ahead was strewn with shoal areas, and not having any experience in the art of navigation, he was unsure of the significance of the slight turn to the left made by the sailboat. Gant began to adjust his course to cut the corner and reduce the distance to the yawl.

"No, keep it straight. It might be a trick to lure us across some rocks. Don't turn until we get to where they turned," the boss ordered. As a result, the aluminum boat bearing Captain Small and his crew remained hidden from view by the sails of the yawl for a few moments longer.

July 22, 1125

"Alright, in a normal rescue we'd bring them along the leeward side of the boat, blocking the wind and giving them a gentler sea for boarding, but right now we can't afford the delay, so when I give the word, you two let go the sheets and dump wind. As soon as the sails go slack, we'll coast up to meet them and bring them aboard on the windward side." Webb was busy giving instructions to the Franklins as he carefully judged the rapidly closing distance between *Water Baby* and the tugboat's aluminum tender.

"Erin as soon as you release the genoa sheet, go forward and be ready to take a line from them. But cast it off as soon as they are all aboard." The nine-ton sailboat slowed gradually once the idled sails began luffing in the wind. At the same time, the tug's crew in the skiff used their one remaining oar to manoeuvre the craft so that it lay parallel to the yawl. *Water Baby*'s momentum did the rest, carrying the two vessels together in a reasonably respectable fashion. A line was passed, and the entire crew transferred to Webb's vessel within fifteen seconds.

"Glad you could make it. Anything of value aboard?" Webb asked Small, as the big man joined him in the cockpit.

"No. Let it go," he said, turning to make sure that his instruction had been heard, and they all paused as the old Prince Craft slid along the yawl's side and drifted away.

"Poor old outboard quit after just an hour," Small continued. "We didn't see a single boat out here till you guys came along. Sure am sorry we didn't get ashore to call for help. I see you've been having a bout of 'good news – bad news' yerselves," he finished as he accurately judged the situation with the closing tug.

"You want to believe it!" Webb said, before turning

back to the Franklins. "Quick, sheet in the sails again. Let's get going." He glanced astern once more, judging the tug now to be less than half a mile back. Once his boat started to accelerate before the fifteen-knot wind, he began to brief Small and his crew.

"Okay, here's the plan, such as it is."

July 22, 1135

Willard Reiger could not believe his luck. From the wheelhouse of *Lady M,* he watched the sailboat pick up Small and the tug's crew and abandon the aluminum boat. As smoothly as the transfer had gone, it had still cost *Water Baby* almost half of its slim lead over the snarling tug.

"Got all the fish in our net now boys," he exclaimed, gloating over his improving fortunes. "We sink that boat, and all the remaining witnesses are gone. Dead men tell no tales." For emphasis, he impatiently shoved forward on the tug's throttle handle as he had already done so many times in the last couple of hours. There was no more power to be gained; the throttle had remained pegged at its limit since the beginning of the pursuit.

As the anticipation grew in the tug's wheelhouse, Goreham gleefully thought this was how it would have felt to have been a Caribbean pirate. Your ship, after the long chase, was gradually overhauling its quarry, all hands ready to overwhelm the prize ... yeah. His blood was up — he was ready for a fight. And he really had a hankering to get at that woman. She was hot.

July 22, 1140

With Mike Small's crew briefed and Small himself steering the yawl, Webb hauled his tool chest out of the portside sail locker and handed it down the companionway to Billy Manion. Returning to the cabin himself, he removed the companionway steps and went to work on his crippled engine. While he had not felt there was much hope of reviving the old beast on short notice, Hank, the tug's engineer, was more optimistic, and encouraged him to try. And now with extra hands aboard — and a skilled mechanic at that — it might just be possible.

"You know your way around the engine compartment, so you work in there. Give me the spark plugs and I will dry them out while you replace the hose." The old Dutch engineer knew how to organize a work party, and while Manion handed requested wrenches to the boat's harried owner, Hank was measuring, by eye alone, the length of replacement water hose needed. He cut it with his pocketknife from a spare piece that Webb kept on board for emergencies and traded him for the wet plugs.

While the two of them worked to revive the engine, Ray Ethier, though somewhat in the way, huddled over the battered VHF radio sets lying on the chart table, trying to determine if there was a way to jury-rig an emergency set. The Franklins distributed the arsenal of homemade weapons to strategic locations around the boat. Some were placed on the V-berth below the forward hatch from which one person could pop up and throw or fire. The bulk of them would have to be deployed either from the cockpit or out on deck. Charlie, the tug's cook, said he'd forego the high-tech defensive gear and use his fists when the bastards came aboard. He sat out of the way in the salon, petting Heywood, the cat.

July 22, 1200

Aboard the tug, Gant and his men were out on the port side deck waiting for Reiger to close the remaining distance to the yawl which appeared to be sailing without engine power now. He had little knowledge of running a tug, but he correctly assumed that the only direction the sailboat could dodge away and still use the power of the wind would be downwind to their right. With the shoreline looming steadily closer, he couldn't risk prolonging the chase any longer. He planned to limit their defence by coming alongside to the right of the yawl, and had directed Gant to hold fire until they were in that position.

10. THE GOOD FIGHT

July 22, 1205 hrs

Even with five additional crewmembers aboard and without engine power, *Water Baby* was still making over five knots. But that was not going to be enough to avoid a clash with Reiger's gang very soon. Although the tug was still handicapped by its fouled propeller, it was now less than one hundred yards behind them and quickly narrowing the gap.

In an operation that would have done a pit crew proud at the Indianapolis 500, Hank had cleaned and dried out the spark plugs in no more time than it had taken Webb to bleed the carburetor and replace the broken hose. With all the parts reinstalled, they now crossed their fingers.

Webb bounded quickly up into the cockpit and pushed the starter button, playing the choke and throttle settings at the same time. With the transmission already in forward gear, the thrust of water past the propeller gave the starter some help, gradually forcing the lifeless engine to turn faster. But after the starter had been whining without any result for almost thirty seconds — it seemed an eternity to everyone aboard — Webb was about to give up on his engine restarting at all. Looking back over his shoulder at the nearby tug, he knew he would soon have to turn all hands to face the attackers.

Just as he was about to quit, one cylinder began to fire.

With renewed hope, he continued to hold his thumb on the starter button — there was no point worrying about damaging the starter motor at this stage. As the tug loomed still closer, the starter, the propeller's thrust and the first of four cylinders now firing pushed the engine's revolutions even faster. Soon a second cylinder fired occasionally, a third joining in strongly just seconds later.

Knowing that the engine, as rough as it sounded, would keep running on its own, Webb let go of the starter button. He opened the throttle the rest of the way, then turned to deal with the threat from Reiger and the *Lady M*. The tug was now less than thirty yards behind the yawl. But as he had hoped, within the next twenty seconds the Graymarine engine was once again pushing strongly on all four cylinders. They weren't going to go down without a fight.

At Webb's suggestion, Mike Small had already latched open the heavy steel lazaret locker lids. Propped up at around sixty degrees, they would provide some protective shielding if Reiger's bullets started flying from astern.

"Stay below and down low until I give the word," Webb shouted to the others gathered in the cabin. At the same time, he released the genoa sheet from its cleat and nodded to Small.

Taking his cue, the big tug captain let the mizzen halyard go free and turned the yawl smartly to port, into the wind. The small aft sail slithered down its mast track, half of the sail draped across the boom and the rest lying on the poop deck, covering his next move in which he made record-breaking time cranking on the genoa furling winch, also located on the poop. It wasn't a pretty job, but the big headsail was rolled in and put out of business in a hurry.

Even before Small completed that task, Webb reached forward onto the cabin roof and pulled the brake release for the mainsail halyard winch, bringing the big centre sail roaring down onto the cabin top.

"*Go, go, go, go!*" Webb bellowed down the companionway. Under engine power alone, the sailboat resumed its tight turn to port, and it appeared to him that whoever was at the wheel of the tug was unprepared for the sudden manoeuvre. *Water Baby* briefly gained back several desperately needed yards of separation and was now headed back in the opposite direction with the two boats each presenting their port sides to the other.

Webb was thinking that in the days of sail-powered navies this would have been a perfect opportunity for the opposing ships to trade broadside cannon shots. And at just that instant, Jim Franklin, self-appointed captain of *Water Baby*'s 'marines,' made a perfect football throw of a gasoline-filled scotch bottle which smashed against the deckhouse aboard *Lady M*.

This action triggered a brief but withering barrage of handgun and shotgun fire from Gant and his two remaining goons aboard the tug. But with *Water Baby*'s main boom sheeted tight along the centreline of the boat, the downed sail hanging from it created a curtain running fore and aft along the cabin top, hiding the defenders. Aside from Webb and Small, they were all crouched on the starboard deck, with the steel cabin structure between them and the guns on the tug. The two skippers squatted low in the cockpit, also surrounded by steel. Despite the intense gunfire, only half a dozen rounds actually hit anything solid aboard the yawl. The boat's steel skin did not allow the small-calibre rounds to pass through. One round from the shotgun made a dozen pea-sized holes in the mainsail, but Goreham wasted his other four rounds in the excitement of the moment, shooting holes in the sky.

As soon as the wild firing subsided, Webb popped up from the safety of the cockpit and let loose a 12-gauge flare at the tug which was now beginning its turn toward them. Before the glowing projectile had finished its arc onto the deck of the *Lady M*, Webb had a second round chambered in the little plastic flare gun.

July 22, 1212

If Reiger had not paused to try to interpret the sudden and simultaneous dousing of sails aboard *Water Baby*, he would have been in a near perfect position for his men to pour a hail of bullets down into the people on deck before they could gain cover. However, mesmerized by the unexpected and neatly executed turn, he had failed to give the order to fire until he saw the incoming whiskey bottle hurled by Judge Franklin. That delay was to prove costly for the arrogant owner of Mid-Con Waste and his enforcers.

As they opened fire at the sailboat, Gant and his men moved quickly away from the patch of gasoline that the shattered bottle had splattered harmlessly over the deck and deckhouse bulkhead.

Stopping to ram a fresh magazine into his 9-millimetre pistol, Gant was amused to think that some overeager dope had thrown his Molotov cocktail without lighting the wick. He looked up just in time to see Webb's flare ignite the gasoline-soaked area. He felt the wind generated by the whoosh as the fuel lit up, but he was not in immediate harm's way. In fact, although none of the men suffered any injury from the mild explosion, the resulting fire now separated him from the other two shooters.

Gant was alone near the bow while Mitch and Goreham had moved toward the aft deck. The sheets of flame shooting up past the portside wheelhouse doorway temporarily blocked Reiger's view of the yawl. He immediately tightened the tug's turn toward the sailboat, but by doing so, the two gunners astern were unable to bring their fire to bear on the target and lost valuable time scrambling around to the starboard deck to join their leader forward again. They arrived just as the next whiskey bottle slammed into the base of the wheelhouse, right above their heads.

Panic-stricken by the uninvited gasoline shower, Goreham hurled himself over the rail, jumping ship and losing his shotgun in the process. Gant and Mitchell, not wanting to give up the relative security of the tug's deck, scrambled away from the newly soaked area just in time to feel the searing heat when Webb's next flare touched off the fuel there. They had moved far enough back down the starboard-side deck that they avoided being ignited themselves, but were again in no position to return fire. Several more of Franklin's homemade devices continued to pin Gant and Mitchell on the wrong side of the tug. A spectacular blast was created by the ignition of an aerosol can full of engine-starting ether pitched into the flames by Billy Manion. That kept the bad guys hunkered down still longer. At almost the same instant, Ray Ethier had managed to direct an acoustic firework called an 'Air Bomb' through the wheelhouse door of the tug as it passed. Way louder than a shotgun blast, the resulting detonation in the confined space immediately deafened Reiger. But only temporarily stunned by the device, he redoubled his demonic efforts to sink the yawl.

Goreham, now kicking and sputtering in the water, was panic-stricken by the battle raging all around him. When he had jumped overboard from the starboard bow, the tug was digging hard into its tight turn to port. With the aft end of the tug moving more sideways than forward, he had been forced under water, passing completely under the hull, and only narrowly missing the churning propeller. With the two boats still engaged in their savage manoeuvres, he was in mortal danger of being run down and he tried desperately to swim away from the field of battle.

July 22, 1215

For the skipper and crew aboard *Water Baby*, the situation was still tenuous. Mike Small had turned the tiller over to Webb, knowing that the sailor's intimate knowledge of his own boat might be the touch that could save the moment. The tug skipper then began anticipating the tug's ability to carry out the crude moves Reiger was putting it through, and in turn, suggesting appropriate actions for Webb to take in response.

Although Jim Franklin, Billy Manion and Ray Ethier were keeping the gunfire from *Lady M* subdued with a non-stop delivery of well-placed incendiary devices, the tug was threatening to run them down at any moment. Reiger was getting better at handling the big boat, and several times the only factor that saved *Water Baby*, was Small's long experience handling the tug, allowing him to predict where Webb should place the yawl to avoid disaster.

Ultimately however, the tug's tighter turning radius and slight speed advantage was to put *Water Baby* in the wrong place at the wrong time. Having learned from several previous missed approaches, Reiger's razor-sharp mind finally had the right moves figured out. And try as he might, Small, giving commands to Webb on the tiller and a series of swift engine-control orders to Erin, just couldn't make the old yawl turn tightly enough, nor could she be made to accelerate or decelerate in time to stop the ultimate disaster. Everyone aboard watched it happening as if in a dream — at the point where the action goes into slow motion.

The snarling tug had turned on them once more, but this time Reiger had allowed a little extra space to build between *Lady M* and the yawl before beginning his approach. And *Water Baby* had ended up facing nearly head-on to the tug at the end of her last defensive dodge. Heading toward it, not away, she was in no position to be able to outrun the bigger ship. For each steering change Webb applied to the sailboat, Reiger had only to make a minor course correction to keep it in his sights. Only twenty-five yards now separated the two boats. Webb had the rudder hard over to port, trying once more to make a slow-motion turn away from the charging tug, but the closing speed was too great for the old sailboat to be able to pull away. Erin, working the throttle and gear selector, kept a steady watch on the tug as the distance closed between the two boats.

A piercing, hair-raising scream filled the air. It was so close that it had no apparent direction. Webb's first thought was that Erin, who had been a tower of strength until now, was in a final moment of despair — but no, it was a mechanical screeching, and she was still right in front of him, though starting to stand up. Obviously, it had to be *Water Baby*'s engine. Not really surprising, he figured, considering what they'd put the old machine through over the past four hours. Not wanting to leave the tiller, he fixed his eyes on the tug and braced for the impact.

"Hard-a-starboard! Hard-a-starboard! *Hard-a-starboard*," Small's insistent yelling broke into Webb's slow-motion dream. "She's dying in the water!"

Webb, heaved the tiller over in compliance with Small's last order, dreading the worst as he looked once again down to where he had just seen Erin beginning to stand. But she was still there … still quite alive.

"No, look. The old diesel has finally seized," he said. Pointing at the tug, Small could see Webb's obvious confusion.

Following the tug man's gaze, Webb saw *Lady M* still

advancing toward them, but clearly slowing as she lost headway. Black exhaust had ceased to pour from the stack. More than twelve hours of engine time had elapsed since Hank had last topped up the crankcase in the tug's oil-thirsty diesel. And after straining full out for the past four hours without the conscientious Dutchman aboard to continuously tend to its needs, it had finally run out of its last available lubricant.

The wide, squat hull of a tugboat does not coast very far once propulsion stops. *Lady M* had been countering the oncoming yawl's desperate manoeuvre to port with a matching gentle turn to starboard and was lined up for a collision with *Water Baby* when the engine had seized. The tug was only ten yards away from striking the sailboat squarely amidships when the propeller completely stopped turning. Small's quick assessment of the situation, and his orders for a sudden change in course saved *Water Baby* from certain destruction. Despite Webb's momentary lapse in attention, the change in turn from port to starboard began to swing the yawl's stern section, the area now in line to be hit, away from the still-moving blunt bow of the tug. While she didn't quite clear the advancing attacker, *Water Baby* received only a glancing, low-speed blow, which quickly spun her around parallel to the tug's hull. The two boats rubbed together, *Water Baby*'s hull squeaking and squealing against the tug's old rubber tire fenders, until friction and the yawl's engine, responding to an order for "full astern" brought her more or less to rest.

July 22, 1218

As *Lady M* wallowed to a stop, Reiger burst out of the wheelhouse in a rage. Looking down on the tug's decks, he tried to find Gant and Mitchell through the black smoke. But before he could direct his men through the fires toward the starboard rail — even before the two boats had come completely to rest hull to hull — the *Water Baby* marine corps, led by Judge Franklin, swarmed over the rail and onto the tug. The only person left aboard *Water Baby* was Erin, who agreed to ready the lines and, if the battle went in their favour, tie the two boats together.

Reiger, still half-deafened by the firework explosion, was looking out the scorched portside doorway yelling orders at his two remaining warriors when the judge, with Billy Manion and Ray Ethier close on his heels, charged up the starboard ladder and into the tug's wheelhouse. Almost caught off guard, Reiger grabbed for a pistol he'd left near the tug's big wheel. Franklin threw his football-player frame at the Mid-Con boss, ramming into him just as the gun barked.

Although he'd heard victims in court describing the sensation of being shot, the effect of the bullet's impact amazed Franklin as he fell on top of the man. He hadn't expected the searing heat. Reiger, staggered by the impact of the charging judge, was slammed against the portside bulkhead in the wheelhouse and the pistol discharged once more before falling from his hand.

That second shot just barely missed Billy Manion before ripping through the wheelhouse radio. When the young crewman grabbed the gun off the deck, he was shaking with both terror and rage. Pointing the pistol at Reiger, he screamed, "*Freeze fucker!*" Though the man could barely hear him, it had the intended effect. Ethier immediately rushed over to check on the judge.

Aboard *Water Baby*, Erin Franklin hastily tied the yawl to the tug. Despite the commotion of battle aboard *Lady M*, she thought she heard someone splashing and choking astern of the yawl, just around the other side of the tug's bow.

"Over this way," she called. She was concerned that it

189

might be one of the good guys in trouble. Slowly, a yard at a time, the struggling figure of Gant's man, Dwayne Goreham, dog paddled into view. Not wanting to rescue the enemy — especially that jerk — but being too humane to let him drown, she threw him a life ring tethered to a line and instructed him to hang on to it and float away from the boats until someone else was available to haul him out. The authority carried by her order held its effect only until Goreham had a minute to regain his breath.

Aware that his side needed help, Goreham soon ignored Erin's repeated shouts to stay put and he swam to the side of the tug. Using one of the fender tires as a ladder, he heaved himself clear of the water and climbed back on deck.

Unable to draw the attention of her team aboard the tug, Erin knew that she would somehow have to delay Goreham on her own. He was on the fourth step up the companionway ladder to the tug's wheelhouse when Erin got behind him with the boathook she'd brought from the yawl. With no time to waste, she caught the bottom of the pant leg of his weight-bearing foot. Jerking hard on the shaft of the hook, she brought her opponent skidding back down to the deck; his knees and one side of his face bloody from the slide down the expanded steel mesh of the steps. Now he was in a flaming rage.

Seeing the man rising angrily from the tug's deck, Erin knew it was time to retreat to a safer position. She slipped and almost fell between the two boats as she dashed for the haven of the yawl. Recovering her footing, she quickly scrambled into the cockpit and down the companionway into the cabin. She paused in the salon, desperately looking for something to use as a weapon when Goreham, with both hatred and lust burning in his eyes, jumped down into the galley. Without a word he began to move toward her. There was not enough distance between them to allow Erin to escape by the forward hatch, and unless she could stall the terrible thug, she was trapped down there at his mercy. And he was showing no signs of mercy in his present frame of mind.

As her eyes fixed on it, she hated herself for what she was about to do, but the desired effect was immediate as Webb's cat, Heywood, startled from his resting place on the settee, was picked up by the scruff of his neck and flung at Goreham. In an instinctive effort to escape the indignity, the surprised cat instantly engaged his full 'traction control' system, rapidly clawing his way up and over the goon's face.

While Erin's would-be attacker stood yelling in pain, the cat scampered unharmed, into one of his hiding places beyond the chart table. Meanwhile Erin made a hasty escape out the forward hatch. When Goreham's face, a livid blood-streaked mess, began to emerge from the hatchway, she slammed the steel lid down on his head with all her strength. The man crumpled unconscious, onto the forward cabin sole.

On the aft deck of *Lady M*, dodging around the dwindling fires, Rick Webb and Mike Small picked up on movement through the thick black smoke just ahead of them. They finally recognized Gant's man, Mitchell, discharging a fire extinguisher at a particularly stubborn blaze he was trying to get around.

"Hey!" Webb shouted. The outlaw looked over his shoulder, half-turning to face the 12-gauge flare gun held cocked in Webb's extended hands. "Drop it," the officer ordered as his opponent began to swing the extinguisher around. Instinctively, the CO's years of self-defence training took over, and as the red steel object continued to swing toward him, he squeezed the trigger.

Although a 12-gauge flare fired from a three-inch barrel won't cause much damage with its impact, it still smarts like hell. And the surprise of being shot square in the chest by a bright red flaming projectile caused Mitchell to flinch and drop the fire extinguisher uttering a panicked yell as he did. Taking his cue, the big tug captain approached Mitchell from the side and gave him a swat on one shoulder, just enough to spin him around. A body slam threw him against the hot, fire-scarred bulkhead of the tug's deckhouse. As the criminal began to wilt and slide down toward the deck, Small and Webb each grabbed him by an arm and pitched him into the open storage locker which had served so recently as a cell for Webb and the Franklins.

"You are under arrest for a whole lot of shit," began the conservation officer, as they slammed the hatch closed. "And when we have time, I'll give you the rest of the spiel," Webb called through the steel door before turning to go and look for big John Gant.

But Gant had found them. Small and Webb were caught fully off guard. While they were busy incarcerating Mitchell, the big security chief had danced around the edge of that same fire and was closing in on them with his pistol at the ready. Turning from the storage locker hatch, they came face to face with the man's 9 mm Browning.

"You sons-o'-bitches really screwed things up for us," began the giant, focussing intently as he closed in on them. "But now we've got you."

"Wrong, Mr. Gant. *You* are under arrest. Get into that locker," ordered Webb, seeing an opportunity to put the big man off his pace.

"Dumb ass, I got the fuckin' gun. So I give the fuckin'... oouufff." The giant and his last sentence collapsed together as Charlie, the cook, came lumbering quietly down the deck, stooped over and threw himself into the back of Gant's tree-trunk legs. The big security chief didn't even get off a shot and was disoriented enough for Webb and Small to turn the tables on him.

"Man, that was a classic schoolyard move Charlie," Small complemented his cook as he stepped on Gant's right arm — the arm that was on its way to retrieving the dropped pistol.

Webb scooped up the firearm. Finally able to take control of the situation, he ordered Gant to stay quiet and lie face down so he could be searched. The substantial bulk that was Mike Small knelt on the giant's upper back. Despite his own size and strength, there was little that the criminal could do to resist under the tug skipper's weight, in fact he could hardly breathe. In less than a minute, Webb had his pocketknife back and came up with a second gun, an old snub-nosed .38 calibre revolver Gant had hidden in an ankle holster.

"Great takedown Charlie," Webb offered, then looked with concern at the older man who was now resting on the rail and nursing a sore shoulder. "Are you alright?"

"I'm okay, but I only got here when I did 'cause the mate sent me to tell yous guys that the judge got shot in the wheelhouse."

"Oh, Jesus! Mike, you watch Gant." Webb didn't even wait for any details or take time to ask whether or not Franklin was alive, but immediately turned the 9 mm over to Small. Armed with just the snubby, he raced up the portside companionway ladder to the tug's wheelhouse.

He was relieved to see that Franklin was still alive and was sitting on the deck with his back against the bulkhead. Part of his shirt, a bloody mess, had been cut away. Ray Ethier, Hank the engineer and Erin Franklin were working on bandaging up his right shoulder. On the other side of the ship's wheel, Reiger was standing with his hands clasped together on top of his head.

Billy Manion, standing in the wheelhouse starboard doorway as far back from the Mid-Con man as he could get, was still aiming the gun at him. The young tug crewman was no longer nervous and held the arrogant businessman in a cold, withering stare. Reiger knew he was in no position to escape or take back control.

"Good work lad. Hang on a minute longer and I'll give you a hand getting him out of here," Webb said. Then he turned his attention to the judge.

"How's he doing?" he asked Erin, who was looking a little pale at this point.

"It's made a real mess of his shoulder, but you'd be better off asking Dr. Hank. First aid was never a strong point of mine."

"Ha! I am just the repairman. Ask the patient," quipped the engineer.

"Feeling a little crapped out right now … I've never been attended to by a diesel mechanic, before." Franklin gave them all a slow grin. "It hurts like hell, and I'll have to swing the gavel with my left for a while, but I'll be okay. I think John Wayne would have said something like, 'Aw shucks fellas, it's just a little flesh wound'."

"As soon as we get Captain Contaminant out of here, we'll get you moved below to more comfortable quarters." Webb said as he placed a reassuring hand on Franklin's good shoulder and extended a reassuring smile toward Erin. Then he turned to face Reiger. He didn't yet know of the battle Erin had been through with Goreham just moments before.

"Turn around Mr. Reiger, and get down on your knees. *Do it now!*" he ordered. Being careful to stay out of Manion's line of fire, Webb stepped quickly across the small wheelhouse and grabbed Reiger, who had paused for a half second too long. Allowing the older man no time to react, Webb firmly spun him around to face the forward wheelhouse window less than two feet away. Standing beside and slightly behind him, the CO placed his left foot in front of the prisoner's ankles and pushed the man forward, tripping him to his knees.

"You are under arrest for kidnapping, uttering threats, attempted murder, depositing deleterious substances in waters frequented by fish and a whole raft of other criminal *and* provincial offences. Anything you say may be given in evidence …." Webb began to recite the official prisoner's caution from memory as he professionally bound the criminal's wrists behind his back with heavy-duty nylon cable ties. He had grabbed a handful of them from *Water Baby*'s electrical equipment drawer just before he and the others had boarded *Lady M*. They were the modern peace officer's choice for spare handcuffs.

Relieving young Manion of the pistol he'd been aiming at Reiger, the two men escorted the company's owner down toward the newly designated 'Ship's Brig'— the infamous paint storage locker.

"Nice job Rick," Jim Franklin called after him. Watching from the sidelines, he was entirely impressed by Webb's performance, thinking to himself, 'the man has just been through a vicious battle … a fight for our lives … and yet he handled the arrest of this despicable character in a professional manner … just enough force to gain compliance, but not vindictive.'

Down on the tug's main deck, Webb handed some of the nylon cable ties to Mike Small and the group finished securing Mitchell and Gant after full-body searches. One more inspection of the locker itself turned up no additional concealed weapons or means of escape. They even removed the old tarp, Webb commenting, "We don't want any of them hanging themselves in their cell now, do we?"

"That creep, Goreham is out cold in your forward cabin, Rick," Erin Franklin called down to them from the wheelhouse door. "And I'm sorry about the blood," she finished, pausing to watch the man before she turned back to help her father.

And for Webb, that triggered a quick flush of concern. He suddenly recalled that even with the guy down in *Water Baby*, there was still another one of Reiger's troops unaccounted for.

Picking up on the same thought, Small added, "Yeah, and we're still missin' Morris too. Did they both go overboard in the fight?"

Raising the alarm with the others, Webb quickly hopped over the tug's rail, landing lightly on his own deck. With Reiger's seized pistol held at the ready, he was just approaching the cockpit as Goreham climbed unsteadily up the companionway steps. Seeing that the fight was over, the battle-scarred lady's man raised his hands in surrender.

"Jeez, did you shave with a weed trimmer this morning, fella?" Webb queried the damaged warrior.

Goreham, feeling the humiliation of being bested by a woman, came up grumbling, "Fuckin' cats. They should all be tied in a fuckin' bag and thrown off a bridge!"

Asked about the remaining man, Goreham told of the demise of Jay Morris who had disappeared when the squall hit. According to his buddies, Morris might have been pulled overboard by a loop of the hawser when it was snatched by the tug's propeller. It appeared that that had likely been the case, as Mitchell gave them the same story when he was questioned shortly afterward. Reiger and Gant took their right to remain silent very seriously and said nothing.

Just to be sure that Goreham and Mitchell were telling the truth, Webb joined Mike Small who had already started to search the tug for any sign of the missing man. The hunt ended quickly enough when they found traces of rain-diluted blood spatter and some bone fragments at the tug's stern bitts — the place that Webb himself had last seen Morris.

"Well, I'm no coroner, but that sure looks to me like a fresh piece of a skull," Webb suggested, nudging a concaved piece of bone with his toe. "See the shape of it?" None of the others cared to disagree with him.

11. DISASTER

As soon as Hank started the diesel generator aboard the tug, an electric deck-wash pump made easy work of extinguishing the last of the dwindling fires aboard the *Lady M*. In fact, the old tug was so badly in need of paint that the rust-stained steel of the deckhouse bulkheads and the worn checker plate decks alone did not begin to provide enough of the fuel needed to support a raging shipboard fire. It was primarily the flares and flammable liquids thrown by the *Water Baby* marine corps that had fed the flames.

Meanwhile, Charlie, the cook was scurrying about his galley, laying on a quick snack for the hungry warriors. Wolfing down a sandwich on the fly, Webb picked up a tray of food and carried it forward to join the others in Small's cabin where Judge Franklin was somewhat comfortably established on the tug skipper's bunk. Handing the tray to Erin, he looked apologetically at the judge.

"Sorry Jim, but this is for your famished daughter who refuses to leave your bedside. 'Dr. Diesel' reminded me that the patient can't have anything to eat. You can only have sips of water in case they have to do surgery on you later. I think I remember hearing that once in first aid training too."

"Oh that's bullshit. My *dentist* could fill this little hole," the judge grumbled and then, changing the subject, he forced a grin and asked, "So what's next? You've got your villains rounded up … the survivors anyhow. You want me to try them right here and now and then perhaps hang them from the yardarm? Or did you have something else in mind?"

"I like your line of thinking, but Mike and I figure since no one's come speeding out here to welcome us home, we're close enough to Britt that we can use *Water Baby* to push *Lady M* into port. Then we'll get everyone to town at the same time and the good guys sorted from the bad at the docks there. We probably won't make much more than two and a half or three knots, but lashed to the starboard quarter of the tug out of the wind, my boat'll do alright. After today, she's going to need a major paint job anyhow, so a bit more chafing and scuffing will just save me some time on the sandblasting work.

"In the meantime, his first mate is still in my navigating station trying to reinvent the radio." Between the two boats there were no functioning lines of communication with the outside world. They had found Erin's cell phone in her backpack where Gant had thrown it under the desk in Mike Small's cabin — the pack being one bit of evidence they'd missed in their morning purge. But the battery was dead and her charger was at home. The judge's phone was nowhere to be found. The tug's radios were already known casualties. And none of Reiger's gang had a working phone with them either — they had pitched them all overboard along with the tug's satellite phone to avoid any possibility of being tracked after the tug's crew had abandoned them. All they'd really needed to do was shut them off.

"So, Mike," Webb said as he prepared to issue instructions to the gathering in the tug's little office. "When we get *Water Baby* lashed into position, you take command of the tow from your wheelhouse, and Hank and I will handle the helm and propulsion from the deck of my boat. We'll just have to yell back and forth or use hand signals to keep things coordinated."

"Look, y'all seem to be forgettin' that officially, I'm still on the shit-list. Remember, I'm one of the bad guys," said Small, totally ashamed of his role in the whole mess. "I'm willin' to help, but I don't know about commandin' the tug anymore."

"Mr. Small." Despite the pain he was enduring, James Franklin spoke in his most judicial voice. "I believe your actions and those of your entire crew today go a long way toward easing at least some of the legal difficulties you might be facing. If this were a bail court hearing, I would be strongly inclined to release you on your own recognizance. That means I trust you to continue working with us, whatever we finally decide to do here. I think I speak for Officer Webb as well?"

"Yes, Your Honour," came automatically from Webb, momentarily back in a courtroom frame of mind.

Small was genuinely relieved and quietly mumbled his thanks.

"Now, while I didn't realize that a sailboat could move a tugboat, I agree with the plan hatched up between you and Webb. So let's get this show on the road. We need to get back to civilization and let the rest of the world know what's been happening out here.

"And I want it understood by everyone on this boat: Reiger, Gant and their accomplices are very dangerous men. We've got to get them into police custody at the earliest opportunity. In the meantime, nobody, and I mean *nobody*, is to open that locker. If they are hungry or thirsty, show them the same consideration they extended to us … absolutely none!

"Considering the events of the last twenty-four hours, I'm beginning to understand why the general public seems to think that sometimes the courts today are too soft on criminals."

July 22, 1240

The bulk carrier *Blue Mountain*, finally loaded with 18,000 tons of crushed limestone, backed herself away from the dock at McGregor Bay. Skilfully applying repeated short bursts of forward power with the rudder hard over, alternating with short bursts full astern to keep the ship from actually advancing forward, Captain Henry persuaded the old lake freighter to pivot end for end in a circle hardly larger in diameter than its own length. Though many modern vessels had the luxury of bow thrusters to make this an easy manoeuvre, Henry always loved to demonstrate his ship-handling prowess using the traditional 'back and fill' method, as it was called. It was the only technique available to his aged lake boat. Once facing the channel out of the small harbour, the captain set about the task of threading the big freighter amongst rocky islands and cocky pleasure boaters for the nineteen-mile run back to the open waters of Georgian Bay.

July 22, 1250

Following a quick check for oil level, cracked hoses and frayed water-pump belts, Webb had the engine aboard *Water Baby* restarted, and the yawl was now lashed in position along the starboard quarter of *Lady M*. Mike Small carefully checked all the securing lines and verified that the assortment of fenders cushioning Water Baby were placed in the optimum locations before suggesting that Webb apply power to the tow. Gradually, the thrust from the yawl's old engine began to inch the tug forward through the water.

July 22, 1255

"Skipper, the chief wants you to call him," announced the man at the wheel of *Blue Mountain*. Captain Henry had just returned from a quick trip to the head.

He picked up a portable radio. "Chief, you there? Captain here." The officers and crew preferred using the small handheld radios rather than the ship's antiquated telephone system.

"*Yeah, Skipper, while they were working on that conveyor at McGregor, Anderson and I did some poking around down here and found bearings on a few of the rollers on our own conveyors that look like they are getting close to timing out. They should be changed while we're on passage. Be a real bitch to work on if they packed it in with a load of stone going up the chute.*"

"How long do you figure it'll take to change them Chief? Do you have spares aboard?"

"*What's that Skipper? Your signal is bro…*" Static, then silence, were all that came out of the little handheld radio. Repeatedly clicking the transmit button did nothing to revive it.

"Damn thing's gone dead." The captain was being frustrated by one technical failure after another. To the helmsman, "Wasn't this on the charger when I picked it up?"

"Yes sir, but I think the battery on that one's cooked … first officer was complaining about one of them not holding a charge a couple days ago."

"And no one thought to put a new battery pack on it. Leave it for the next poor bastard to deal with," he vented. Impatient to hear the rest of what the chief engineer had to say, but not wanting to play games with another handheld, Captain Henry walked straight over to the bridge VHF radio and punched in the 'on board' frequency they used on the marine-band portables. He neglected however, to switch the VHF set from its 25-watt setting down to 1 watt. "Chief engineer this is *Blue Mountain* bridge. Over."

"I can read you real good now Skipper. I heard you ask about how long to change the worn bearings. Shouldn't be more than six or seven hours to do them all. Your next question was broken up and cut off, but I'm guessing the answer you're looking for is, 'Yes, we do have spares aboard'. My question to you is, how much time 'til we hit Midland? Do you want us to change 'em now, or chance it and get at them on the next long crossing?'

It didn't take Henry more than a heartbeat to weigh the odds of being plagued by further mechanical gremlins sooner rather than later. The ship was way too far past her prime to go more than a day without something breaking down.

July 22, 1255

Lady M was being pushed by Webb's old yawl which was lashed to her starboard quarter. Her speed gradually crept toward two knots, and she was still accelerating. For the moment, an exact course was not essential — for the moment it was enough to know that the sailboat was up to the task she'd been assigned, and the vessels were headed in the right general direction. Mike Small, Rick Webb and Hank the engineer stood in *Water Baby*'s cockpit discussing a simple system for relaying helm and engine orders between the tug's wheelhouse and the yawl. At the same time, Webb was getting a feel for steering the big tug using the yawl's tiller. Pretty impressive performance for less than thirty horsepower he decided.

Erin Franklin was in the sailboat's cabin delivering sandwiches and coffee to Ray Ethier. He had been hunched over the chart table aboard *Water Baby* almost continuously since they had retaken the tug. He was muttering to himself in a combination of French and English. The remains of Webb's two VHF sets were now spread across the table's surface, the individual components having been tenderly removed from their battered cases. A number of the pieces were held down to the table by strips of masking tape. Working carefully, twisting wires together to make one connection at a time, the tug's mate was attempting to assemble a scratch-built radio set. He had put together plenty of electronics kits as a hobby when he was up north on the Hudson Bay tugs, so this was just a little refresher course for him. There had been lots of spare time up there and little else to do outside of the brief shipping season.

He finally sat up straight and smiled as he flipped a toggle switch bringing 12-volt power to his desktop creation. A loud static squawk filled the yawl's cabin. Everyone aboard but Ethier himself was startled. He looked over the top of his reading glasses, found the volume control, and turned the static noise down to a tolerable level.

"'Ere we 'ave a simple radio receiver. It cannot transmit yet, and I don't know what channel h'it is on, but we do one t'ing at a time, eh? The V haich F sets on *Lady M* h'are too new to work on. Everyt'ing der h'is digital … no user serviceable parts h'as dey say."

Erin looked questioningly at the tangle of parts taped to the table, and the men in the cockpit crowded together looking down through the companionway offering cautious encouragement and flooding Ethier with questions. But he held a hand up to silence them as he started to turn the tuning knob salvaged from the older of the two destroyed sets.

He had gone through twenty of the twenty-six possible frequencies on the old tuner without hearing a thing, and just when everyone was beginning to feel that Ethier's efforts were all for naught, they heard a faint signal, "*No Chief, get at it right away*." Ethier turned up the volume. The signal was still thin and overlaid by static, but the occupants of *Water Baby*'s cabin and cockpit could all hear it.

"*We're just abeam of McGregor Point now. It'll take us an hour and fifty minutes to thread our way through this weekend boat traffic to Campbell Rock buoy, then we'll set a direct course for Hope Island, just skirting the outer shoals of the Western Islands. Should be in Midland harbour in just over eight hours. I want that conveyor serviced and running the minute we dock there. We've already lost too much time on this load to chance a breakdown of our own.*"

Ethier's scratch-built desktop radio had picked up the transmission from the VHF on the bridge of *Blue Mountain*. He was wearing a proud smile that ran from ear to ear, and the rest of those on board were congratulating him on his miraculous technical achievement.

A dark frown suddenly clouded over Mike Small's face. As fluid as a professional dancer, his massive bulk swept down the companionway steps and forward to the dinette table where he began to rifle through the nautical charts moved there earlier to give Ethier a place to work. Laying a straight edge on the big Georgian Bay chart, he lined up the course planned by the bulk carrier's skipper.

"Jesus H Christ!" he muttered audibly, and then he called up to the cockpit. "Webb!"

Rick immediately sensed the tug man's urgent tone. "What's the problem?"

"We gotta cast off our tow! That carrier on the radio is on a headin' to pass right over Dawson Rock. That's where we've been dumpin' the illegal product. We've got to turn that ship away."

"They wouldn't intentionally run a big ship like that over a shoal, would they?" Erin Franklin joined the conversation, alarmed by this latest development.

"Normally, if the drums weren't down there, there'd still be plenty of depth for them to pass with more than ten or twelve feet to spare. But it sounds like they're runnin' behind schedule, so straight lines save time. If they go right over that barrel dump at fifteen knots, the bow wave will suck the drums up off the bottom with a lot of them gettin' chewed up by the prop after they pass down the hull! Or they'll just break free from their weighted pallets and go adrift, endin' up anywhere around the bay."

Erin gasped at the thought, dramatically elaborating for the others the probable consequences of such an event. "If enough of those toxins are released into the water, that stuff will contaminate all the fish … oh God … depending on what's in them, all the *aquatic life* in Georgian Bay and probably the rest of the lake, *and* the lakes downstream for years to come. This is terrible!" Even then she didn't know that over half of the dumped product consisted of deadly PCBs.

"That's a big wide shoal Mike, what makes you so sure your waste dump will be overrun?" Webb questioned.

"There's a thirty-five-foot-deep trench that runs across the shoal northwest to southeast. It's where I dumped the product to keep it safe from tumbling winter ice; some of those big sheets get pushed over pretty bad in winter storms. But I've never known the lake boats to cross there. That's why I chose that spot. But if they were going to do it, that'd be the route across the shoal for them. It's wide enough." The man was close to tears.

Word was quickly passed to the judge aboard the tug and the game plan was immediately rewritten. Even before Webb had a chance to assign new roles, Mike Small spoke up.

"I gotta go with you," he stressed as he returned to *Water Baby* with half of the tug's supply of impressive commercial-grade emergency flares. "It's my mess. I know exactly where the dump site is and I have to do everything in my power to avoid a disaster, or all the judge's pardons in the world ain't goin' to mean spit." The tug skipper, so buoyant just a few minutes earlier, was now in a big sweat.

"I had every intention of taking you along, Mike. I need a crew — and you've proven yourself more than worthy. And I need a guide and a fellow who can talk persuasively to arrogant ship captains, if that's what we happen to run into out there."

Billy Manion, Hank the engineer and Charlie the cook were to stay aboard the disabled tug with Judge Franklin and the criminals. Manion and the engineer would drop the anchor to keep *Lady M* from drifting down the bay, or worse, onto the rocks of the nearby coast. And it was their job to activate the remaining supply of flares if either a passing vessel or an aircraft was sighted.

Ray Ethier insisted on staying aboard *Water Baby* to continue his attempt to assemble a working transmitter if it could be done. He said that if he had to move what he had done so far, he would lose time redoing what he had already accomplished. And if he did get something working, he wanted to be as near to the lake freighter as possible to have a reasonable chance of establishing contact with it.

It was assumed by most of them that Erin would stay with her dad aboard the tug. And although she was torn both ways, she said she had to finish what she had started. She wanted to do whatever she could to help the others turn the bulk carrier away from the toxin-filled drums on Dawson Rock.

In fact, Webb was pleased that she wanted to come along. She too, had proven herself a capable sailor and although he still resisted the idea, he felt a growing attraction to the woman, despite how prickly she'd been at first.

The judge was also relieved that she wanted to go with

Webb and Small. He didn't want his daughter sitting idle on the same boat as the thugs who had already put her through hell, even though they were locked securely in the storage locker. That would be just plain cruel.

12. INTERCEPT COURSE

The lines securing the yawl to the tug were hurriedly cast off and Small took the tiller. He immediately engaged forward gear and advanced the throttle to its best smooth power. Rick and Erin soon had the sails set and drawing well as they headed off once more, this time in a desperate bid to intercept the bulk carrier. They had to stop it before it could blunder into the toxic chemical dump lying along its course to Midland.

Dawson Rock lay west-southwest of *Water Baby*'s current position and the wind was still coming from the northwest, somewhat forward of abeam. On that point of sail, even powered by both the engine and sails, the yawl was making just barely over six knots. The waves had grown slightly higher since their earlier dash to the northeast. But fortunately, they had also lengthened considerably between crests. The boat was essentially climbing long hills on the diagonal, not smashing through short steep banks of water. That was a help, but those long hills required energy to climb, and the heavy yawl did not accelerate quickly down the backs of the waves. So, while the motion was reasonably comfortable, the classic yacht just couldn't motor-sail as fast into the wind as it could with the wind abeam.

Turning the tiller over to Erin, Small followed Webb down into *Water Baby*'s cabin to help plot their course to Dawson Rock, and too, plot the anticipated course of the southbound freighter. They hadn't heard the ship's name yet over Ethier's receiver, but Webb remembered something from his night sail to Club Island.

"Man, that was only about thirty-six hours ago, but it feels like a week," he said. "There was a bulk carrier transiting eastward … what was her name?"

"Oh, shit … ah … no, sorry, it's on the tip of my tongue, but I can't remember off hand," Small answered and looked at Ethier who just shrugged his shoulders and kept on working.

A quick check of that evening's entries in his now badly trampled ship's log gave Webb the answer. "This is it, *Blue Mountain*." Now he remembered. "They were headed up to the top end of the bay. If you hear any radio traffic, either for or from *Blue Mountain*, monsieur Ethier, écoutez bien s'il vous plaît," Webb tried his limited French, advising the tug's mate to keep his ears open. Ethier grinned and nodded an acknowledgement.

Looking at the chart with the tentatively drawn course lines, Webb and Small consulted on their best approach to the situation once they got close to their destination.

"Mike, it just struck me that if we go straight toward Dawson Rock, and then start setting off flares, they're going to come straight across it towards us to affect a rescue. Wouldn't we be better to…."

"Yeah, yer right," Small cut in. "We gotta pinch a bit north of Dawson and draw them aside of the shoal water before they're onto it. Based on whatever ETA you have come up with, do we even have time for that? Or will they have already passed by the time we get close?"

"Well, using the time frame we picked up from their radio conversation, the ship should arrive at the northwestern edge of Dawson Rock by 1610. And I was just about to calculate our own ETA. But without the GPS to direct us to the exact spot, the actual result could vary a little from what we put on paper."

In addition to the clock and the cabin compass, the yawl's cockpit compass and speed log were the only navigational instruments that had survived Reiger's wrath. And the speed readout varied slightly depending on which tack the boat lay, as well as the angle of heel of the boat. Webb had never bothered to create an actual table of corrections, but was reasonably confident that he could adjust, from memory, the log readings to actual speed made good. His main concern was that overestimating their speed in this particular crisis could put them some distance short of their intercept point at the critical moment. And he knew too, that pinching closer toward the wind was going to cost them some precious speed.

"We've got to come up close to fifteen more degrees into the wind, Erin," he called out from the cabin. "Put us on a compass heading of two-seven-zero, and after she settles on course, give me the new speed … she's going to slow down a bit I'm afraid."

"It reads just under five and a half, Rick," Erin reported shortly. "Call it a steady five point four knots".

"Okay, thanks. That's actually closer to five point one on this tack." Returning to the chart, Webb quickly spanned the distance with his dividers and declared that they would still be about three miles east of the ship as it came to within the last two miles of Dawson Rock.

"How much room do you think she needs to come to a stop Mike?"

"Oh, shit, she'd need more than that to do a straight-line

stop but remember that we're goin' to be about sixty or seventy degrees off her port bow, and far enough away that they'll be able to turn towards us, then take off the power, losin' speed as they approach. They'll have turned clear of the shoal water by then. Yeah, that should work out fine … as long as everything goes as planned."

July 22, 1335

Red, the water taxi operator, was huddled by the smoldering remains of his small fire on the beach ridge at Halfmoon Island. For the second time in less than twenty-four hours he was engaged in a battle to fight off hypothermia.

Following the passage of the three PWCs early that morning, the only other boat to pass within reasonable signalling distance was the tug to which he had delivered the guy with the code name 'Kingfisher' — who turned out to be a judge. And that was sometime around seven. The tug was towing a sailboat southeastward, not its own barge. With the knowledge contained in the urgent note left by this judge fellow, Red had made no attempt to attract the attention of the tug.

After the squall and cold front had swept through, he saw nothing more of either the tug or the sailboat. And there'd been absolutely no other boat traffic pass by the island all day. Pleasure boaters usually stayed put in the cold windy conditions that followed such a squall. As a result, he'd spent the rest of the day cold, wet, miserable and undiscovered. And while he did eventually manage to get one of his signal fires started, he'd burned up every scrap of burnable wood he could find on the island.

Finally, it looked as if he had caught a break. Some guy was rowing ashore from an old express cruiser that was done up in a colour scheme like a coast guard boat, but without the big lettering. 'Of course,' Red thought, stirring from his funk. 'The guy must be a member of the Coast Guard Auxiliary.' The auxiliary was a civilian volunteer water safety training and rescue organization that worked in conjunction with the Canadian Coast Guard. With renewed hope, he hustled his cold and stiffened limbs down to the water's edge.

The auxiliary man, who had seen Red's apparent situation from some distance out, had anchored his old cruiser as close to the leeward side of the island as he could. From there, he rowed an inflatable dinghy in over the shoal water for the remaining couple of hundred feet. As soon as his dinghy ground gently on the small island's course gravel beach, the bearded, silver-haired rescuer handed Red the blanket that he had already guessed the poor shivering soul would need.

"Afternoon. Name's Alex Galt. I take it you don't live here full-time," he said, in an effort to lighten up the situation a little. And then on a serious note, "Is there anyone else out here with you?"

Too cold to talk any more than a shivering stutter, Red just shook his head.

"No? Okay, then let's get you aboard my *Angel* where you can warm up."

During the brief introduction, Red passed the man the tattered scrap of paper with the judge's note on it. Galt stroked hard on the stubby oars to get the little inflatable quickly back to his cruiser. Franklin's scribbled message, when put together with a news item he'd heard that morning about a missing judge, added up to the need for a major police presence somewhere out here on Georgian Bay — immediately!

As Red settled in the cruiser's warm cabin, he sipped on a mug of coffee hastily poured from an ancient Thermos by his thoughtful host. Galt listened to Red's abbreviated story, and then immediately began to relay the information to the coast guard on his VHF. He would have preferred to use his cell phone to call the police directly, but out here, there was no signal.

Galt was transmitting on a duplex working channel, which was at least in part, away from prying ears. The duplex system meant that all calls transmitted from boat radios would be sent on one frequency, and all calls sent back by the coast guard radio were transmitted on another. Other boaters, if they had tuned in to listen, would only be able to hear the coast guard operator's side of the conversation, not the information transmitted by Mr. Galt.

However, on hearing the nature of the information, the operator wanted to take the message immediately back to channel 16, broadcasting it in the clear, for all to hear as a Mayday message.

"No, no, no. You mustn't do that! As a retired police detective myself, I assure you that the police *will* want to broadcast to other boaters for assistance, but they may wish to keep some information out of the public domain for now. Just get them on the phone and let's get this moving forward. Over."

"Roger, Angel. Understood. Please stand by on this channel."

July 22, 1355

The police investigation suddenly took on new life. At first it had just been Judge Franklin missing without a fresh trace — other than his car mysteriously turning up in Owen Sound. Then on the same day, some water taxi operator vanished with his brother-in-law's muscle boat. The place and approximate timing gave credence to there being a possible connection. But the trail had stayed cold since then.

Now word had just arrived that the water taxi skipper had been rescued following a mysterious boat explosion. His urgent message for the police tied the judge to the tugboat *Lady M.* Another piece to the puzzle dropped into place, thanks to Red O'Reilly.

Detective Constable Tina Stambury was struggling to manage her fatigue. Coffee can only go just so far in keeping a dead tired person awake, let alone alert and thinking clearly. But as soon as O'Reilly's message arrived, she returned to her computer. Despite being red-eyed and exhausted, she quickly traced the ownership of the tug to Mid-Con Waste Management Inc. And that rang a bell for her.

She recalled Friday's coffee room chatter about an environmental court case in town that didn't go well earlier in the week. And to think she'd skipped right over that one last night when she'd ruled out the judge's dismissed cases in her research. 'Well, that's a lesson learned,' she'd told herself wearily.

Stambury quickly devised an action plan and the day shift sergeant immediately agreed to it. She phoned back to the coast guard communications centre asking them to broadcast several messages on channel 16. The operators in Thunder Bay were more than willing to assist.

July 22, 1400

On the bridge of the bulk carrier *Blue Mountain,* Captain Lorne Henry had pretty much reached the boiling point. The freighter had just passed Heywood Island on the second-last leg of the route back to the open waters of Georgian Bay when several weekend boaters transiting nearby Lansdowne Channel began calling each other continuously on VHF channel 16. Apparently, neither boat could hear the other's transmissions.

But despite the blunt warnings from the coast guard radio operators, the annoying repetitive calling continued.

Shortly however, that particular chatter was cut off. Aboard a vessel with an even stronger signal, someone's child had picked up the microphone and started talking to an imaginary friend — without taking a break for many long minutes.

Livid at the ill manners of the so-called adult boaters who started the ruckus, and furious that the parents of a child would not be paying attention to the fact that their kid was tying up the airwaves, Henry reached up and turned the radio volume right down. Only gradually did his blood pressure begin to subside, and although the big lake boat was not yet out into open water, Henry excused himself from the bridge, leaving Second Officer Latham in charge. The young fellow had, after all, shown good judgment rerouting to the wider passage when faced with the squalls the other night. He'd be fine.

July 22, 1410

"*The tug Lady M, the tug Lady M, the tug Lady M, this is Thunder Bay Coast Guard Radio, Thunder Bay Coast Guard Radio.*" One minute went by, then the broadcast call was repeated.

Calling the tug was stage one of Stambury's action plan. For the next twenty minutes the coast guard operator made the broadcast with a five-minute interval between each pair of attempts. No reply was received from the tug.

July 22, 1430

"*Pan pan, Pan pan, Pan pan. This is Thunder Bay Coast Guard Radio, Thunder Bay Coast Guard Radio.*" A 'Pan pan' call was just one level short of issuing a Mayday.

"*The Canadian Coast Guard is attempting to locate the eighty-five-foot black and white tug named Lady M in regard to an urgent family matter. Vessel was last seen towing a blue sailboat in a southeasterly direction this morning at 0710, approximately three miles east of Halfmoon Island. Any vessel with knowledge of the whereabouts of the tug Lady M, please contact this station immediately. Thunder Bay Coast Guard Radio out.*"

Stage two of DC Stambury's action plan let out the sort of information that was most likely to draw on public sympathy without actually showing their hand. Almost everyone has family, and most people would want others to help if there was an emergency situation in their own family. Most would willingly reach out to help others. Boaters are particularly good about such things.

The coast guard communications centre immediately received two calls. The first revealed that *Lady M* had been in Club Island harbour earlier the previous night, had left and then returned before dawn, the events being described as peculiar. There had also been a blue and white sailboat anchored in the cove overnight. The second caller reported having passed a tug of that description towing a blue and white sailboat, with two wooden masts. It was headed southeasterly at around 0745 about ten miles north of Cabot Head.

The radio operator who took the calls thought that something out of all that information sounded familiar. He clicked on the sailing plan icon on his desktop monitor and looked up the check-ins for the previous day. Yes, there it was. Blue and white yawl with wooden spars … *Water Baby* … closed his sailing plan at Club Island yesterday at 0505 … no new plan filed. 'Ah ha! Two plus two … just maybe …' thought the operator as he picked up the phone.

July 22, 1440

DC Stambury was outside for another smoke break when the sergeant called out the door and told her of new developments. She crushed her smoke on the sidewalk, dumped the last of her coffee in the flower bed and hurried back inside. The marine broadcasts had born fruit and the reports coming back from the coast guard indicated that a boat owned by a Richard Webb of Parry Sound, was somehow possibly caught up in the picture too.

Tina knew Rick Webb from curling and had seen him in court quite often too. She knew him to be a dedicated game warden who would do everything he could to solve an environmental crime.

At first, neither she nor the sergeant had any idea why either Franklin or Webb might be involved with the Mid-Con people after a case had already been disposed of in court. But Stambury went back to the courthouse computer records she'd skipped over last night. What she learned there, quickly tied all three together — Franklin, Webb and Mid-Con. And the record also provided the name of the company's owner.

'So, the judge, the lead investigator and the defendant were all in the same courtroom just a few days ago,' she pondered. 'But those facts alone still don't explain if, or why the judge and Rick would be abducted. They weren't on the winning side. So what's going on here?'

And then she suddenly recalled Ridley's comment about the judge moving heaven and earth for his daughter — his daughter the environmental activist.

She quickly tried another call to Erin Franklin's two phone numbers. She'd been calling periodically all night and even more frequently as the new day had worn on, but each time there was no answer — just her voicemail message. That had left the detective with a bad feeling about things. And now that feeling was suddenly getting worse, but she still didn't have enough pieces to complete the puzzle.

While Erin's second number started ringing, the detective went on-line and Googled news reports on past court battles between the government and Mid-Con Waste.

"Bingo!" she exclaimed aloud. Two years earlier, convictions were registered against Reiger and his company in a Toronto area trial. Charges had been laid by the natural resources ministry based on a complaint put forward by a member of the public — a member of the public named Erin Franklin.

It was still just speculation on Stambury's part, but she suddenly felt the last pieces of the puzzle falling in place with a sickening thud. "Erin's in trouble, her father is trying to 'move heaven and earth' to help her and somehow Rick Webb has joined the fight," she spoke aloud again as she locked that conclusion in her mind.

Quickly pushing away from her desk, she called to the day shift sergeant and laid out her hypothesis. She admitted that there still weren't enough facts to make all the pieces fit together. But the sergeant agreed that it was worth acting on. It was one of those times, he said, that a gut feeling might be all they ever got to act on. Jumping over the detachment commander's head, he phoned straight through to the district superintendent. The minutes they saved could be critical in a possible hostage situation.

July 22, 1455

The first of two police helicopters hastily dispatched by the district superintendent to begin the search, immediately headed for the southeastern end of the extended course line provided by the coast guard. Hours had passed since the sightings of the tug and Webb's boat, but they had to start looking somewhere, and the far end of the last course the vessels were observed on was the logical choice. Meanwhile, an RCAF Hercules search-and-rescue plane was called into the search as well. The first thing that the police asked its pilot to check out was the cove at Club Island, before swinging south to work with the choppers.

July 22, 1535

While the police helicopters scoured the rocky, island-dotted eastern side of southern Georgian Bay, the crew of the air force Hercules reported that the only vessel at Club Island right then was a loaded barge with the badly faded name, 'Mid-Con Waste' painted down the sides. The vessel appeared to be aground in the northeast corner of the cove. That first Hercules was joined shortly afterward by a second one and they began to conduct a systematic grid search of the open water portions of the southern end of the bay.

The Ministry of Natural Resources operated its own air service. As well as providing aircraft for the province's forest fire-fighting organization, the Ontario Provincial Air Service was also used by the conservation officers for aerial surveillance and detection work both inland and on the Great Lakes.

The district inspector of the police spoke to the air service director about the emergency developing on the bay. The director immediately volunteered a Twin Otter aircraft on amphibious floats to join the search. He personally knew some of the COs, and it went without saying that the ministry would join in on the search for one of its own people.

Coordinating with the police dispatcher, the Twin Otter

started from its Sudbury base almost immediately and began to fly southeast to close the gap with the other aircraft. Flying a thousand feet above the northeastern corner of Georgian Bay, the yellow twin engine plane flew past *Lady M* about four miles east of her location. Their mission instructions were to begin a search of the inlets and channels off of Parry Sound and then work their way south to link up with the police choppers. The pilot and his engineer-observer paid little attention to the area immediately around them. They were impatient to get to their starting point twenty-five miles farther down the bay.

July 22, 1537

"Jeez, I don't know, it's a long way off, Hank. Shouldn't we wait till there's one goes by closer?" Billy Manion was leery about wasting a flare on a plane so far from their position.

"Now or never, boy. We haf more of them. Set it off quick now," the old engineer urged. The yellow plane, just a tiny dot above the eastern horizon, was not getting any closer.

After the thump and whoosh of its launching, the flare seemed to take forever to climb to where it would ignite, and each second was taking the aircraft farther away.

July 22, 1538

The pilot and observer aboard the Twin Otter were kibitzing about the day back in May when the boss, busy making a point about a maintenance issue, walked backwards right off the end of the dock into the ice-cold water.

"Yeah, and you silly boneheads were laughing so hard he damn near died of hypothermia before *I* hauled him back up on the dock," Dale Moses laughed as he looked over at his passenger in the right-hand seat. He was about to make another point when he caught a glimpse of a bright red light out of the corner of his eye. Whatever it was — and he was pretty sure he knew — he'd seen it through one of the side windows near the back of the plane. And then it had just as quickly been obscured by a windowless section of the fuselage.

"Well, that's interesting," the pilot said as he began a sweeping right-hand turn out toward the open water. "If you'd been using those eyes in the back of your head like any decent observer, you would have seen the parachute flare that just went off on our starboard quarter. Keep your eyes peeled for anything down on the water … it'll still be a few miles ahead."

Moses increased the power slightly to climb another five hundred feet for better viewing as he steadied the plane in the northwesterly direction toward where he thought he'd seen the flare. Just two minutes after finishing the turn, observer Sandy Brandon pointed ahead and down to the right.

Whoever had sent up the parachute flare knew what they were doing. Seeing the plane turn and begin to approach, they were now burning a bright red handheld flare on deck so the plane could pinpoint their exact location. The big yellow float plane began a gliding descent toward the flare and the pilot radioed the sighting back to the police dispatcher. Five minutes later, a slow, low altitude pass down one side of the tug revealed the name, *Lady M.*

"Boy, that's one tough lookin' old Hell ship," Moses said. "Looks like they've had a fire too. And she's sure a long way from where everyone is lookin' for her. Someone on board knows their signals … they're flyin' the flag upside down … ye olde international distress signal.

"It's way too rough to land down there. And if there's bad guys aboard, I have no desire to get into that kind of a jackpot, even if we could put down. See if you can raise them on the marine radio Sandy."

Brandon spoke up after several minutes of calling the tug on channel 16. "No answer on the radio, Dale,"

"One more pass, real slow then. It looked like one of them was trying to do semaphore or something."

"And do you speak semaphore?"

"Not a word of it, but let's see how distressed they look anyhow," Moses finished as he took a wide sweeping turn to line up for another pass by the tug. With the flaps extended, the Twin Otter's stall speed was rated at fifty-eight knots. Moses set full flaps and applied sufficient power to keep the plane flying at sixty-five knots, just to be safe. Flying straight into the fifteen-knot wind, they passed the tug doing barely fifty over the water. The floats were just yards above the wave tops and Brandon wondered if the wingtip would even clear the tug's wheelhouse.

"One guy's got his fist in front of his mouth, and another beside him has his forearms crossed in an X," reported the observer. "Third guy's just waving his arms in a distress type of wave."

"Fist in front of mouth, and an X. C'mon Sandy, even you should be able to interpret that sign language!"

"Ummm ... well ... oh! No radio?"

"Ha, give the man a cigar. Grab one of those little personal communicator walkie-talkie thing-a-ma-jigs and stuff it into a waterproof drop bag, will ya? Use lots of bubble wrap. I'm hoping to give it a hard landing. We should have a chat with these boys before we report in."

Dale Moses was one of the best in the air service when it came to dropping message bags. The trick in this situation was going to be that the folks on the tug weren't going to be able to run across a clearing in the forest to retrieve the bright orange pouch. If it ended up in the water, which was pretty likely to happen, either they'd have to swim for it, or let it go.

July 22, 1550

Nearing the end of their anticipated three-hour dash toward Dawson Rock, those aboard *Water Baby* were finally rewarded by the sight of the bulk carrier, *Blue Mountain.* She appeared to be on her predicted course, still some miles to the northwest of them.

Their urgent westward passage to meet the lake freighter had gone as well as could be expected. The yawl's mixed crew had worked flawlessly together, each taking half-hour turns at the tiller. And Ray Ethier had stayed at the navigating station stubbornly intent on creating a radio transmitter. To the others it just looked like a hopeless jumble of wires and stuff, sitting alongside the other jumble of wires and stuff that had already become a working receiver.

They were all tired after a full day of physical challenges and emotional hardships. But Rick Webb was impressed that after a quick tidy-up he'd started in his dishevelled cabin, Erin had continued the job in earnest during her next break from steering. Her expression appeared to him to be more one of determination, rather than of enthusiasm. She wasn't all sunshine and sweetness like Melanie had been, but he realized that he had still warmed to her as the day had progressed. That thought still disturbed him. While steering his boat toward their intended rendezvous point, he kept wondering what Mel would want him to do. While part of his mind strongly suspected that she would have wanted him to move on — to fall in love with another woman and start a new life, the other part of him still felt guilty about letting her go and leaving her behind.

Meanwhile, Erin was thinking that she'd been pretty harsh in her preliminary judgment of the guy. He'd managed to pull off their escape from Rieger's clutches, and he'd sure handled himself well during the morning's chase and the sea battle. She just didn't know how to smooth things over with him without sounding flakey. The cabin clean-up bee was about the best thing she could think of, and by the time she had finished doing what she could (Ethier still had the navigating station in an uproar) she was pretty impressed with Webb's old yawl. In spite of the abuse it had taken that day, it was a really classy looking antique. The cabin just needed some repairs, some paint and varnish touch-ups and a detailed cleaning. An industrial strength vacuum cleaner would do wonders on the mess left by the Mid-Con gang.

During the crossing, Ray Ethier had experienced several setbacks in his quest to build a radio transmitter from the salvaged pile of parts. But he finally felt he was within a few minutes of a breakthrough.

"H'each time I try to transmit on de twenty-five watts power, she blow de fuse," he explained to his anxious onlookers. "I only 'ave one fuse left, so I rewire de set to just use one watt to transmit. We need to be really close to de ship before dey can 'ear us." And with that, he clicked the microphone once, causing a squeal of feedback to come from the speaker of the receiver he'd created earlier. He grinned from ear to ear.

"De receiver, she doesn't cut out when she transmits like when she h'is built, so I 'ave to turn down de volume h'except for when we receive. But dat was h'a good test. We know she works," he proudly pronounced. It was still a mystery as to which frequency the radio was set on, so for now Ethier said they'd leave it on the channel they had first heard the ship transmit on.

Up in the cockpit, glassing the bulk carrier with Webb's binoculars, Mike Small suggested it was time to begin launching parachute flares. Rick and Erin agreed. Each flare would climb to about one thousand feet, then ignite and deploy its chute. The bright red flare, which would burn for forty seconds or more, would be impossible for anyone aboard that ship to miss unless they were all asleep — or dead. If needed, they would launch successive flares every five minutes, although Small doubted they'd need to set off all four of them to get a reaction.

July 22, 1554

On the bridge of *Blue Mountain*, Second Officer Don Latham was engaged in an animated discussion with Thompson, the helmsman about yesterday afternoon's game between the Blue Jays and the White Sox. Each was an avid fan of the opposing team. Each was trying to make a point about the umpire's call on a particularly close tag at second base. The lake boat was running along at fifteen knots on a steady southeasterly course pre-set into the auto-helm. Captain Henry was in his cabin, either catching up on a mountain of paperwork, or taking a nap — the young second officer couldn't really recall what the old man had said when he had left the bridge earlier near Heywood Island.

"Holy shit!" Latham exclaimed as a red flare ignited in the sky four or five miles to the east. Despite the bright afternoon sky, the flare's brilliance was impressive. "Someone's in trouble out there."

Thompson, who was supposed to attend only to the helm — automated though it was — made it first to the big long-range binoculars. He quickly carried them from their storage rack out to the port bridge wing. Latham, annoyed that the man should try to get first look, moved in behind the eyepieces the instant the helmsman had fixed the heavy glasses to the rail mount.

"Well that's odd," he said. "There's a sailboat out there … can't see much detail from this distance … but it looks to be under full sail and moving right along … coming this way. I don't see any indication of trouble … no smoke … nothing. And there are no other boats out there. Take a quick look for yourself, but then you'd better get back to the helm … the helm that you shouldn't have left in the first place … and keep an ear on the VHF for any distress calls. I'll watch here for a few minutes more. The captain's blood pressure will go through the roof if we decide to stop for a weekend Romeo who was just putting on a flare demonstration to impress his girlfriends."

July 22, 1559

Everyone aboard *Water Baby* was disappointed by the lack of any sort of response from the fast-approaching bulk carrier. Every minute the lake freighter continued forward at speed used up precious manoeuvring space between it and the toxic waste dump.

The crew aboard the yawl fired off their second parachute flare. At the same time, Ray Ethier decided to send out a continuous message on his cobbled-up VHF transmitter.

"Bulk carrier *Blue Mountain* standing h'on for Dawson Rock, turn h'aside immediately. Dis is de sailboat on your port bows. h'Uncharted h'underwater obstacle 'as been detected. After repeating his message twice he stopped transmitting and turned up the volume on the receiver. No response. Again he turned down the volume and resumed transmitting.

July 22, 1601

On the bridge of *Blue Mountain*, just as Thompson saw the

second parachute flare blaze red in the sky, the walkie-talkies on the charging stand squawked out sounds of static, along with the faintest trace of a human voice.

"Oh shit again. Mr. Latham, get in here quick," he hollered as he reached up and turned the volume up on the bridge VHF. They'd forgotten to do that after the captain stomped off the bridge earlier.

But the action on channel 16 was all coast guard and police chatter about something going on somewhere else down the bay. As the second officer quickly returned to the bridge, Thompson punched in channel 10 on the VHF. That was the channel the walkie-talkies were hissing and burping on.

" *...Dawson Rock, turn h'aside immediately. Dis is de sailboat on your port bows. h'Uncharted h'underwater obstacle 'as been detected.*" The poor quality, low-power signal, overridden by static, left the two men riveted to the deck. A long moment of indecision elapsed before Latham reacted. After what seemed an eternity he reached for the VHF mic.

"Vessel calling *Blue Mountain*, please try calling on channel 16. Your signal is weak and broken up. Over."

"*Radio damaged. Don't know what channel we h'are on. Turn away from Dawson Rock now. We 'ave no times for chattering,*" came scratching back at him.

"Thompson, quick, helm hard to port, engine full astern," Latham finally ordered as he finally began to react to the emergency, at the same time, pushing urgently on the call button to the captain's cabin. "He's sure going to be pissed if this is a crank call." The last comment was drowned out by multiple short blasts from the ship's horn.

July 22, 1605

It was with a mixture of both relief and horror that the

occupants of *Water Baby*'s cockpit finally detected urgent action aboard the bulk carrier. Its horn bellowing, a welter of white foam boiling up from under her stern, the ship was still charging steadily toward the outer edge of Dawson Rock — still headed for the illegal toxic chemical dump.

Erin kept exclaiming that she couldn't bear to watch — but stared intently, just in case even from two miles away now, she could see any chemical drums rolling to the surface.

After checking with the binoculars, Mike Small realized that the ship was not turning, but forging on, straight ahead. He quickly told Ethier to call the ship and order "hard to starboard." The natural reaction of a ship's engine going hard astern while the vessel was still moving forward is that 'paddlewheel effect' of the propeller will pull the stern to port, forcing the bow to go to starboard. With *Blue Mountain*'s rudder trying to turn the ship the opposite way the paddlewheel effect was largely being cancelled out.

"Steer 'ard to starboard you fool," Ethier called into the microphone. Proper radio etiquette fell by the wayside.

July 22, 1610

"Latham, the man's right. Hard to starboard!" Captain Henry, his blood pressure spiking once more, had caught the beginning of the radio conversation after turning up the volume on the repeater speaker in his cabin the instant the ship's horn had started blaring. He completed his dash to the bridge just as Ethier's command from the ether suggested the steering change. Picking up the mic he said, "Vessel calling distress, exactly where and what is the nature of this obstruction?"

Upon hearing Ethier's hurried reply, Henry took a quick look at the depth sounder reading. Forty feet of water at the bow. The ship was already starting over the shoal and was still pushing forward at about five knots. Although Thompson had taken the rudder full over the instant the captain ordered it, the lake boat hadn't yet begun to swing into a starboard turn. As with the people watching from aboard *Water Baby*, Henry knew he was quickly running out of time and distance.

His nautical mind whizzed through the calculations. By their estimate, barely a quarter mile ahead — a mere two boat lengths — well over two hundred drums of toxins sat in thirty-five feet of water. 'If any have landed down there double stacked on top of another pallet allowing say, four feet of height for each pallet ... oh crap, that eats up about eight feet of clearance ... only two to four feet left below the keel ... shit, shit, shit, shit, shit!' Quickly coming to a decision, he ordered the only thing that could be done — besides praying.

"Center the helm ... *now!*" A long pause, and then after he'd mentally measured the progress of one of those two boat lengths through the water, Henry barked, "Engines all stop!"

July 22, 1612

"What are they doing? They're not reversing anymore," Erin exclaimed, astonished by the sudden silence that fell over the bulk carrier.

"I think that's his only option," Small suggested, going on to explain what the ship's captain had likely decided. And all four spectators aboard *Water Baby* held their breath watching the freighter in nervous anticipation.

July 22, 1614

At just over three knots, *Blue Mountain* glided silently over Reiger's toxic waste drums. No longer spinning at full panic speed astern, the giant propeller created no turbulence. But even at that low speed, the ship's forward motion continued pushing a huge volume of water ahead of the hull, creating considerable turbulence beneath. A number of the pallets of drums teetering on top of others tipped off and fell the remaining four feet to the lakebed as the ship's bow passed nearby.

Most of the pallets deposited in Small's drop zone, though they were weighted down, still shifted violently across the bottom. At first, they were pushed away from the ship's path by the force of the water being pushed ahead of the hull, but once the bow had passed, they were sucked back toward and underneath the hull as it continued over the area. Pallets and drums tumbled and bumped into boulders as they were forced across the rocky bottom. The only immediate evidence of the ship's passage over the illegal dump was a dense cloud of bottom silt suspended in the water. Several dozen drums, broken free of their steel strapping, had surfaced and were now floating barely awash. These were visible from the aft deck of the ship after it passed — and they were visible from the air too.

July 22, 1620

"*Having a good vacation Webb?*" The voice of pilot Dale Moses startled everyone aboard as the low-flying Twin Otter buzzed the yawl from less than a hundred feet above them. "*You sure know how to put on a good show!*"

"Jeez Moses, you scared the crap out of us. What are you doing out here?" Webb queried the government pilot after a quick dash into the cabin to work Ethier's scratch-built radio. "And how did you find our frequency? Even we don't know it yet. Over."

"Ah, that's for me and the Blue Mountain boys to know," came back the cocky reply. *"Anyhow, we saw your flares after leaving the tugboat. And by the way, Judge Franklin sends his compliments. Says all is well aboard that fine luxury yacht. And, in case you were worried that somehow the bad guys had retaken the ship, he says to tell the 'Iron Maiden' that he's real proud of her and he'll see her when she gets back home."*

Webb flinched on hearing that awful name spoken in front of Erin. She'd joined him in the cabin when she'd overheard the news from the tug. As much as the name grated on him though, hearing it was the reassurance that he had hoped for. None of the other participants in this wild adventure had been made privy to the name, so it did come from her dad.

Glancing cautiously in Erin's direction, Webb saw a tear sliding down her face. Unsure of what to say, he reached out for her hand. Erin squeezed his in return, and smiling, she quietly mouthed, "I'm okay." She was touched by the gesture, and he was lost for words. It was a long time since he'd had the opportunity to show that kind of sensitivity toward a woman. It felt good. But it still worried him.

"So what does the outside world know of our situation here Dale?" Webb asked, returning to the business at hand, but still savouring Erin's electric touch. She hadn't let go yet. It was reminiscent of Mel's touch, but strangely, that similarity didn't bring unhappy memories with it. It just felt good.

"Oh, we're all up-to-date on your adventure Rick, and everything's been looked after. Your whole vacation, at least for the rest of the day, has been planned by Sunshine Air." Sunshine was an in-house nickname for the air service, generally invoked by staff upon having a flight cancelled by their pilot over concerns about bad weather — two days away — somewhere out over the prairies. Of course, because of their collective caution, the

air service pilots possessed one of the best safety records of any Canadian commercial air carrier.

"*We've got one of the cop copters on the way to the tug after they hit a gas station. They're going to meet the coast guard light tender that's going to tow the tug into Britt. And the Blue Mountain skipper says his schedule's been so badly fucked up ... oh, sorry, can't say that word over the airwaves ... ah ...badly delayed already, that they'll stand by now to receive the other chopper here ... briefly. They, the police, want to talk with your tug guys, but they know that the judge has released them on a recognizance thingy.*

"*Judging from the terrible signal you are putting out, and the ugly scuff marks I see on your nice shiny yacht from up here, I'm guessing you had quite a duel with the devil back there. So stand by for a message bag. I'm lending you my company satellite phone and a hand-held marine radio. The judge has the number for the phone and will call as soon as he has access to a land line. The big coast guard ship is an hour and a half away from this location ... coming to scope out the cleanup job down there. After the police are done with him, they want your tug skipper as a guide, so a working VHF will make you sound a little more professional when they arrive.*

"*I guess that's about it then. Can I fetch you some gas or rum or anything like that before you head off on the rest of your vacation?*"

"No, but thanks, Dale. Got plenty enough of everything I need to get back home. I think my vacation will have to go on standby for a bit. My poor old *Water Baby* has been rode hard and put away wet, once too often today. The bad guys beat her up pretty badly inside, so it's a haul-out for the ship, and shore leave for me I guess, until I can get her prettied up again."

Only then did it really hit Webb, the whole impact that the day's events had on his poor old boat, not to mention his vacation plans. Despite the victories of the day, the ravages endured by his lovely yawl suddenly left him feeling sad and empty — a return to the same sort of emptiness that had haunted him much of the time since Melanie's death. The yawl had been a happy part of their short, married life together. The abuse taken by the old boat had re-opened the wounds of her loss. He sat on the settee, disconsolately surveying the damage.

They were alone in the cabin now, and sitting across from him, Erin easily picked up on his sense of loss. She was kicking herself for the cold attitude she'd shown him for so much of the short time they'd been together. Despite the fact that circumstances had kept stacking up against him, he'd pulled it off. He had saved their lives several times over and received little in the way of acknowledgement from her. She looked at him thoughtfully before she spoke.

"Rick, thanks. For everything." She smiled briefly, then she continued sheepishly, "I feel terrible about the way I treated you so ... so horribly, right from the beginning. I pre-judged you because of the poor behaviour of some other people, and that isn't the way I was raised. I'm really sorry."

"No Erin, there's no apology necessary. You've been through absolute hell in the last few days. Worse than what I've had done to me. My rescue plans sure didn't work out the way I'd hoped last night, and I wasn't happy about that either. I'm just glad we all made it. And I need to thank you for all your help today ... taking watches, bringing down that Goreham character, this cleanup ... everything. It's kind of difficult tidying up after a tornado has hit, but it looks a lot better down here than it did earlier. That means a lot to me."

He realized that she was calling him by his given name, no longer just 'Webb'. As tough an image as she had originally projected, when she smiled, he found that he just wanted to be close to her. He watched her wistfully, half wishing he could somehow connect with her but still reluctant to abandon Melanie's memory.

Heywood chose that moment to snuggle up against her and start purring. "I didn't think he'd want to be near me after what I did to him earlier," she said, stroking the big tom's head.

"He's a very forgiving creature. And I think he was just glad to be able to help save a damsel in distress," Webb smiled in reply. He felt warm inside. But in the next instant his caution caused him to subconsciously withdraw from her. And then a summons from up on deck interrupted their private moment together.

"Webb, I'd like to start rounding up some of these loose drums if we can, before they drift away from here. You got any spare lines?"

"We'd better give those two a hand," Erin offered, seeing Webb's building discomfort. She wondered if it was she who was the problem — there was a good chance of that, considering her earlier performance — or was he just shy maybe? Along with his apparent discomfort, she detected a look of longing in his face. And she was left with that thought as she followed him up to the cockpit to help start corralling the stray floating drums that had broken loose from their pallets.

Committed to standing by for the incoming police chopper, Captain Henry launched an inflatable runabout from *Blue Mountain* to help with the roundup, and between them, within half an hour they had all the loose drums they could find, rafted together. The police landed on the laker soon after and briefly interviewed the tug men, leaving them each with a summons to attend the Parry Sound detachment for finger printing and processing.

July 22, 1930

The Canadian Coast Guard ship *Samuel Risley* was 'hovering' on station over Dawson Rock. The 230-foot multi-task vessel was being kept in place using its GPS system linked to its thrusters. The captain had no desire to drop anchor so near to all those drums of toxins. The risk of damage to any of them with either the anchor itself, or the heavy chain rode, was just not worth it.

A team of MNR divers, who'd boarded the ship in Tobermory, had just finished a preliminary assessment of the situation on the lake bed. Surprisingly, although pallets of battered drums were scattered for hundreds of yards every which way across the shoal, only a couple of them appeared to be damaged to the point of leaking.

As expected, Mike Small and Ray Ethier would be staying with the coast guard ship during the salvage operation. Small, while being thoroughly condemned by the coast guard crew and ministry divers for his role in the illegal dumping, was at least being commended for having the foresight to dump where he did — it would have been a secure location if not for the unfortunately routed ship traffic — and they were impressed with his ability to keep an accurate mental inventory of everything he'd deposited there, too.

It was burned into his memory, he explained to them, and it replayed over and over again whenever he tried to sleep, ever since the first load went overboard. He promised to turn the tug's log books over to them if the police hadn't already seized them.

Everyone from *Water Baby* was invited to use the shower facilities aboard the ship and Erin got to run her wet 'prison' clothes through the laundry when they first came aboard. Freshened up and pleased to be back in her own clothes, she and Rick dined with everyone else aboard the *Risley*. At dinner she related the gist of the phone conversation she'd had with her father earlier.

"He said that the police arrived in force, by helicopter, to take charge of the Reiger gang, but kept them locked up until the tug reached the dock. Apparently, the prisoners were not happy with their treatment while in holding. Big brave Gant crapped himself when the pilot's message bag slammed into the steel side of the tug's 'lockup'. They all had to put up with the stench for almost three hours. It couldn't have happened to a more deserving bunch!

"Anyhow, Dad's okay, and an ambulance is taking him straight to the emergency room in Sudbury to have his gunshot wound taken care of. But he still insists he is going to his dentist in the morning to have the hole filled properly. He's still got his sense of humour, so I know he's okay."

July 22, 1940

The effects of the cold front had passed quickly and that evening there was just a light breeze blowing warmly from the south — a harbinger of the next heat wave already forecast for the region. The water was almost completely calm again.

With dinner over, the crowd at the captain's table gradually broke up and Rick and Erin moved to the ship's rail just above where *Water Baby* was rafted alongside. The coast guard captain had asked Webb to delay his departure for another few minutes while his radio tech installed a loaner VHF aboard the yawl. It had better range than the handheld unit that Moses had dropped for them.

They leaned on the rail and looked out over the peaceful lake that had been the scene of so much trouble just hours before. Webb broke the silence just the instant before Erin was ready to speak.

DAVID G. FERGUSON

"The coast guard skipper says you've turned down a chopper lift to Parry Sound. Are you planning to stay here while they do the salvage job?"

Erin looked suddenly crestfallen. "I, um … I was sort of … well … I thought maybe you'd want someone to sail back with you. I mean … your vacation's been ruined, and that's my fault, at least partly." With a sinking feeling, she continued, "I guess I could stay here … if they have room for me."

"No, none of it's your fault Erin, and I'd really like to have you sail home with me," he said. It would give him some time — well a day anyhow — to get to know her a little better. Then, maybe he would know if he was finally ready to leave his past and move on.

"Anyhow, if you've got the time, I'm going back to Club Island tonight to pick up my dinghy and they're lending me a VHF so I can report back to the *Risley* on the situation with the barge. We can overnight there … I've got the V-berth and also the pilot berth in the salon … so there's lots of room aboard for both of us. Then tomorrow we'll sail back to Parry Sound."

This wasn't working out the way she had hoped it would. Everything was threatening to unravel because he'd opened the conversation before she had. She was on the point of losing her nerve, but decided to jump in with both feet.

"Rick, there was something else Dad told me when we talked on the phone earlier, but it wasn't meant for the dinner table crowd." Still leaning on the rail, she looked at him standing beside her and spoke cautiously. "He told me what happened to your wife. I'm really sorry. I didn't know that before … I knew she'd died, but not the horrible circumstances of her crash. It must have been terrible, what you've gone through ever since." Rick's chest tightened at the memory of Mel's loss. A lump formed in his throat.

"Dad thought you were pretty reluctant to start a new

relationship and he said he recognized that from himself. His first and only girlfriend was my mother. They didn't get married until he was almost thirty and after Mom died, he couldn't bring himself to get involved with anyone again.

"So I think he understands how you feel and he told me not to expect … oh, this is coming out all wrong," she turned away from Rick and looked down at the water again, thoroughly embarrassed. Tears were forming in her eyes, and Webb was quick to realize that, like him, she was having trouble expressing what she really felt. In that moment of mutual torment, he suddenly felt a bond form between them. Now he knew for sure what Mel would have wanted him to do and he turned to face her. Pulling her toward him, he wrapped his arms around her in a reassuring hug.

"Erin, it's okay.…"

"Please … let me finish," she stopped him. The hug gave her the courage to go on. The tears were still in her eyes, but were not flowing and she wiped them away with her fingers.

"I haven't ever done this before, and I didn't plan on asking to sail back with you until after I'd said it all. But everything got out of order when you brought up the chopper ride." She paused again and then suddenly the rest of it came out in a rush. "I've never felt close to a guy before. And I'm sorry it took me almost twenty-four hours of pure hell to see it, but you've really got me hooked."

She was even more embarrassed by how rash that must sound, so she cautiously added, "But if that's a problem for you, or it's happening too quickly, I don't want you to feel pressured."

"Erin, I've been living in the past for way too long and I needed a good push from someone to point me toward the future. You are the only one who's been able to do that." He finally felt the kind of joy he thought he would never get to experience again.

"And no, as much as I've been dragging my feet, it isn't too sudden. Maybe it's not even been twenty-four hours we've known each other, but we've faced more life-threatening challenges in one day than most couples face in a lifetime. I think we've gotten to know each other better than we realize. And besides," he finished with a grin, "I love the way you handle my boat."

She gave him a heart-melting smile and put her arms around his shoulders, pulling them even closer together. And they held each other tight.

Ten minutes later they were back aboard *Water Baby*. They were surprised by the change from what they'd left earlier. His smashed GPS, Loran and RDF receivers were all tidily removed from the navigating station, leaving no loose dangling wires. And Ethier's scratch-built radio transceiver had been removed from the chart table. A handheld GPS sat in its place on top of a note written on coast guard letterhead. It read:

To: Rick Webb and Erin Franklin:

In appreciation of your successful apprehension of a very wicked operator (and his henchmen), and for your crucial role in saving our lake from a horrific disaster today, we thought a bit of a tidy up was in order. Your damaged gear will be available for pick up at the base next time we are in port. (Your insurance company will probably want to see the evidence.) Like the radio we've lent you, the GPS is strictly a loner – in this case it's the personal gear of our comm. tech. But please feel free to keep it for a few weeks. We ALL think you deserve that vacation more than ever.

Capt'n & Crew
'CCGS Samuel Risley'

As well as the tidy-up of the ruined electronic gear, someone from the *Risley* had laundered the sheets and remade the bed in the forward cabin. Goreham's blood stains were no longer there. And the stains had been removed from the cabin's carpets too. Someone had been busy while they were dining aboard the ship.

"Wow, it really *is* a beautiful boat Rick," Erin said as she looked around. "My tidy up didn't even begin to make it look this nice."

"You faced a much bigger mess than they did, Erin. And you didn't have a ship load of cleaning supplies and equipment. I mean, I *am* impressed, and it was really good of them to do all this, but your efforts this afternoon helped win my heart.

"This however," he smiled as he picked up the coast guard note. "This begs the question: Just how did they know there would be two of us here to read this Ms. Franklin?"

A cautious smile crept over her face before she spoke. "Well, the captain asked me if I wanted a chopper ride ashore, but I said I'd try to catch a ride with you … that part I already told you. Anyhow, the captain knows my dad — they curl in the same men's league — and he talked to him on the phone after I did. And then I saw him and Mike Small talking furtively on the bridge after the phone call ended. I wondered if maybe they were cooking up something, but they said nothing to me. I think Dad and Mike had us pegged even before we figured it out. Honest, the cleanup and the note were a surprise to me too."

"Okay. So, you're only guilty by association then … and I love it." His next hug came with a passionate kiss, willingly accepted and sustained by the receiving party.

"Now, let's cast off. We're on the wrong side of the *Risley* to catch the sunset, and there's nothing more beautiful than … no, scratch that … there can only be *one* thing more beautiful than seeing the sun going down from the deck of this old yawl. And that will be watching it go down with you beside me," he said.

Pulling away from the ship, they called up their enthusiastic thanks to the waving crew. Standing apart from the rest, a beaming Mike Small gave them a double thumbs-up.

"Are you sure you really want to sail back home tomorrow, Rick?" she asked after they were clear of the *Risley*. "I mean, you've just barely started your vacation," she continued. "And the boat still floats, the engine still runs, and the sails still go up and down. Then there's all this good food you've still got onboard."

"So I take it you want to go on vacation with me?"

"Yes … that is … if you want me to."

"I'd love that, Erin. But what about your father? We should probably get back to Parry Sound and drive up north to see him at the hospital."

"Day surgery stuff," she countered. "Even if we went full bore, he'd be home before we were. At the very most, they'll keep him overnight. Besides, we've still got your pilot's government phone. I can call Dad and tell him. He'd be pleased … for both of us."

"What about your business?"

"Voicemail. And maybe it's time that more people started calling your ministry with their pollution complaints. Actually, I can change my message to tell them that. Then afterwards … well, I'll see what the future brings."

"What about your lonely little car?"

"If you really don't want me along, I can jump off right here, you know," she grinned. "Otherwise, I can courier my keys to a friend in Toronto when we get to Little Current, and she and her husband can pick it up for me. Any more questions?"

"You don't have any spare clothes." He said, still contemplating the logistics of resuming his trip.

"Do I need any?"

"You might get cold."

"I've got you to keep me warm."

"I guess I'm going to have to get those guys in the Toronto office to cut out the 'Iron Maiden' comments then," he said, smiling.

"One thing at a time, my newfound love, one thing at a time," Erin replied. "I was thinking, after the coast guard ship is out of sight, maybe we could just drift for a while. Then we could work on cancelling the 'maidenly' part first."

EPILOGUE

Immediately after his release from hospital and return home, Judge James Franklin reported the situation to his boss. He was forgiven by the Chief Justice for succumbing to influence and throwing the case against Reiger and Mid-Con Waste. Being a dispassionate adjudicator was one thing, the chief said, but anyone who could ignore a threat of that nature, made against his own family, would be a cold-hearted son-of-a-bitch and not well suited to the role of a provincial judge.

Over the course of the next five weeks Franklin decided that his experience at the hands of the Reiger gang was going to affect his ability to provide unbiased judgement on serious criminal cases. Jim Franklin retired from the bench, effective September 30th.

His new goals in life were: more golfing, more gardening and maybe even some grand-parenting duties — if recent suspicions were confirmed.

—

In a widely publicized trial, Willard Reiger, John Gant and their surviving enforcers were all found guilty on nine counts of attempted murder; each one of them having been involved in their potentially murderous rampage. Reiger and Gant each received a life sentence with no chance of parole for twenty years. Their followers were treated slightly more

DAVID G. FERGUSON

leniently but would still be approaching middle age by the time they were free men again.

In a separate trial, numerous convictions under provincial environmental laws and the Fisheries Act of Canada were registered against the same group and the company, resulting in fines large enough to render Mid-Con Waste Management Inc. insolvent. The business was completely stripped of all assets. Equipment, buildings and even real estate were ordered forfeited to the Crown.

In turn, a group of the company's former employees who had not been involved in Reiger's illegal activities, negotiated to buy the company back from the government and start doing business under another name. This relieved the province of the burden dealing with the large inventory of toxic substances remaining at the former Mid-Con facilities.

—

Mike Small and Ray Ethier both pled guilty and were convicted of illegally depositing deleterious substances in waters frequented by fish; one conviction for each of the six occurrences carefully documented in the tug's logbook by Small himself. While the judge in their case gave them a royal dressing down for their part in the illegal dumping scheme, he went on to express the province's appreciation for their gallant efforts to help turn the tables on Reiger and his co-accused. In the end, he gave the two relieved and apologetic tug men an absolute discharge.

Small got to stay in Canada and accepted an offer to take the transportation manager's position with the newly formed waste management company. He did so, on condition that a replacement tug would be purchased and Ethier and the rest of the tug crew would be hired to run it.

Also by David G. Ferguson:

BEAR RUNNERS

AVAILABLE ON AMAZON

Another bear brought down with just one shot. Pleased with his latest kill, the man who calls himself Eagle Feather is carving out a new career in the northern wilderness while hiding from the law, and a past cloaked in dark secrets.

Conservation Officer Robert McNabb and government pilot Sam Williams team up in an attempt to bring the murderous polar bear poacher to justice in the depths of a particularly harsh James Bay winter.

In a vast land of bush planes, blizzards, remote communities and lonely winter roads, McNabb and Williams face a string of extreme challenges which make for slim odds of their success, let alone their own chances of survival. And a budding romance hangs in the balance.

For a sample of the adventure, read on...

The man who called himself Eagle Feather bent down and used the crusted snow at his feet to wipe the blood off his knife. The vapour of his breath was torn away by the bitter wind. He had just finished skinning the fifth polar bear he'd taken in the past ten days. Although the local Cree people had once told him that most of the big males would be hunting seals on the ice farther offshore by January, he had found the hunting along the northern edge of Polar Bear Provincial Park to be most rewarding.

The bears were still hunting along the shore because the seals they preyed on had not yet moved offshore onto Hudson Bay. And that was because climate change was affecting the normal distribution of species in the food chain from the tiniest plankton up to the fish species sought by the seals. In addition, the ice cover along the coast was still poorly formed with plenty of open leads allowing the bears and the seals easy access to their respective prey.

Eagle Feather was pleased with his harvest. As with his first hunt of the winter, this trip had been a simple matter of following the coast and finding where the seals were hanging out. If the bears weren't already there, they usually came along within hours. It was almost too easy.

At the same time, he felt he was being cheated by the men who were buying his products. Unlike the hunters and trappers of three hundred years ago or even as recently as thirty years back, Eagle Feather did not live in isolation without news from the outside world.

At his cabin, just a day-and-a-half snowmobile ride from this remote corner of Ontario's Arctic coast, he had a satellite connection to the Internet, and he could track the fur auction sales online. Top grade specimens of the big white bears were selling for anywhere between ten and twenty thousand dollars apiece. It had become all the rage in Russia and Asia for the rich to decorate their homes and offices with Arctic wildlife furs and taxidermy mounts. And all the combined bear quotas in the Arctic nations that still allowed a hunt couldn't begin to keep up with the demand.

After repeated complaints to his buyers, they had grudgingly agreed to increase his share by thirty percent, but he was still convinced he was getting shortchanged. He figured that if they'd been willing to bump his share by that much, then there must be an even greater payoff that should be coming to him. With that in mind, he'd already decided it was time to make some changes. This winter he had come up with a scheme to bypass the middlemen.

Eagle Feather kept his real name a secret because of his checkered past and the interest its revelation would generate amongst a number of North American law enforcement agencies. In fact, it was the intense interest of the police that had caused him to leave his previous occupation — stealing and exporting high-end cars and SUVs to offshore clients.

With the law finally closing in on him, he had needed to disappear. He had used the proceeds from his final auto shipments to relocate and assume this new identity.

With his dirty-blond hair dyed black, the half of his genetic line with north Asian ancestry gave the man a facial resemblance and skin tone close enough to some North American Indigenous people to pass off as one of them — or so he felt. He wasn't worried about the blue eyes inherited from his Scandinavian ancestors. He knew there were plenty of genetic anomalies amongst the aboriginal populations after five hundred years of close association with European settlers.

He had drawn his assumed name from his childhood. As a boy he had created an imaginary friend he named Eagle

Feather, and of course, as is the fate of so many imaginary friends, he blamed the little Indian boy for any and all mischief he was accused of. Since the young version of Eagle Feather never got caught it seemed fitting that needing to disappear from his former life, he should assume the name and identity of his make-believe childhood friend.

He also had a strange affinity for the story of the Englishman, Archie Belaney, who in the early 1900s passed himself off as an Indian trapper and conservationist by the name of Grey Owl. Eagle Feather had hoped the James Bay Cree might somehow transpose that benevolent imposter's values onto his own reincarnation.

The allure of big money in the trade of polar bear and other Arctic wildlife furs led him to choose the seclusion of the northeastern corner of Ontario where he would start his new life. He set up camp on Sutton Lake in a remote and sparsely populated area, but by chartered bush plane within easy reach of Moosonee and Timmins. And there were trees there unlike the barren Arctic coastlines of Canada's three northern territories. He knew he could easily survive in a wilderness with trees.

Thirty-five kilometres long and less than a kilometre wide, Sutton Lake was a pristine body of water located in the only high country of the Hudson & James Bay Lowlands. It stretched from north to south, draining at its north end through the spectacular Sutton Gorge into Hawley Lake, another narrow lake, twenty kilometres long. Both lakes were known for their fly-in summer trout fishing, but there was little human activity there during the long winter months. It was just such isolation that Eagle Feather sought for conducting his nefarious new trade....

ABOUT THE AUTHOR

David Ferguson is a retired Ontario government employee who invested 24 years of his career working in three diverse regions of the province as a conservation officer with the Ministry of Natural Resources. And to be clear, being a CO is a vocation, a calling — it is not just a 'job'.

In that profession, he learned that successful law enforcement is an intense study of human behaviour. On the job, he met and dealt with a wide variety of people — a great many good, law abiding folks and then some others who landed on the wrong side of the law. Even the people who broke the law included an assortment of characters ranging from those who accidently 'slipped' over the line and maybe deserved a bit of a break, to outright bad guys you wouldn't want to turn your back on. Many of the latter group are also known to the police.

Dave and his family, plus cats and dogs, have sailed Georgian Bay aboard a yawl that bears a remarkable resemblance to *Water Baby*. They have sailed to, and visited the islands and coves detailed in these pages.

As an avid reader of fiction himself, Dave knows that his career provided him with a wealth of human characteristics and a variety of geographic locations that could be woven into fictional characters and places in some exciting imaginary adventure stories. This one is his first.

Dave lives with his wife Pat in northern Ontario, and when they are not on the road touring the continent, he can be found out on the lake in the summer, or feeding the wood stove in the cooler seasons while conjuring up his next story.